Mad Love

colet abedi

Copyright © 2014 by Colet Abedi
All rights reserved. No part of this publication may be reproduced, stored in a retrieval system, or transmitted, in any form or by any means, electronic, mechanical, photocopying, recording or otherwise without the prior permission of the publishers.
e-book isbn 978–0-9967088–2-1
Book Design: Hagop Kalaidjian, Shawn Tavassoli
Layout: Cassy Roop at Pink Ink Designs
Jacket Photos: iStockphoto / Michael Langhoff
Second edition edition 2015

For my husband
I love you madly

"When love is not madness, it is not love."
-pedro calderon de la barca

Acknowledgements

My special thanks to Lisa Gallagher, my amazing agent and friend, for her love, support and encouragement. You are a true gem and I feel blessed to have you on my side. I hope you think of me and laugh when you hear our "special" word.

To my editor, Jane Cavolina. Words can't express how incredibly lucky I feel to have met and worked with you. I don't know what I would have done without your guidance and wisdom. I wish I could superglue you to my side! PS- If you don't mind, I'm keeping you.

To my family. Mom, Dad and Jasmine you've always encouraged and taught me to believe in my dreams. Love you more.

Mina. I'll never forget the trip to the library with you where I checked out my first romance novel. That was the moment I began to dream.

Giuliana & Bill. I don't know how to thank you both for all that you've done for me. I will never ever forget it. I love you guys.

To the real life Erik & Orie. Sophie and I are so grateful to have you in our lives #forrealz #forever.

My friends. In no particular order . . . Cathea, Andrea, Nicky, Carlton, David, Sally, Rana, Amal, Giannina, Christina, Shawn, Mary, JD, Tana, Jorge, Bob, John, Lauren, Annalynne, Angel, Ally, Rob, Rick, Brandee, Ariana, Cori, Matt, Toby . . . Each one of you is so special to me. Love you all long time.

To Amanda . . . thank you for all your support.

Thank you Paul Almond. For everything.

Here's to being madly in love, and loving madly, forever.

Note to the Reader:

This is a work of fiction. Names, characters, places and incidents either are products of the author's imagination or are used fictitiously. Any resemblance to actual events or locales or persons, living or dead, is entirely coincidental. Any and all product names referenced within this book are the copyright and/or trademarks of their respective owners. None of these owners have sponsored, authorized, endorsed or approved this book in any way. The author and publisher specifically disclaim all responsibility for any liability, loss, or risk, personal or otherwise, which is incurred as a consequence, directly or indirectly in relation to this book.

Chapter One

I AM IN COMPLETE darkness.

I panic for a moment, forgetting where I am. The quick jolt of turbulence instantly reminds me. Right, I'm thirty-two thousand feet in the air on my way to a vacation that people only dream of. The Maldives. One of the world's most beautiful and remote destinations. I try to get excited. But right now the feeling is nonexistent. I grimace as reality starts to wash over me like a tsunami. *Try to be grateful, Sophie,* I silently snarl to myself. *Who wouldn't trade places with you right now?*

I flip the eye mask off my face and stretch out in my seat. The cabin is darkly lit and a quick look at the television monitor tells me that we are still a few hours away from Male. I click the button on my chair and move from the flat bed to a seated position. Yes, I know I'm lucky. To be in a window seat in first class and not crammed in coach is a blessing. I used to appreciate these kinds of moments more, but now I'm just bone weary. I feel older than my twenty-three years. But then, so much has happened in the past few weeks. So much has changed in my life. Some for good, some not so great. I try not to dwell on negative thoughts, but it's hard. I can't seem to help myself.

I force myself to think about the self-help and spiritual books I've read and downloaded on my iPad to help me become a more well-rounded person. There's *The Power of Now* by Eckhart Tolle, who teaches you to live in the now, which I personally find really hard to do. I mean honestly, who can always be present besides Buddhist monks in remote villages in Thailand? I realize my cynicism is getting the best of me. I need to be fair. I *used* to believe you could live in the now. Maybe you can. *Try now,* Sophie, *I think to myself.* I take a deep breath and focus on the seat I'm sitting in, the television screen in front of me, the sound of the plane humming through the sky. That's the now, right?

Then my inner voice chimes in. *This vacation is costing you a fortune,* it says. *And,* I ask myself, *your point is?* The point is, *Do the math. Your bank account can't handle this.*

Whatever!!

Okay, so living in the now is really not working at this moment. I continue to mentally flip through the catalogue of books. What about Don Miguel Ruiz's *The Four Agreements?* That's a good one. What are the agreements again? Oh yes, *Never Make Assumptions, Do Your Best, Be Impeccable with Your Word* and *Don't Take Anything Personally.* Well, shit. I'm sitting here right now because I've taken everything in my life personally. And if I consider the rest of Mr. Ruiz's agreements, I've definitely made a lot of assumptions. According to my parents, I'm not so impeccable with my word, and I can't honestly say that I've always done my best. Umm, that's zero out of four.

Yikes. I clearly need to do some spiritual work on myself.

I sigh and grab the remote for the television. I'm just so tired. When did this happen? *How* did this happen? I'm only twenty-three, for the love of God. I shouldn't feel like I'm carrying a five-hundred pound weight on my back. I expected this general feeling to occur later, when I'm married with four kids and have a mortgage I can't afford and am drowning in credit card debt. I fidget in my seat in agitation.

There is just so much going on in my head, so many different problems I need to sort through. This vacation is supposed to be my saving grace, my salvation from all the real-life drama I've faced in the past few weeks. My family is angry with me for becoming "a stranger overnight," as my mother so dramatically said. First, I broke up with Jerry—the man they wanted me to marry—because he never kissed me with the passion that I'd read about in romance novels. And then I dropped out of law school to pursue a career in art. Lord Almighty, just thinking about it makes me break out in a sweat. No wonder my mom tearfully told me that she was going to disown me, that she didn't know who I was, and that I had disgraced the family.

I hit the call button for the flight attendant. It's a good time for a drink, right before panic starts to envelope me. In a second the flight attendant leans over me. I can't believe she looks so good after fourteen hours in the air. But then I was told that Singapore Airlines has the best looking and most accommodating flight attendants in the world.

"Gin and tonic, please," I whisper in a voice, slightly embarrassed that I'm asking for a drink at what is breakfast time in Los Angeles. If she disapproves, she doesn't show it. She simply nods and hurries off to get me my drink.

I guess if I'm going to have my own eat, pray, drink vacation, I think with some amusement, I should do it with a bang. I used all my precious air miles to book the first-class ticket. I even cajoled my best friend and his boyfriend to join me on my extravagant vacation—*except they didn't need to max out their credit cards to find themselves,* my mind annoyingly reminds me. I'm instantly angry with myself for going down this dark path. I hit the button on the remote to find a movie.

"Did you just ask for a gin and tonic?" Erik asks me as he rolls over on his flat bed to look at me. He pushes the blanket off his body and runs a hand through his thick hair.

"Yep." I can't help but smile at how gorgeous he looks.

His blond hair is slightly tousled and his big blue eyes are earnest in his handsome face. *Why can't he be straight,* I ask myself for the thousandth time. He moves his seat into an upright position and studies my somber demeanor.

"Are you going to cry again?" He's clearly afraid of my answer.

"No," I say, but my voice wavers. God, I hope not. The amount of crying I've done in the past few weeks should be a crime.

"Honestly, Sophie, if Orie and I are going to have to cajole you out of bad moods the whole vacation I'm going to be really pissed off."

I laugh. His candor is biting, but real. Okay, borderline offensive, but what can I say? I love the guy.

"It's not like I don't have anything to cry about," I say a bit defensively.

"The only thing you should be crying about is that outfit you have on." Erik checks out my pajamas, courtesy of Singapore Airlines.

"What's wrong with it?"

"There's a reason they're free. And given to you in a small plastic bag."

"Oh, please. They're comfortable. And besides, who's seeing me on this plane?"

Erik turns his overhead light on and looks straight at me.

"First of all, *I'm* seeing you. Second of all, and almost as important, you should dress every single day, *every single outfit,* as if you're going to die in those clothes."

It's hard not to laugh out loud but I want to be considerate to the sleeping passengers. The funniest part of the conversation is that Erik is dead serious.

"Trust me when I say you wouldn't want to be caught dead in *that*." He points at me and turns the overhead light back out.

"You're obsessed."

"*And?* You're the girl who was wearing boot-cut jeans until last year. I found jeans in your closet that you used to wear in high school. The only reason you don't have them on right now is because I threw them out!"

"If you love me you won't talk about those four years of hell." The thought of high school makes my skin crawl. I *so* didn't want to relive Sophie Walker's *Wonder Years*. Because seriously, there really wasn't anything wonderful about them.

"If you didn't want a reminder of how completely uncool you were, why keep the hideous jeans?"

"I loved them," I tell him honestly.

"Sophie, that offends me. On every level."

I lose the battle to stay silent and burst out laughing. Erik is a stylist to the stars in Hollywood. He's considered to be one of the best, and every celebrity he works with instantly falls in love with him and can't get enough of him. I don't blame them. He lives and breathes fashion. His love for clothes, handbags, shoes, and accessories comes a close second to his love for Orie. And sometimes, depending on what designer he has on, he might even love the outfit more.

Before I can answer, the flight attendant brings my drink.

"May I get you anything else, Miss Walker?"

"This is great, thank you," I say politely.

"I'd love to have one of those as well," Erik asks her with a smile. She nods and walks away.

"Are we drinking our sorrows away?"

I stir my drink and shrug. "Maybe."

"Sophie, your parents are assholes." Erik just rolls right into it. I know what's coming next so I take a giant sip. "Instead of supporting their daughter and her dream of being an artist, they act like pricks."

The thought of my parents makes me sick to my stomach.

"I mean, look at you. Not at this moment, of course. I'm talking in general. Your parents should be so proud of you. Of how brave you are. Of being so confident in your ability as an artist. I mean, it's your choice if you wanna be poor," I almost smile. Erik looks so indignant. "Your mom should support your artistic endeavors. She was a dancer for God's sake! Your dad is a stiff lawyer, but your mom? She's got a lot of nerve to be pissed at you."

I bite my lip and hope my face doesn't betray the pain of his words. I wish I made my mother proud. Instead, I'm the cause of her anxiety and heartache. But then I could never be as perfect as her. When my father first set eyes on my mother she was a ballerina in *Swan Lake*—of course, she was the swan queen. He watched her perform and was instantly smitten. He had to meet her, so he bribed his way backstage and came face to face with my mom. They both say that when they set eyes on each other they knew instantly that they were meant to be together forever. And to this day, they are still madly in love.

They compliment each other in every way. My mom is small, petite, perfect. My dad, a former football player in high school, is the epitome of the all-American, with his wholesome good looks and easy smile. My mom quit the ballet company and followed my dad to Los Angeles, where he was enrolled in law school at USC.

Now he has a successful criminal law practice and my mom is his rock. She has dedicated her life to him. They never had any other children so all they do is focus on me. Obsessively, I think. They expected me to pursue a career in law and take over the family business. And being the pleaser that I am, I dutifully did as I was told and applied to law school—in Los Angeles, because my parents couldn't bear the thought of me leaving them. I got into my dad's alma mater and was on my way to following in his footsteps. That was the plan. *Was* being the operative word.

And then there's Jerry. Perfectly coiffed, immaculately dressed, and knowledgeable about everything, he is the perfect man. And he looks like George Clooney. I've known him since I was five years old; we played hide and seek when we were kids. He taught me how to ride a bike, spit like a man, and catch frogs. We drifted apart in high school because of our three-year age difference, but we always talked and always remained friends. When Jerry came back from Harvard Law—where else?—he started working for my dad's firm—of course.

I interned there almost a year ago, and one night when we were both working late, Jerry looked at me seriously and said, "Should we just give it a go?"

"Give what a go?" I had no idea what he was talking about.

"Us." He smiled at me, showing perfect dimples. "It seems kind of natural, huh?"

My heart dropped. What was I supposed to say to him? We were friends. I didn't want to lose that.

"I don't know—"

He leaned in quickly and kissed me softly on the lips. I was frozen.

"We're perfectly matched. Our families know one another and like each other." He shrugged as he brushed his hand across my cheek. "It just feels—comfortable."

Comfortable? Huh?

Before I knew it, I was in a comfortable relationship with comfortable kisses, comfortable handholding, and nothing uncomfortable about it.

Two weeks ago. Erik made me see the light. I may not have been ready to have sex with him, but I at least wanted to know that the man

I was going to marry at least *wanted to*. I tried to break up with Jerry via text, I was so chicken shit. But Erik made me do it in person, and even drove me to Jerry's house. He waited down the street while I took a swig of vodka from a flask, a first for me, and walked up to Jerry's house at three a.m.

I rang the doorbell and after a moment Jerry opened it, his hair disheveled from sleep but still looking good in sweat pants and a t-shirt. He was immediately concerned, which made me feel even worse.

"Sophie? What's wrong? Do you know what time it is?"

"I'm breaking up with you," I blurted it out like projectile vomit.

It took a moment for him to register this piece of information. Then he said, "What?"

"I hope we can remain friends," I said and turned around to run straight back to Erik's car, but Jerry took my arm.

"What is wrong with you? We are not breaking up!"

"Yes, we are, Jerry." I pulled my arm away and mustered up what little courage I had. "You can't really tell me that you want this for the rest of your life." I pointed at my body for dramatic effect. I knew I was insulting myself but I didn't care.

"I do. I want you."

"No, you don't," I told him, shaking my head emphatically. "You can't even bear to kiss me! Am I going to stay a virgin *forever?!*"

I'll never forget the look on his face. He was mortified by my question, but then I was humiliated that I even had to ask.

"I was trying to be considerate."

"Considerate?" I practically shouted at him. "Do you know how completely horrible that sounds to me?" *He's Just Not That into You* popped into my mind. Clearly I could have been a case study.

"Yes! There's a family relationship here, Sophie. I'm being respectful. Try to get a grip and understand."

But I felt like sex-starved nymphomaniac.

"There's no passion between us."

He looked so offended by my words that I felt even worse than before.

But for once, Jerry was quiet. How could he deny it? There was no way he could.

"You know I'm right," I rushed out. "I love you like a brother. And if you're honest with yourself, you only love me like a sister."

That was about all I could handle before turning around and running to Erik's car like a bat out of hell. This time, Jerry didn't try to stop me.

The next battle, my parents. I didn't want to disappoint them, but it was inevitable. Jerry is what my dad likes to call "a rising star." He says Jerry exhibits this in his social life and in business. Unfortunately for me, they adore him even more than what the average person would deem normal.

My mom was so upset by the break-up that I think if she had to choose between us, she would have chosen Jerry.

The night I told them, I went home to their place in Brentwood for dinner. I walked through the front door and felt the familiar feeling of home and security, as I always did when I entered their cozy domain. The house is a traditional Cape Cod and my mom had designed the interior as if it were in the Hamptons. As was our ritual, she greeted me at the door.

She always looks so good, never a hair out of place, always immaculately dressed. She's like a little porcelain china doll.

"Where's Jerry?" she asked as she looked over my shoulder.

"He's not coming," I managed to say through my dread.

"Oh? Is he working late, dear?" she asked as she wiped her hands on her apron.

I tried to muster up as much courage as I could.

"Mom, Jerry is never coming with me to this house again." There it was. Out in the open.

"Whatever do you mean, dear?" My mom stopped in her tracks to turn and look at me, a brow raised in surprise.

"I broke up with him." I felt relieved.

My mom was quiet for a moment, then she shrugged and said, "Lover's quarrel. You'll make up."

I hadn't expected that. I needed to be clearer about this. Brutal. It was the only way to get through to her. "No, mom. We are never making up. I'm not in love with him."

"Yes, you are."

"No, actually I'm not."

"*Yes, you are.*"

"Are you really trying to tell me how I feel? I don't love Jerry!" I told her. I couldn't believe we were even arguing about it.

"Oh." I could tell my mom was devastated. She didn't say anything else, but walked to the bar and poured herself a healthy glass of scotch. She downed it in a second, like a pro. I was impressed.

"Are you upset?" I asked as I watched her pour another drink, tap the bar with the cup, and take it down in one swig.

"Why would you think that, dear? It's your life, your choice." I knew she wanted to add *your mistake.*

"Well, thanks for understanding, Mom." I tried to keep the sarcasm out of my voice, but I hoped that my innocent comment would make her feel bad.

"Of course, dear. You know we'll always support you in every decision you make," she said as she headed into the kitchen. I thought I was home free, almost at the finish line, but then my mom can't ever seem to help herself when it comes to me. "Even if you'll never ever find someone as kind, intelligent and handsome as Jerry," she said over her

Mad Love

shoulder before disappearing into the kitchen.

Nice.

I chose not to respond with an equally biting comment because I knew that if the two of us started down this road it would end in tears—only mine, of course—and in my mom inevitably convincing me of the error of my ways.

I'm sure she wonders sometimes if I'm really her daughter or if the hospital made a mistake and swapped me for her real child. If you really analyzed us you would notice that the only similarity we have are our toes, and even those are questionable.

"Speaking of your mom, where did she come up with name Sophie? It's not like she's French. She should have named you Maria or Monica." Erik brings me back to the moment in a second. I'm so glad for him.

"I'm named after my dad's mom."

"I always wondered," he says as he pulls out a Chanel face mist. He gives himself three sprays then holds it out to do my face.

"Close your eyes." I do as I'm told. The mist actually feels great on my skin.

"Thanks." I open my eyes and smile gratefully at my friend.

Erik stares at me for a long moment. He knows me well. He has sat with me through endless tirades about my family, about Jerry, about my desire to be an artist, the many nights all blurred into one, giant, alcohol-induced haze.

"So what's on your mind? Why can't you sleep? Please tell me you're not thinking about Jerry the fairy." He says the last part with a great deal of animosity.

I snort out loud. "He's not—"

"So is. The man never ever tried to have sex with you—"

"Lower your voice!" I hiss at him in agitation as I look around the cabin." He says he was being considerate."

"Considerate?" Erik pauses for a moment. "Do you believe the lies he tells you?"

"Whatever."

"Oh honey, there is so much you have to learn." He pulls a lip balm out of his Goyard make-up bag.

I finally ask out loud the question that has plagued me since the moment Jerry and I started dating. "Maybe he didn't find me attractive?"

"Spare me the mental anguish! Have you looked in the mirror lately?"

I look away from Erik. "You're my friend."

"What I find so damn puzzling about you is how you can be so strong and confident about certain things and so insecure about your own beauty." He shakes his head at me in disappointment.

"Strong and confident because I don't want to live a lie? I can't stand law. I'm just so done with doing what my parents want. I want to live my own dream. Nothing makes me happier than painting. *Nothing*."

"Exactly. You walked away from law school in your second year and then you dumped the man your parents wanted you to be with because it didn't feel right in your heart. That's confidence, babe. That's someone who knows what she wants and won't settle. And yet you don't see the hot woman looking back at you when you look in the mirror. I'm at a goddamn loss."

"*Hot?* Please." He's right about the confidence part. But come on, hot? Me? That's not an adjective I would ever use to describe myself.

Erik looks like he wants to strangle me.

"You're a knock-out. You've got an amazing body. You have perfect brown hair, which happens to have its own natural highlights. Most women pay a hair stylist a lot of money to get that color. You're blessed with great skin, beautiful green eyes, spectacularly long, naturally curly lashes. If you were five inches taller you could have been a model."

"Thanks, I think." I laugh again.

"What? Five feet four inches isn't so bad." He leans over and whispers, "Maybe I can look into those surgeries that stretch people out. I think they do that a lot in Asian countries."

The flight attendant arrives with Erik's drink.

"Thanks." He says and takes a sip.

"I'm totally serious about the surgery, by the way."

"I know you are. But I'm completely okay with being average height."

"Actually, it's called petite, babe."

Erik looks over at his sleeping boyfriend. His jet black hair peeks out from underneath the blanket he has draped over him. "Orie could use a few inches. Maybe we can get a two-for-one deal."

"You're terrible." I shake my head at Erik as I look on the sky map.

Only three more hours to go.

Chapter Two

MY EYES ARE CLOSED again and I'm stretched out in the waiting lounge of the W Spa and Resort. After we landed, we were ushered here by the welcoming committee, which would take us out to the resort in a seaplane. I changed from my plane pajamas into loose pants and a tank top because it's really hot. Orie, who happens to be a famous hairdresser, has braided parts of my hair and artfully pulled it back, a look he tells me will make me blend right in with the island girls. I just go with it.

It's early morning in the Maldives and all I want to do is sleep. Jet lag sucks. I'm using my carry-on bag as a pillow, and Erik and Orie are to the left of me chatting away, completely adjusted and okay with the time difference. They look good. Really, really good. It's unfair. After almost twenty-four hours of flying they look fresh and flawless. Orie's black hair is perfectly combed back from his good-looking face and Erik looks immaculate. On the other hand, it'll take a good scrub and a nap to make me feel like myself again.

I hear voices and know that more guests have entered the resort's private waiting room. I assume they'll be on the seaplane with us to our destination. The guys are quiet for a moment and I know they're checking out the new arrivals, evaluating the other people who'll be at the resort. I decide to take a quick peek myself. I'm instantly glad I have my sunglasses on to conceal my blatant appraisal of the guests.

Wow.

Let me rephrase that. Holy shit.

A vision of a perfect male specimen is in the room. He's standing in a corner and talking to what I assume is one of his friends. He has light brown hair and cerulean blue eyes that are so bright they make my heart skip a beat. His lips are full, sensual, and he's got a straight, perfect nose. His face is utterly masculine and hot. He's tall, really tall, well over six feet, broad shouldered, and is sporting a natural tan that hints at a life spent out in the sun. He looks like he's in his early to mid-thirties and he exudes worldly sophistication. I stop breathing. I can't help it. I think I even might have forgotten how. He is the most good-looking man I've ever set eyes on. He literally looks like a walking piece of art. Erik puts his hand on my leg and squeezes hard. He sees what I see. I ignore him.

But Erik's movement catches the gorgeous man's eye and he glances over him at me. His gaze slowly moves along my outstretched body, lazily assessing me, from my sneaker-clad feet to the top of my head. He stops at my face, staring intently, almost like he can see through me, and I hold my breath again. Does he know I've been looking at him? He can't, I tell myself. He isn't Superman, he can't see through my shades.

But his gaze remains fixed on me, staring so intensely now that it makes me incapable of movement. It's the kind of look Daniel Day Lewis gave Madeline Stowe in *Last of the Mohicans,* when he literally devoured her with his eyes right before he dragged her off for the epic love scene. It is still one of the best love scenes of all time. I used to imagine what it would be like to have someone give me that Hawkeye stare. And now it's happening, for the very first time, from the drop-dead gorgeous stranger.

Erik has a death grip on my leg, clutching it so tight that I think I'm losing circulation. Clearly, he's witness to this most incredible moment, so it can't just be my jet lag or runaway imagination.

The stranger's bright gaze moves to my lips and they part of their own accord.

He smiles.

Oh my God! He knows I'm staring. I close my eyes and try to control the mortification that comes over me. How embarrassing!

I count to ten then open them again.

Shit. He's still looking.

Is my heart still beating?

Since I will just look back I try to save myself the embarrassment and flip around so my back is to him. I need to get a grip. Good Lord, this has never happened to me before. I've seen hot men before. LA is filled with good-looking men and women. What is wrong with me?

I hear a chuckle. *His* chuckle.

It's deep, masculine, and totally sexy. I know it's him. I just know it. Oh Lord, is he laughing at me? Erik leans down nice and close to my ear and whispers in a not-so-very-subtle way.

"Turn around and just stare, babe. He's a shining example of what a sperm and an egg can come up with if they try really hard. He gives me a reason to contemplate breeding. Flawless. Impeccably dressed. And confident as hell. What more can you ask for?"

Lord, Erik is right on the money. I slowly turn around to take another quick peek. My gaze meets his penetrating blue eyes. Oh my. I smile slightly and try to act cool as I look over at the people I think are his friends. He's standing with three other men and two women. They're all expensively dressed with designer handbags and luggage. They reek of sophistication and clearly come from a world of privilege. Suddenly I feel self-conscious in my baggy harem pants and tank top.

There's no smile, no welcoming look, just a piercing gaze like he's trying to see into my soul.

I take my glasses off and turn to Erik and Orie.

"Have. You. Ever?" Erik asks me in a low voice.

I shrug my shoulders. No, I have never. But do I want to say it out loud? What if Mr. Adonis hears me? Before I'm further tortured by my friend a woman from the resort enters the waiting room.

"Welcome to Male. The seaplane is here to take you all to what we know will be a fabulous holiday. Please follow me."

I stand quickly and pick up my carry-on bag. Erik and Orie get distracted gathering their things and I'm blessedly given a reprieve. I keep my head down and start to walk toward the door. His friends follow the woman but Mr. Gorgeous lingers, almost like he's waiting for me to catch up to him. But I know that's just got to be wishful thinking on my part. I try to walk slowly, but I'm next to him in a second. He towers over me but in a good way. A really, good way.

"Can I help you with that?" he asks me politely.

I'm so startled by his question that I'm incapable of speech. I look up at him and hope my mouth hasn't dropped open. Up close he's even better looking. More appealing. How's this even possible? It's so unfair. It's like dangling a piece of chocolate in front of a contestant on *The Biggest Loser*. I look around quickly to be sure he's even talking to me.

"Pardon?" I manage to stumble out.

"Your bag. It seems heavy. Can I help you with it?"

He *is* talking to me. I'm so floored I don't answer him.

"Allow me," he says.

His voice is lyrical, low, sexy. He has a faint accent. Very faint. I wonder where he's from. Even though he's said only a few words, I could listen to him talk all day long. God, maybe being a twenty-three-year-old virgin has made me incapable of small talk with the opposite sex.

"I'm good, thanks," I respond as calmly as possible.

He looks at me for a long moment as if he's weighing my words then cocks his head to the side.

"My name is Clayton Sinclair."

Clayton, I think dreamily to myself. *Clayton*. It's a good name. Strong. Regal. The kind a hero usually has in a period romance novel. And I should know, considering the closest to sex I've ever gotten is from guilty-pleasure reading. I'd die before I'd ever admit that, thank you. I snap back to reality.

Speak, Sophie. Words. Now.

"Sophie Walker," I say back softly.

"Nice to meet you, Sophie," he says with a smile then proceeds to take my bag from my hands. "My mom would be really angry if I let a woman carry a bag I'm perfectly capable of carrying."

He takes it from my hands and I just watch him in bewilderment and say the only thing that comes to mind.

"You really don't have to."

"But I do," Clayton says smoothly. "After you."

Oh my God. Oh my God. Oh my God.

I try to smile, but I can't. I'm just a quivering mass of nerves. I walk past him, acutely aware of my size and his, and wonder what it would be like to be wrapped in his arms. I know it would be a pure, masculine embrace one that envelopes you, sucks you into warmth and passion, then culminates with the kiss you've dreamed about all your life.

Stop. Oh God, stop Sophie, I think in annoyance. My mind is like a bad drunk. Once it starts there's no end in sight. Ever.

I turn around to look for my moral support, Erik and Orie. But they are suspiciously absent and I'm left all alone with the most handsome man I've ever met in my entire life.

I look up at Clayton, who cocks a brow.

"Forget something?"

Just my sanity and the ability to breathe properly. *God, why are you so damn good looking?*

I shake my head. "No. No, I think I'm good," I say again.

"You're fine, Sophie. Don't worry. You'll be taken care of."

My heart flutters at his words. For the briefest second I think what it would be like to be taken care of by someone like him.

Five minutes later I'm sitting across from Clayton on the seaplane. It's hot as hell and I can feel the sweat dripping off my face as the propeller's noise roars through the small cabin. Instead of enjoying the view outside the window, I'm worried whether I'm sweating in a really unattractive way. We're all wearing life jackets in case the plane goes down—not a very comforting thought—and the additional heavy layer doesn't help the heat situation. Erik and Orie are across the aisle taking pictures and having a ball but I'm so nervous about being in such close proximity to this man that I can't even manage a smile or enjoy the experience of being on a seaplane for the first time in my life. His legs are so long they practically cradle mine. It's so intimate I get an adrenaline rush. The windows are slightly cracked in the seaplane to allow a light breeze. Clayton's white linen shirt billows in the wind, exposing a beautifully sculpted, tanned chest. He leans back and laughs at something with his friend, revealing his perfect white teeth.

Seriously? Where's the flaw?

"Take a picture, baby!" Orie shouts out to me. "*Smile, girl!*"

The two lean over their seats and pull me in close. Erik lifts me up with an arm and puts a hand on my leg, squeezing me into his body as Orie takes a snap shot. I'm surprised when I feel another hand on my thigh and it's not Erik's. It literally burns through the thin material of my pants. Hot electricity rushes up my leg. What the hell? I've never felt anything like that before in my life.

"That's really dangerous. You should sit in your seat." I look from Clayton's hand to his face. He's leaned in nice and close to me. I stare at his perfect lips.

Oh Lord, there goes my breath again. Erik doesn't say a word as I move away from him and sit back down. Clayton assumes his position, legs inches from mine, and smiles like he's won something. And I realize he kind of has. I just listened to a complete stranger's orders. What in God's name is wrong with me?

He puts on a pair of dark aviator sunglasses and stares at me. Jesus. They look really good on him.

The short flight to the resort is fast and bumpy but I don't really mind because of the company I'm in. When the plane lands smoothly on the water I'm saved from the possibility of embarrassing myself again. I take a moment and just look at the sheer beauty of the tiny resort island. It is breathtaking. The water is crystal clear, heavenly, and looks extremely welcoming in this heat. Straw-thatched bungalows stretch out over the ocean and I'm struck by the allure as the sun hits the water in a perfect way, creating shimmers of light, like jewels in the sea. It could not be better. If I pictured heaven this is what it would look like. I can't wait to pull out my sketchpad and start a Maldives-themed series. This place is a painter's dream and is already giving me a feeling of sensory overload.

Once the seaplane pulls up to the dock, Clayton gets up and holds out a hand to help me. I blush again from the attention.

"Thanks."

His grip is sure, strong, completely enveloping my hand and sparks shoot through my body. I tingle all over. His touch, a single touch, makes me feel more alive than I have ever felt in all my life. Is this what real attraction is like?

He helps get me out of the plane, which is not so steady on the water as it sways in the current, and I end up falling right into his arms. My hands instinctually reach out and grab his chest for support and I gasp. The man is made of steel. And heat. I feel like I've been burned. Branded. I think I hear his breath hiss and I'm afraid I've landed too hard against him.

"I'm so sorry," I say lamely.

"Don't be." He helps me regain my balance on the dock and then clicks open my life vest. "Let me help you with this."

I keep reminding myself that I just met this man and here I am letting him hold my bag, take my life jacket off, and generally act like he's known me forever.

"I've got that," I tell him shyly. My hands move up and are instantly entangled in his. It happens again. The jolt runs up and down my spine. I look up at him, wondering if he felt it too, but I can't read him.

"It's done," Clayton says softly as the jacket comes open. I step away from him quickly, needing space to breathe properly again. And not to be consumed by the heat of him.

Chapter Three

WE STAND UNDER THE canopy next to the seaplane and wait for the W Maldives staff to take us to our villas. I look over at Erik and Orie and step close to them, needing their protection. Clayton stands a few feet away, stares at me for a second more then turns toward his friends, who've been watching the entire scenario closely. The women, I note, don't look too happy with me or with him.

Three women from the resort walk over with wet towels and drinks. I take both gladly. I wipe my face with the towel and then take a long sip of the drink. I notice that Erik and Orie are suspiciously quiet. I raise a brow.

"What?"

"You know what," Erik whispers.

"I think you might get laid on this trip," Orie says a bit too loudly.

I almost spit out my drink.

"Orie!" My face turns red as I quickly look around to see if anyone heard him. And by anyone, I mean *him.*

"What? It's about time, girl," he says innocently. "You're the last of your kind. Who else do you know who's a virgin at twenty-three? It's a sacrilege."

"He's right, you know," Erik chimes in with a smile. "It's kind of like the worst thing I've ever heard."

I can't even manage a response.

"There's gotta be cobwebs in there by now," he continues as he sips his drink. "It can't be too pretty."

Orie holds out his drink and clinks with Erik. "Here's to our girl finally arriving at the party."

I choke on my drink this time and Erik hits me on the back. Are they serious? I look over to where Clayton is standing with his friends and notice that his arms are crossed and his head is tilted slightly to the side. Almost like he's listening. There's a small smile on his face, maybe from something his friends said or from the TMI that my friends have blurted out to the world. Who knows? But in any case, I feel like Renee Zellweger in the movie *Bridget Jones's Diary,* when she walks into the party wearing a bunny costume when it wasn't a dress-up party and everyone else was wearing normal clothes. Except in my case, girl in bunny outfit means VIRGIN. Oh my God, I think I really am going to die.

"Would you guys *please* lower your voices?" I manage to mutter. Erik raises his brows and shrugs his shoulders.

"You can't fault a guy for being honest."

Before I can give them both a proper lecture on the merits of abstinence, a nice-looking gentleman dressed in white linen pants and shirt walks over to us.

"Miss Sophie Walker?" he asks with a smile.

"Yes."

Mad Love

"I'm Iain Summers, the general manager. It is a pleasure to have you here with us at the W Spa & Resort."

"Thank you so much. These are my friends, Erik Johnson and Orie Pratt."

"Lovely to meet you all." Iain motions toward a young Indian man. "This is Bikram. He will be your butler for the duration of your stay."

A butler? This resort really is no joke. Bikram smiles at us cordially. I like him instantly.

"Nice to meet you, Bikram," we all say.

"Miss Walker, Mr. Johnson and Mr. Pratt, welcome to our island. If you're ready, I would like to show you to your bungalow now." Bikram speaks with a thick accent. He has a general sense of calm about him that you don't see too often. Who wouldn't, I think to myself as I look around at the general splendor. Working in heaven every day would be anyone's dream.

We grab our carry-on luggage and follow Bikram to the golf cart that he's using to take us to our bungalow. We pass Clayton and his friends, who are now talking to Iain. He is laughing, but looks over at me and nods. I blush and look away. He's too good looking for words. I'm thankful the golf cart is waiting to take me away from drooling over his perfection. Bikram gets in the driver's seat, Erik and Orie take the middle seats, and I am unfortunately left at the back of the cart facing behind, which happens to be toward Clayton and his friends. I pretend to study my manicure so I won't stare. Again.

"Isn't this unbelievable?" Erik says in excitement as the cart drives off.

"It's heaven," I agree.

I turn around to face them and smile as Orie and Erik lean into each other, holding hands. They are so in love. I'm so happy for them. This is the perfect setting for romance and it makes me long for what they have. A companion. A lover. A mate. I wonder if it will ever happen.

Bikram takes a left off the dock and heads away from the overwater villas, which have a panoramic view of the Indian Ocean. We've booked a beach bungalow because it's a bit cheaper. I'm happy with it but I do kind of wish that we were staying in an overwater one. Perched on top of the ocean every day like that would surely be the experience of a lifetime. My gaze settles on a giant villa that sits at the end of the long wooden path that leads along a row of villas that rest on the sea. Bikram motions toward them.

"Those are the Seascape Villas and at the end is the Ocean Haven."

"It is enormous!" I'm sure he can hear the awe in my voice. What kind of people get to stay there?

"Yes, it is unbelievable, too. The villa is fifty-two hundred square feet, with a living room and two bedrooms. It is really fantastic. Very luxurious. It is the jewel of the Maldives."

"How much does it go for?" Orie asks curiously. I'm glad he does because I'm dying to know.

"It is about fifteen thousand American dollars a night right now, in high season."

"Wow," I say.

"So it's like the Hope Diamond of villas?" Orie says to Bikram, who laughs at his comparison.

"Yes, I guess you could call it that, Mr. Pratt." Bikram says.

"Is it booked?" Orie is never afraid to ask anything. Nothing fazes or embarrasses him. Another one of the amazing qualities I love about him.

"Yes, sir, a guest has just booked the villa for fifteen nights. I believe he's checking in today. He is a returning guest. He stayed with us last year for fifteen days as well."

"That's . . ." Orie whistles softly.

"A lot of fucking money," Erik finishes.

My thoughts exactly.

Bikram smiles. "Yes, Mr. Pratt. It is *a lot* of money."

"Must be nice," Orie says with a smile, but I know he could care less. Money has never been a driving force for him. He's more of a live-your-passion kind of guy.

We head down a white sandy path, off the beach and deeper into the lush, tropical island. I marvel at all the foliage and vibrant colors of this small paradise. The beach villas blend in well with the jungle vegetation. I'm struck again by the awesome picture, the live canvas of art that is right here every day for guests to see.

Bikram continues down the velvet sandy path and gives us a quick tour of the resort. Almost all the restaurants are centrally located in one pocket of the island next to the main u-shaped beach and are accessible on foot. All the restaurants and the gym are clustered close together. We're surprised to hear that there's a small underground dance club on the island that is open three nights a week. We're told that we can ask for bikes, but honestly everything is so close that I can't imagine why you'd need them.

The spa is located in a giant villa across from the overwater guest villas. It looks like the ultimate sanctuary. I can't wait to have a massage.

Everything is so tastefully done and just reeks of relaxation. Bikram tells us that they have yoga and water classes for free every morning in the main guest pool, which is next to the restaurant where they serve breakfast. We all quickly decide to attend the following day.

"I can book any treatment for you at the spa at any time. There are many wonderful options. And we are very pleased to have Noom with us right now."

"Who is she?" I ask.

"She is a crystal energy healer," Bikram tells us. "She is very famous here on the island. Lots of Hollywood celebrities come to see her."

"Really?" Erik asks. "Hollywood celebrities, huh?"

"Yes, sir. She can cure anything, from physical to mental ailments."

Erik immediately turns to look at me. "You've gotta see her."

Gee, thanks. Do I look like I need that much help, I think.

"Yes, you do," Erik says, obviously reading my mind.

"Would you like me to book a session with Noom for tomorrow, Miss Walker?"

"Yes, please," I say. If I don't do it, I know Erik will for me. Who knows? Maybe Noom will be able to help me.

"Around ten o'clock, after your breakfast?" Bikram asks me pleasantly.

"That sounds perfect." Well, great. I haven't been here for a day and I'm already in therapy. I guess I can't complain, because I did come here to have an awakening of sorts.

Bikram makes a quick turn and heads down another path, away from the main resort buildings but still along the sea. He soon pulls up to a straw-thatched bungalow.

"We have you booked at the Beach Oasis."

We jump off the cart and follow Bikram as he opens the door to our bungalow. I gasp in pleasure. It is spectacular. We have a cozy living area that leads into the master room with a king-sized bed that looks welcoming and plush with its crisp, white bedding. There's a staircase in the living area that goes up to a deck with views across the sea, for daytime or an evening of star gazing. We also have a private sundeck with access to the white sand beach. And our own circular daybed that sits next to a plunge pool I can't wait to jump into.

We walk back into the living room and Bikram opens another door.

"And this is your connecting oasis, with a twin bed for Miss Walker. You also have your own private bath." The room is pretty and I'm really happy but I can't help but frown at the twin bed. Will I always sleep on a twin bed alone?

How sad.

"This is *so* cute," Erik says as he comes up behind me and puts his hands on my shoulders.

He's no dummy. He knows how this looks. He knows what I'm thinking. *You are pathetic,* my mind screams at me. What were you thinking? Coming to the Maldives, the most romantic place in the world, all alone?

"You don't like it?" Bikram asks in concern. He can't miss the frown on my face.

"Oh no, no, Bikram. It is unreal. This is all so wonderful. Thank you," I quickly answer, hoping I haven't offended him in the slightest. It's not his fault I'm a spinster. Or a loser. Or a twenty-three year old virgin loser.

Bikram doesn't look convinced, so I smile brightly at him and hope I'm a good actress. "I love this."

He nods slowly then motions toward our luggage, which we notice is already in the room.

"Please enjoy your stay, and if you need anything, I am at your service. I will confirm your appointment with Noom for tomorrow, Miss Walker."

"Thank you, Bikram."

Before he leaves, he pauses at the door. "I almost forgot to tell you that tomorrow night is our end of days party on the beach. I would be more than happy to book you a table."

"End of days?" I ask curiously.

"Yes, tomorrow is a holy day. According to the old island-dwellers, it is either the end of the world as we know it or a rebirth. It is a very spiritual time. We will celebrate life tomorrow night."

Huh. If it's the end, I'm dying a virgin. I know Erik and Orie will be more than happy to point this out.

"Please make a reservation. We will be there to celebrate with you all," Orie tells him.

Bikram leaves us to our oasis. We are all quiet for a moment.

"Sophie, there's hope for you yet. Maybe the Holy Ghost will pay you a visit tomorrow night." Erik says to me with a mischievous grin.

"That's just rude," I tell him pointedly. "And blasphemous."

"Oh shit. Did our girl just throw a five-dollar word at us?" Orie laughs.

I look for something tangible to throw at them both and then the reality of where we are settles in. This is really paradise. We are the luckiest people alive. The three of us immediately start jumping up and down in pure happiness.

"Let's put our bathing suits on right now and jump in the pool!" Orie says eagerly.

"I'll pop open a bottle of champagne!" Erik chimes in.

I stop myself from demanding that Erik check the price before he does anything drastic. *Sophie, you chose this place. You wanted to come here,* my mind scolds. *Okay, okay,* I say back grouchily, I just don't want to blow my wad, considering my parents were adamant about not giving me a dollar for this trip. Alright! I'll forget my finances just for the day.

I walk into my room and look at the twin bed and actually start to laugh. It's pretty funny. Well, funny in a sad kind of way, but I can't dwell on it. It is what it is. I quickly change into my favorite black bikini, unbraid my hair, and let it flow down over my shoulders. I go back into the main room. Erik and Orie already have their swim trunks on and are sipping champagne. Erik hands me a glass.

"Cheers, bitch. Here's to having the time of our lives."

Mad Love

"Cheers." We all take a sip.

"Let's get in the pool!" I shout out happily.

As we head out, the phone rings. Orie runs over and grabs it as Erik jumps into the pool with a loud splash and I follow him. The water is cool and refreshing and feels great. I dunk my head in the water. I feel good now. This is exactly what I need. Orie walks over to the edge of the pool holding the cordless phone in his hand and a look of amazement on his face.

"You guys are never going to believe this."

"Tell me now," Erik demands.

"They're upgrading us to an overwater villa. Sophie gets her own villa and so do we, babe!"

"No way." I don't believe him. It's impossible.

"The resort has room and I guess the way we booked our reservation we qualified for an upgrade or something," Orie quickly explains.

"But I don't understand. How?" I'm definitely excited but I just don't know how it's possible.

"What's there to understand?" Erik says as he jumps out of the pool and grabs a towel from one of the lounge chairs. "Let's take it before they change their minds!"

"So get out of the pool, Sophie! Bikram is coming to get us now." Orie yells at me as he starts throwing their items back into their luggage.

I laugh at the two of them. As if there was a chance in hell that we wouldn't take it?

"Okay, okay! I'm coming." I'm happy. Fine, really happy about this sudden change of fortune. It's like I wished for it by the dock and got it. Why can't everything in my life work this way?

I'm standing in my overwater villa staring out into the sea and can't believe our luck. Erik and Orie are next door and the happiest I think I've ever seen them. They've put us at the very end of the dock, right next to the giant Ocean Haven. My personal villa is unbelievable. I have a king bed, my own private plunge pool overlooking the ocean, and a sitting area, complete with every amenity a girl could ever desire. Bikram informed me that I can order a barbeque at my villa for dinner if I want. He tells me it's a very popular way to dine. I think I'm going to try and convince the guys to partake tonight, although I'm pretty sure they're going to want to check out the other guests in the restaurant and scope the general nightlife situation.

I look out on the ocean and take a deep breath. The sea is so soothing. Talk about Zen and being able to find my very own peace here, I'm already never wanting to leave. Is eleven days enough? I can't wait to pull out my pencils and sketchpads and get started on my view.

The phone rings and I'm jolted back to the moment. I walk inside to answer it, knowing it's probably Erik and Orie freaking out in joy.

I pick up the phone and gush. "I know, I know. I'm dying too. This is incredible!" I say, giddy with excitement. "It's like early Christmas!"

"I'm glad you like your room," a sexy voice I remember oh so well says back to me.

Oh. My. God.

I can't seem to find my voice. How did he find me? Okay, easy enough. *Why* did he find me? Why on earth is he calling me?

"Sophie? It's Clayton."

"Uh. Hi." I try to sound calm and cool. "I'm so sorry, I thought my friends were calling me." My voice wavers unsteadily and I know I must sound like a complete idiot.

"That's not a problem," he says. I can almost feel his smile through the phone. "This place is quite spectacular."

You're spectacular, I think to myself as I smile like a cheeseball. My mind wanders to dreamland. I try to think of something clever to say back but I draw blanks.

"Yeah."

Yeah? That's all I can think of? What a loser. There's that awkward silence again.

"Are you staying in an overwater villa?" I quickly ask.

"Yes. I've stayed here once before, so I knew what to expect when I arrived."

He's stayed here before? Probably with a girlfriend or something.

"Alone?" I spout out before I can stop myself. Oh no. What is wrong with me?

"I'm so sorry! You don't have to answer that," I quickly blurt before he can speak. Why am I so awkward? Why would I even ask him that question? I have no right. I don't even know the guy!

He laughs into the phone. And it sounds so sexy, even though it's at my expense. "It's quite alright. It's an appropriate question. I did come with someone the last time I was here."

Probably a model, I think sullenly. I bet he only dates Victoria's Secret models. The crème de la crème. The ones in the Angel fashion show televised every year. The ones who make every hot-blooded heterosexual man drool with desire.

"It is a very romantic place," I say. Understatement of the century. Try, it's like the most romantic setting a couple could ever wish for.

"It is. But I was here with the wrong person."

Oh?

I can't stop the rush of pleasure I feel from those words. Visions of me being the right person flash through my mind. I picture us holding hands, walking along the beach, staring into each other's eyes—

Sophie! I quickly pull myself out of my reverie and give him a suitable answer.

"We've all been there." There. That sounds cool. To be honest, I've never actually traveled on vacation with a man before so I have no idea what he's talking about, but he doesn't need to know that. And it doesn't take a brain surgeon to know that being here with someone you love or are, at the very least, massively sexually attracted to, would be the vacation of a lifetime.

"Have you?" he asks, and there's a sharp tone in his voice.

"No," I answer honestly, but my hand smacks my forehead in horror. Why did I just say that? Me and my verbal diarrhea! I'm supposed to make myself sound worldly!

"But I've heard stories from my friends."

"Ahh." The amusement is back. I throw myself on the bed and close my eyes with the shame of it all. Why don't I possess the skills of a cool chick?

"Yeah, well, I hope you have a better experience this time." This is the lamest thing I can say, but all I want to do is get off the phone now before I embarrass myself even further. And let's be real, it is entirely possible, given the conversation so far.

"I think I will. It's definitely looking better already."

Did I hear him correctly? Is it possible that he could be referring to me? The thought is too good to be true.

He continues smoothly, "I'm having my friends over to my villa for dinner and drinks tonight. I'd love for you and your friends to join us."

My heart stops.

Am I dreaming? He's inviting me over for dinner? In less than three seconds I picture myself arriving in a long, beautiful gown, with my hair perfectly curled, fake lashes and all. Oh shit. Did I even bring anything appropriate to wear? I think I only have summer dresses and flip flops. I wonder how late the gift shop is open?

"So what do you think?" He asks when I don't answer.

"Umm, sounds great." I hope I don't sound too excited.

"Great. Everyone is arriving from their rooms at seven pm. I'm in the Ocean Haven. It's the bungalow at the end of the walkway. From your room number I think you might be close by."

Close by?

Try right next door. *He's staying in the Ocean Haven,* I tell myself. That's fifteen thousand American dollars a night! Forget that! He's right next door to me.

Right. Next. Door.

I get up off the bed and walk out to the deck and stare at the wooden wall separating us. Okay, there's some water separating us too, but still, we are really close.

"Umm, yeah. Okay. Sounds good," I manage. I try to keep my voice down, thinking in paranoia that he can hear me walking around the deck. He obviously can't, but I do have an active imagination.

"See you tonight, Sophie."

"Bye." We both hang up at the same time. I let out the breath of air that I've been holding inside. Of all the odds?!

He's the best looking man I've ever seen in my life. He's staying in the biggest villa on the same damn resort. And he's right next door to me. I have to tell Erik and Orie. I grab the phone and before I can hit the talk button, it rings again. This time, I answer way more coolly.

"Hello?"

"Did you plan on calling your mother and me to tell us you got there safely?" my father's voice practically screams through the phone.

Oh shit.

I totally forgot to call my dad.

"Sorry dad. We literally just got here."

"That's not true, Sophie. Your plane landed three hours ago. We tracked your flight." Ugh. I forgot how anal retentive my father is.

"Dad, you should have been CIA."

"I find no humor in that statement."

"I'm sorry, dad. I've just been overwhelmed by this place. You and mom would love it here. It's so unbelievable," I tell him apologetically.

"It should be. You're spending your life's work on this vacation."

Really?

"I wouldn't have to if you had paid me more as an intern," I argue back. "I'm lucky I was even able to save a dollar with the salary you gave me."

Silence.

Okay, maybe that wasn't the smartest thing to say to my dad when he's already pissed off at me. But let's be real, it's not like I got any special treatment because I was his daughter. Still, he is my father and I love him and I've thrown a lot at him and my mom these past couple of weeks.

"I'm sorry. I didn't mean it. I'm just tired from jet lag." My tone has lost the bite.

"I accept your apology." His voice is filled with concern as he says, "Your mother and I just want what's best for you."

"I know, daddy," I tell him, sighing loud enough that I hope he can hear. "But what you want and what I want are two different things."

"Sophie, do you know how hard it is to make a living as an artist?"

Here we go again, I think to myself. The gates have opened and my dad is definitely going to attack. I walk outside and lay down on a sun chair. I stare out at the ocean and prepare myself for the argument he's been giving me since I shocked the shit out of him with my decision.

The glimmer on the water distracts me. It is really quite spectacular. I think of Clayton and smile. I should paint a profile shot of him staring out over the sea. That would be a pretty hot painting.

He doesn't notice that I haven't answered him.

"Being an artist is not an easy dream. How many Van Gogh's were there? Picasso? Warhol? Only one. Those are the names you know and remember. Success like theirs is like winning the lotto."

I state the obvious. "I know it's not easy, dad. I'm not saying it's going to be." He's right, of course. My logical father has a rational way of looking at things, but still. Nothing is easy in life. And as my father, shouldn't he be encouraging me? Telling me that I'm so talented that if I work hard enough I could potentially be one of the greats?

"I love you, honey. But listen to me. Pick something that you have a fighting chance at, for the love of God!"

"Shouldn't you be encouraging me to follow my dreams?"

"Not if your dream is barely going to support you and cause needless heartache from all the rejection."

"Gee, thanks for believing in my abilities, dad."

"I do believe in your abilities. Your mother and I think you're exceptionally talented. But honey, you live in Los Angeles, a city where you see struggling actors, actresses, writers, directors, every day. Being a painter is no different. I thought you were smarter than they are."

"I've never claimed to be smarter than anyone. All I know is that I'm good. And it makes me so happy, in a way that nothing else does. Don't you want that?" I fight the tears that threaten to fall from hearing the censure and sting in my father's voice.

"Of course I want that. What kind of person do you think I am? If it makes you so happy, paint on the weekends." That's *his idea* of a compromise.

"Dad, I've watched you all my life. You are prepping for cases on the weekend or if you're not doing that you are so exhausted you just want to relax. And I don't blame you for it." He needs to hear this. I need to make him really hear me. "I don't love law like you do. I just don't. Please understand me. None of this is personal. None of this has anything to do with you and mom. It's just me. And it's what I want and need to make me happy."

There's a long silence as my father digests my words. Finally, he lets out a breath and sighs.

"I just don't understand, honey. Try and help me wrap my head around this chain of events. A short while ago you were enrolled in law school and doing very well, especially for someone who doesn't 'love it,' as you say. You were dating Jerry, a man you've known all your life. A man your mother and I love—""

"Then the two of you can date him." The words pop out before I can stop them.

"Watch your tone, young lady."

"I'm sorry, but Jerry is none of your business, Dad. That's my personal business and I don't want to talk about it. And honestly, you of all people should at least support me in my decision to break up with him. All my life you've told me the story of how it was love at first sight with mom. And you just knew. Don't you want that for me too?"

There's a long silence again. I know my dad is thinking about all the things I've said. And I know he doesn't appreciate them one bit. But tough. This is me. Or at least, this is the new me.

"For someone who has no interest in being an attorney, you sure know how to win an argument."

"That has nothing to do with law school. I grew up watching my father, who happens to be the best trial attorney around, win almost all the time. It was inevitable that I picked up a thing or two." My voice is raw with emotion and I know he can hear it.

"I love you, Sophie. You know that. Your mother and I just want you to have everything we didn't."

"Everything you didn't, but not everything you did?"

"Sophie—"

"Dad, you guys had the freedom to choose your professions and each other. Give your daughter that same gift."

"We'll talk about it when you get home."

This is code for I'm not convinced and neither is your mom, and we know what's best for you.

"Alright, Dad." I'm only saying what he wants to hear to give him some peace of mind over the next few days. I have no intention of talking about it anymore. "I have to go and meet up with Erik and Orie," I say. I want to get off the phone. "Love you, Daddy."

"Love you, too."

Before I hang up, I can't help but ask, "Does mom hate me?"

"Your mother could never hate you, sweetie." He pauses for a moment. "She's just disappointed."

Knife.

Straight through the heart.

"Bye, Dad."

"Be safe," he says to me before he hangs up. I close my eyes and stretch out on the lounge chair, suddenly exhausted by it all, and let the sizzling sun soothe some of my problems away. I'm dead asleep within seconds.

Chapter Four

A FEW HOURS LATER, I'm awakened by splashing in front of my villa. I look out to see Erik and Orie swimming in circles in the water. They look like you'd picture ancient, exquisite merman. I walk to the edge of the deck and stretch. The nap definitely helped with my mood and jet lag.

I slowly peel off my t-shirt and stand in my bikini. Okie whistles loudly in admiration.

"Hot bod!"

"You look so skinny," Erik says in approval. Erik loves skinny. I joke with him that this disease came over him when he moved from Oregon to Los Angeles, because in LA everyone is obsessed with their weight. It's not uncommon to hear people say things like, "The skinnier the better," "You look amazing . . . Did you lose weight?" "If she's throwing up, it's done wonders for her body," and my personal favorite, "She looks so emaciated, almost like a bobble head. I'm so jealous."

"You have mental issues and suffer from body image dysmorphia," him as I roll my eyes.

"I'm completely okay with that," he answers with a smile.

I change the topic. The last thing I want to do is have a discussion about being skinny. All I want is to have a pizza sent to the villa.

"How long have I been sleeping?"

"Three hours," Erik says as he swims closer to the deck. He splashes water at me and it feels great.

"You're lucky you don't burn," Orie says with envy.

"That's the Italian in me." My mom has told me that her mother and her friends used to compete to see who could lay out in the sun the longest. Apparently, my grandma would always win, and the only protection she used was olive oil, which she rubbed generously over her body. Dead serious. And no joke, my grandma has the best skin ever.

I walk inside and grab my iPhone out of my purse and plug it into the dock in the room. I quickly search for some music and stop on Rhianna's "We Found Love." I blast it and walk back outside to watch my friends.

"Get in the water!" Orie demands.

I look down at the water and shrug. Ocean, especially deep ocean, has always scared me. I think of sharks and sting rays. Mainly sharks.

Okay, just *Jaws*.

"It's too deep over here. I prefer the shallow area where you can see what's beneath you."

"Why?" Orie asks in surprise.

"She's scared of sharks." I can hear the laughter in Erik's voice.

"Girl, there are no sharks here. At least not the ones that bite people. This water is crystal clear."

I shake my head at him and point down toward the sandy beach, which seems far away but in reality is probably a five-minute swim. "It's clear over there. Not here. We're too far out. And there are sharks.

Bikram specifically said they have the black tip sharks here."

"Those don't bite. And they're two feet long," Orie answers.

"They could. They're sharks. That's what sharks do. And the way my luck is going, I'll be the first victim of a shark attack in the Maldives."

"She's got a point, Orie."

I nod at Erik, silently thanking him.

"So you're never going to get in the water? You're not going to snorkel?" It seems that Orie is unable to let this go.

"Of course I am." I roll my eyes and point to the shore. "But I'm going to get in the water over there and I'm going to stay over there."

"Where it's barely even two feet deep?" Orie cocks his head to the side and looks at me like I've grown two heads.

"Uh-huh," I say.

I sit down on the deck and let my legs dangle over the edge.

"Considering the island people think tomorrow is the end of the world and you're a virgin, don't you think you should take some chances?" Erik asks. I can't stop the laughter that escapes me.

"Why are you so funny?"

"I don't fucking know." He swims farther away and I squint to see if I can see any fins. "I'm serious though. What if tonight is your last night in the world?"

"Then she's fucked," Orie laughs.

"Well, we hope she's finally fucked," Erik practically shouts before dunking under the water and disappearing.

That's when I remember who my neighbor is.

Before I can start obsessing, I hear a splash and see a body move through the water, right into our space. The space in front of my deck, to be exact. And it's him. Clayton. He swims up and treads water near Erik and Orie. Holy shit. He didn't hear this conversation, did he? I hear another splash and see his two male friends swim over.

I wave at him awkwardly and am suddenly self-conscious of my half-naked body. I feel exposed on the deck by myself, my figure up for his perusal. I fidget nervously, wondering if it would be weird if I stood up and covered myself with a towel. No, not a good idea. I'd have to walk to get it and then he'd have an even clearer view. What if he thinks my butt is too big? Or too skinny? Or that it's flat? I stop myself instantly by choosing to remain utterly still. I try not to breathe, because inhaling and exhaling, as we all know, makes the stomach stretch in and out.

"Hey man!" Erik says. "I'm Erik. This is Orie, my boyfriend. We didn't get to meet you earlier."

"Clayton," he says politely in that voice that is amazing. "This is John Maitland and Eduard Percy." John is slightly overweight and has strawberry-blond hair and Eduard looks like the famous Ralph Lauren Polo model. The guys exchange pleasantries.

"I know you've met Sophie." Erik says.

"Yes. I had the pleasure." Clayton looks directly at me when he answers the question.

"Nice to meet you, guys."

I start to feel the burn on my skin and it has nothing to do with the sun. It's him. He's staring at me again, in that crazy way that makes me think he's not from this planet or something. How can he make me feel like this from a distance? Just from a look? He holds my gaze while he asks Erik, "Did she tell you about my party this evening?"

"No, she didn't," Orie chimes in, raising a brow at me as he treads water.

"I've invited my friends to my villa for dinner and drinks. I'd love you guys to join us."

The sun hits him in all sorts of delicious ways. His hair is slicked back, his blue eyes are like bright beams shooting out of his face. His shoulders ripple as he easily treads water. His body is perfect, sculpted like he works out hard- and often. It's all a girl can take. I'm about to tell him that of course we'll come and ask if we can bring something, when Erik answers for me.

"We actually have dinner reservations at the restaurant, but maybe we'll stop by after."

If we were in a club, the music would have come to an astounding scratching halt. I look over at Orie, and even he seems shocked. Huh? I think I see a flash of real annoyance on Clayton's face before it's politely disguised.

"That's too bad. Sophie didn't mention that when we spoke."

All eyes turn to me. I stare at all the men in the water, trying to figure out the right thing to say. I'm saved from stammering out a ridiculous excuse from the same friend who put me in the situation in the first place.

"That's because Sophie didn't know the plans. Orie and I made them while she was napping. It's our first night here and we want to celebrate together." I'm wondering what Erik's game is. He's usually the first to be spontaneous. But not this time. This is when he decides to play it cool?

Just my lousy luck.

"Of course. I hope you'll make it after dinner," Clayton says quietly, looking at me in that way that literally makes my toes curl. I want to launch myself at him from the dock and ask that he take me to his villa and have his way with me but I can't. I just met him. I don't even know how old he is. Or what he does for a living. Or his sign. I know nothing about him, and yet I can't deny the intense desire and undeniable attraction I have for him.

"Sophie." Clayton nods at me, then disappears into the water and swims away. His form is perfect, quite beautiful actually. He's like a great God of the sea. No joke. Literally, a god. His friends follow suit and when they're far enough away, I narrow my eyes at Erik.

Orie takes the words right out of my mouth. "I'd like to know why you did that."

"That makes two of us," I whisper furiously. Erik swims up to the deck and Orie follows. He does not look apologetic. He grabs hold of the wooden railing on the stairs that sink into the ocean.

"I have my reasons."

"Care to share them?" I'm annoyed and it shows. "He's the best looking, most spectacular guy I've ever encountered in my life!"

"I know. You've been eye-fucking him the whole time you've been sitting here."

I flush in embarrassment.

"In your defense, he's been eye-fucking you, too." I flush again for all sorts of other reasons.

"Really?" I'm so pathetic.

"Sophie!" Erik is irritated and acts as though he's speaking to a child. "This guy is the real deal. He's got pussy flying at him from every direction."

"I resent that. I'm not that obvious!" I say to him even though I'm not quite sure. But how dare he even insinuate such a thing? Well shit, I was just daydreaming.

"You got caught red handed with your fingers in the cookie jar. I can see it, smell it, a mile away."

I blush. "My version of the cookie jar is way different than yours."

"I know, babe. Your version is the G-rated one where you hold hands and peck, with a goddamn pre-school song playing in the background. But mine and Clayton's is the X-rated one. Hard core. Straight up. Porn."

My heart is in my throat. Visions of Clayton's hands, mouth, and tongue run through my mind.

"Are you serious right now?" I ask in shock.

They both look at me like I'm the crazy one. Erik raises a brow.

"Fine. Since you prefer the lecture, I'll continue." And he does. "You're in way over your head right now and I'm going to bring you back to reality before this turns into a shit storm. You need to play it cool, bitch. Cool as a cucumber." Erik pauses a moment. "And Orie and I need to teach you what to do with that cucumber, by the way."

"Pronto," Orie finally speaks.

"Oh my God. I don't need to know what to do with a cucumber. Actually, I don't *want* to know what to do with one. Thank you for the offer, though." I stand and put my hands on my hips as I stare down at the two of them.

"Yes, you do," Erik says as he climbs onto my deck. "You've been dying to know what sex is like since you set eyes on that man. And I don't blame you. But I sure as hell am not going to let you go to him ready, willing, on a goddamn silver platter waiting to be taken. What kind of friend would I be if I let that happen?"

I try to stay angry, but I can't. Fine. He has a point. But what is all this talk about platters, and willing, and sex? Sex! I dated and knew Jerry for . . . how long? In fact, if I'm honest with myself, I probably could have pushed him into an intimate relationship. But now I think there was a part of me that just didn't want it with him.

And before Jerry there was only one other guy that I ever even came close to being intimate with and it was such a traumatic experience that it scarred me as an undergrad. His name was Adrian and I met him freshman year at UCLA. He was a junior and played for the varsity tennis team. We met at a party on campus and instantly hit it off. He was two years older, super charming, and boyishly handsome and had the cutest dimples. He asked me to go to the movies with him the next night and I agreed. The only film that wasn't sold out was *Toy Story 3* and since we were practically the only ones in the theater we ended up making out through the entire feature.

When the credits rolled he invited me to his fraternity house for an after-hours party. I was too naïve to see the writing on the wall, but Erik later said there was no way I could have anticipated what would happen.

It was a typical college party, everyone getting hammered, couples making out, and music blaring loudly.

Adrian leaned down and had to practically shout in my ear, "Wanna see my room?"

I desperately wanted to be cool so I agreed, against my better judgment. "Sure."

As I followed him up the steps, I was pretty sure I was making a monumental mistake, but then I kept telling myself that Adrian had a good reputation on campus, and if he offered me a drink that I thought might be roofied (yes, I was that paranoid) I wouldn't take it. He ushered me into his room. His walls were covered with Agassi and McEnroe posters and he had a white wrought iron queen-size bed with a hot pink duvet and pillows, which I did find rather odd.

"It's dope, isn't it?" he said to me with a smile.

"It's very pink," I said.

"I dig pink." Adrian shrugged. "I'm totally in touch with my feminine side, ya know?"

"Yeah," I said, thinking how sweet it was that he was so sensitive. "I totally get it."

"You're cute, Sophie," he stroked my cheek. "Too cute."

Was being too cute a good or bad thing, I wondered?

"Umm, thanks," I said as I nervously tugged on my ponytail.

"I'm gonna use the bathroom and I'll be right back," he told me. "Don't disappear."

I shook my head. "No."

I watched him walk into his private bathroom and my gaze quickly scanned the room and found a plastic folding chair in the corner. I moved it as far away from the bed as possible and sat down, crossed my boot-cut jean clad legs (yes, I was wearing those), and nervously waited for Adrian to reappear. My BlackBerry vibrated in my pocket.

I wasn't surprised to see that it was Erik.

Erik: I'M DYING. TELL ME EVERYTHING.

I smiled and quickly texted back.

Sophie: I'M IN HIS ROOM.

I knew that would get him thinking. The phone vibrated back immediately with his answer.

Erik: HOLY SHIT! ARE YOU NAKED?

I tried not to laugh.

Sophie: NO! DON'T YOU KNOW ME? HE'S IN THE BATHROOM.

Erik: WHAT'S HIS ROOM LIKE?

I looked around, trying to find an appropriate way to describe it.

Sophie: HE HAS A LOT OF TENNIS POSTERS . . . AND A WHITE WROUGHT IRON BED . . .

I could feel Erik thinking through the BlackBerry and then—

Erik: WHAT COLOR ARE HIS SHEETS?

I took a moment before I answered, debating whether or not I should tell him.

Sophie: HOT PINK.

The phone didn't vibrate back and I was worried that Adrian would walk out of the bathroom and I'd be caught texting.

Sophie: GOTTA GO. CALL YOU WHEN I GET HOME. LUV U.

Just as I put the phone back in my pocket, the door to the bathroom opened and my worst nightmare was realized.

There he stood, a very naked Adrian in all his glory. His hands were on his hips and he faced me head on (no pun intended), forcing me to take it all in—and by all, there wasn't much to write home about.

"So whaddya think?" he said as he lazily strolled toward me.

I was too shocked to move. Or speak.

"Cat got your tongue?" he smiled as he came to stand right in front of my face, his privates gazing back at me.

I closed my eyes in horror.

"What are you doing?" I stuttered.

"I'm getting ready for sex." His hand patted the top of my head. "With you, kitten."

As if!

I stood up quickly, brushed against his nakedness, and resisted the urge to jump up and down and squeal in disgust.

"Are you crazy?!" I shouted out at him and ran like the wind out of his room.

I never thought of Adrian again.

And now here I am, thinking about sex, imagining it with a man I just met. I wonder what this says about my moral compass? It can't be good.

"You're frowning." Erik points out the obvious as he studies my face. "Wrinkles? Do you want them?"

"What are you thinking? Tell us," Orie demands as he pops up on the deck.

"To be honest, I saw a flash of my night with Adrian."

"Why in god's name would he even enter your mind?" Erik demands.

"It's the closest I've ever been to sex."

"The closest . . ." Erik finds my comment vastly amusing. "That is the funniest shit I've ever heard."

"Fine. It's funny. My experience with Adrian was a joke! I just don't understand why we're even talking about this. You guys are the ones who always point out what a giant prude I am. Why do you think I would have sex with a guy I barely know? I mean, what would that make me?"

"A young, healthy woman with a goddamn need to finally get laid. And let's be honest, Los Angeles does have its share of hot, single men, but none of them have ever even tempted you. But this guy does. So go with it, Sophie. Who cares? I'm not criticizing you, just trying to protect you. Why do you always have to overanalyze everything in your life?" Erik has a point but I still feel the need to defend myself.

"I'm not—" I try to get a word in.

"You can't lie or hide from me. I've known you too damn long. Listen, Sophie, sometimes things happen that are unexpected. You meet someone and you're instantly drawn to them. Like you've known them your whole life." Erik smiles at Orie as he says the last part.

"And you just know it will be right because there's a chemistry that exists from the moment you first stare into each other's eyes," Orie finishes for Erik. I know they speak from experience and yes, they make it all sound so beautiful and romantic, but real life is not a fairytale.

"You guys sound like a Hallmark card."

"You're deflecting. Just listen to me. Sometimes we can't help who we are attracted to. We just are. And you want Clayton. Just go with it. No one is judging you but *you*. My job is just to make sure that you do it as elegantly as possible."

"How can you even use that word to describe what we're talking about?" I can't help but laugh.

"He can use that word because sex isn't the big, bad scary act you think it is. It's usually an incredible special experience between two people who are attracted to one another, no matter the reason or how fast they jump into bed," Orie explains.

I feel like I'm reliving sex ed all over again.

"I get it," I tell them both, hoping they will stop talking about this.

"Do you?" Erik doesn't look like he believes me but he holds out his arms to hug me tightly.

"Yes," I smile as I move into a wet hug. Ugh. "And I love you, too."

"Can I throw you in the water?" Erik asks me.

"Hell no!" I laugh and move away from his embrace. "Sharks, remember?" I look out over the ocean hoping for a glimpse of Clayton, but he's gone.

Hours later, we're at the restaurant on the beach and I can officially say that I'm tipsy. We have a great table on the beach. We watched the sunset and now the stars light up the sky and sea. I'm wearing a short turquoise blue sundress that I bought for the trip. It's simple, with clean lines of soft silk fabric, but it's a dress I could only wear on vacation and it was definitely an impulse buy. I have flip-flops on and I'm happy I have a pretty damn good pedicure. Fortunately, the sun has already given me a little bit of a glow so I think I look okay.

And after three glasses of wine with dinner, I'm having the time of my life. We've splurged and ordered lobster and the catch of the day, along with a delicious bottle of Rosé. I have no idea what time it is, nor do I care, because, guess what, I've got nowhere to go! Time out. Yes, I do have somewhere to go; I just don't know if I should.

Clayton keeps creeping into my thoughts. Every single time Orie or Erik start to tell a story during which I think I can remain silent, my mind wanders to him. I *so* want to go to his villa! I wonder if Erik will deem it acceptable for us to attend the little soiree.

"Get that goddamn look off your face. We're not going," Erik says.

"Huh?" I look at Erik, then Orie, who avoids my gaze. "Why?"

Orie picks up his cocktail and takes a long swig then runs a hand through his thick black hair. He gives me a serious look.

"We talked about it. It's way cooler if you don't show up tonight. You're hard to get. Guys like that."

My heart sinks. "Really?"

Orie takes pity on me and reaches out to take my hand. "Yes. Men are hunters. They like the chase. They live for the chase."

"But I hate running. I suck at it," I mutter as I pick up my drink in annoyance. "What if he doesn't ask us over again? What if I lose the one chance I have?"

"I promise you, he'll come after you." I don't believe Orie, but I appreciate him trying to make me feel better.

"And if he doesn't?"

"Then fuck him," Erik says dramatically. "He doesn't deserve you if he's not going to chase you."

"But . . ."

"You're a goddamn catch. The best of the best. Make him work for it," he interrupts emphatically.

Orie lifts his glass to Erik. "Cheers to that." I know Erik is right, but still.

"And—Bingo," Erik says. "He's arrived. Bow, arrow and sword, ready for the kill."

My breath is literally sucked out of my body. He's here! I begin to turn my head but Orie interrupts.

"Don't turn around, Sophie."

"Close your mouth. You're acting so obvious!" Erik demands.

He's right. I need to get to the bathroom immediately and get a goddamn grip!

"I've got this," I tell him.

I get up, sway a bit from the amount of alcohol I've consumed, and turn to find the fastest route to the bathroom. God, I'm *so* going to have to detox when I get home.

I almost trip over my feet when I see him walking toward the bar looking so hot in tan khaki shorts and a baby blue t-shirt that stretches out nicely over his broad shoulders and happens to match his eyes perfectly. His hands are tucked in his pockets and he's talking to Eduard and one of the women he came with. I notice with some jealousy that she looks like she wants to devour him alive.

Okay. The night just got interesting. I wonder what time it is. Shouldn't he still be at his villa having a party? I look down and push my long hair away from my face and am ready to pretend like I don't see him when I lift my eyes and they clash right into his stormy blue gaze. He stares at me long and hard, and if I were to guess his mood, he doesn't seem too happy. I watch as he coolly looks me over. His gaze lingers on my bare legs, making me acutely aware of just how short my dress really is, and then meets my eyes again.

Heat.

Holy Jesus, do I feel heat. But it's so weird; there's a certain aloofness to him that's as evident as the heat. It's almost icy. And I don't understand it. But hell, I can't even decipher my own psyche—how do I expect to unravel his? I awkwardly nod at him in a silent hello and rush toward the restroom. It's tucked nicely away from the restaurant, down a path facing the sea, hidden and lit up by tiki torches. I practically run in, looking for any haven from Clayton and, lean over the sink to catch my breath. What the hell is wrong with me?

I look in the mirror and barely recognize the face staring back at me. I'm flushed, practically panting, my pupils dilated as I try to slow my breath. My hair is wild around my face in long waves. I look almost—hot?? Am I drunk? Yes. But the way he stared at me made me feel really good. I use the restroom quickly, wash my hands, take one last look at myself, and then walk out. Ready . . . or not.

As I step out the door and start to walk back up the path toward the restaurant, I'm stopped by a voice.

"You didn't show up at my party."

God.

My heart slams against my chest. I look around and see Clayton leaning against a palm tree smoking a cigar. He's lit by the moon and looks sexy as hell. I can't seem to find my voice. I just stare at him. He takes a puff and blows it out. I'm entranced.

"You didn't answer my question." His accent is more pronounced now and sounds very English, I wonder if that's because he's been drinking. I find my voice.

"It sounded more like an observation than a question."

He smiles. "Both."

He watches me like a lion ready to pounce. His gaze moves over my legs again.

"Your dress is too damn short."

I immediately try to pull it down to cover more of my thighs, but it's impossible, so I stop myself.

"I'm sorry, but I don't think the length of my dress is really any of your business." Really, what does my dress length have to do with him?

I don't think he likes my response because his eyes narrow and he has that predator look on his face again. I feel like I'm some tasty morsel he's ready to take a bite out of. He looks me up and down, taking his time, examining every inch of me. If he's trying to make me nervous, he's succeeding.

"I always get what I want, Sophie."

I feel a jolt through my body. I know he's warning me or maybe even commanding me, but God, hearing a man sound so confident is the biggest turn-on ever. I dare myself to reply.

"How would you like me to respond to that?"

"However you like." There's a definite edge to his voice.

I hold my breath and watch him throw the cigar out into the sand and step toward me. Oh my God, he's coming close. He's invading my space. Moving in all around me. His body, his fiery strength, wraps around me like a protective shield against the world. Before I know it, his hand cups my face and he leans into me. I feel the heat move through my body again.

Electricity.

An inner pull. Whatever you want to call it. I'm just drawn to this man in every way. I don't understand it, but there's something about him that calls to me on a primal level. That's the only justification I have for allowing him to get so close to me so fast. I *want* him to touch me. I *want* him near me. My body craves it, calls out to his in a dance as ancient as time.

"Do you know how sexy you are?" His lips, a breath away from mine, whisper like a soft kiss in the wind.

I'm incapable of speech or movement. I'm addicted to the look and feel of him. I've never wanted anything more. He leans in and I'm flush against him, so close that I can almost taste the sweet softness of his lips. I want him so bad it almost hurts. His hand cups the side of my face and I'm literally imprisoned by his grip. His hands move up my cheeks and through my hair, pulling it back softly until my lips are turned up for him to take.

He stares down at me, our eyes intertwined as we just gaze at one another. It is the most intimate and intense feeling I've ever had. I could stay like this forever.

My hands move of their own accord and grasp his upper arms. My lips part. I can't comprehend the feeling I have in his arms or the sense of fulfillment I know this man will give me, but for once in my adult life, I just go with it and trust my instincts. Haven't all the books I've read taught me to believe in what my soul knows?

For whatever it's worth, I know in my very depths that he was meant to come into my life. He calls to me. If it's the alcohol that gives me the extra courage, I don't know. His lips softly brush against mine.

I feel energy surge through my blood and suddenly my entire body is on fire. Erik is right. From one single brush of his lips, not even a deep kiss, I know that Erik is *so* right. This man is completely X-rated, not even R. Straight up X. And I want every last bit of it.

"Clayton? Clayton?" Eduard calls out as he comes into view. I jerk away from Clayton's arms, completely mortified.

Shit. Shit. Shit.

"Sorry, I didn't mean to interrupt."

I'm mortified. I can't look either of them in the eye. What must Eduard think of me?

Many colorful nouns come to mind.

Hussy. Ho. Tramp.

"No, you weren't interrupting! I was just heading back to the table." I know I'm bright red and I need to get away. Clayton's hand reaches out and grabs mine, stopping me from going anywhere.

"We'll walk back together." He doesn't ask me. He commands. I'm all for women's lib, but I have to admit that the way he sort of just takes control of everything is a turn-on. "Do you need something, Eddie?"

"Cigar?" Eduard looks uncomfortable. I think it's the way Clayton's pinned him to the spot with his gaze. I pity him. I'm uncomfortable too, but Clayton's holding my hand, and judging from the grip, I don't think he's going to let me go. God, even the touch of his hand makes me warm inside.

"I left them at the bar."

Eddie nods and lowers his eyes. I guess he even intimidates his friends. I look up at Clayton and am overwhelmed by his intensity. Standing there holding his hand, I feel like a complete hoochie mama, so I try to pull my hand out of his grasp, but he only tightens his grip and I feel that charge again. He looks down at me, his expression serious.

"You're not escaping."

My mouth goes dry. Erik and Orie told me that he's a hunter and Lord, they were *so* right.

I am good and trapped.

Chapter Five

We walk back to my table hand in hand and I almost laugh at the expression on Erik's face when he sees us. It's classic. I know I'm going to get a lecture from him about how I should be acting aloof and I fully intend to defend myself. I try again at the table but Clayton stops me cold when he says, "If you gentlemen don't mind, I'm taking Sophie for a walk on the beach."

I look at him in surprise.

He's what?

Stars? Ocean? Night?

Alone?

That's a recipe for disaster for me. I can't. I won't be able to concentrate on a conversation. I'll just be obsessing about whether he'll try to kiss me. And about how it will feel. Lord, I'm losing control over my mind!

Erik will save me. He has to save me. But wait. *Clayton didn't ask, he just said.* Like it was a done deal. I get the feeling that this man really doesn't ask permission for anything in his life.

"As long as Sophie is cool with it," Orie answers because for once Erik is shocked into silence.

Clayton doesn't wait for me to respond whether I'm cool with it or not. "I'll see her to her villa."

I realize I'm standing there like a deaf mute and that I haven't said two words the entire time.

Erik finally speaks. "We're headed to the club, 15 Below, to check it out. It's apparently the only underground club in the Maldives. It's right over here. Do you guys want to join us before you go on your walk?"

I know he's doing this to make sure I'm okay. And you know what? I love him for it. I need time to think. If I go for a walk with Clayton I won't be responsible for my actions.

"That sounds fun," I answer before Clayton can. I know he's irritated; I can see it. He doesn't seem like the club type of guy, but then I'm not the club type of girl either. Since he always gets his way (or so he told me), this new turn of events can't be sitting too well with him. The pleaser in me wants to make him happy, so I say, "We can check it out and then maybe go for a walk after?" Crap. Why did I say that? *Because deep down, you do want to be alone with him,* my mind says to me in an accusatory way. Well, who wouldn't? Look at him.

"Alright," Clayton says quietly. "We can go to the club for a moment." He smiles at me and my heart flutters again. God, he's good looking, I don't miss the fact that he said "for a moment."

"Great. I'm just going to get the check," Erik says as he holds up his hand to get the waiter's attention.

"It's been taken care of."

We all look at Clayton.

What?

"That is completely unnecessary—" I'm shocked that he's done something so generous and extravagant and so damn *gallant*.

"It's done," he says with finality, looking at me. He squeezes my hand, I think to silently tell me not to argue with him. Erik looks like he wants to, but then thinks better of it.

"Thank you. That was very generous of you and, as Sophie said, totally unnecessary."

Clayton shrugs. "My pleasure. Shall we?"

Erik and Orie get up and walk toward the path that will take us to the club. Clayton starts to follow but I put my other hand on his arm to stop him. I feel his muscle tense beneath my touch and I wonder if he feels the same magnetic pull I do—if he's as in tune with me as I am with him.

"Thank you. You really didn't have to do that," I say softly. When that intense gaze of his meets mine, I have to look away. He makes me so damn shy.

"But I did. And I do. And it's nothing, really."

Nothing? It had to have been at least a five-hundred-dollar dinner.

"Sophie. I thought you wanted to go to the club, or have you changed your mind? Would you rather take a walk and talk?"

No, I'd rather not talk. I'd rather just kiss. But I guess talking is good. Talking will let me ask questions, get to know him before I hand myself over on Erik's silver platter.

"No, let's go to the club first. I don't want Erik and Orie to get upset. And maybe you should invite your friends as well?" I motion toward Eduard and John, who are sitting at the bar. I have yet to meet the women.

Judging by the look on his face, Clayton doesn't seem too concerned whether they come.

"Alright. Let's tell them where we're going."

Downstairs in the club, there are about twenty or so people, including us, but then I guess only the guests of the island would be here so it's no surprise that it's not crowded. For a small island in the Maldives, it's a pretty cool-looking place with a huge, fully stocked bar and a big dance floor with intimate tables set all around.

Clayton has gotten the group a table and everyone's ordered drinks. I'm having a Campari Americano and thoroughly enjoying myself. I've met the two women with Clayton, Jane Billworth and Elizabeth Maitland, John's sister. They both speak with very posh English accents and at least Elizabeth is not as snobby as I originally thought. Jane, on the other hand, is blatantly unpleasant. Her eyes glaze over when Clayton introduces me and I can tell she doesn't like me. Erik and Orie, on the other hand, she clearly approves of. Their comedy soon gets her all giggly and I know she's happy to hang out with them.

I learn from Elizabeth that they're all from London (including Clayton), except for Eduard, who lives in Madrid. I wonder why Clayton's accent isn't as pronounced as theirs. They all grew up with each other and went to boarding school together. She hasn't offered me any further details. I look over at Jane again. She's quite pretty; with her blond hair and blue eyes, she looks like a Barbie doll. She's sitting to the left of Clayton and I notice how she keeps watching him or touching his arm whenever she has a chance. I wonder if the two ever dated and it rubs me the wrong way.

Clayton excuses himself and goes to the bar, where he talks to the mixologist. I watch as he points to a bottle and the bartender pulls it down. My gaze is drawn to his perfectly muscled arms. He's so tall and broad, his body is just not normal. It's like every girl's fantasy. I need to pinch myself because I still can't believe that he's singled me out and has held my hand. He hasn't paid much attention to me since we got here, but he did make sure that we were sitting next to one another. I wish I had chosen to take the walk instead. I feel a hand on my arm, distracting me from my thoughts.

"I've never seen Clayton take to someone so quickly. Or so completely like this. He's usually politely distracted," Elizabeth, who is to my right, leans in to tell me this. Her smile looks genuine, so I think she's being honest. I'm thankful the music is so loud that no one else hears. Jane, I notice, has gotten up and walked over to the bar to Clayton.

"Really?" I can't keep the skepticism out of my voice. Better to be skeptical than hopeful that I'm the first.

"Really." Elizabeth brushes her strawberry-colored hair out of her face and smiles warmly. "And don't worry about Jane. She's tried to land Clayton since they were sixteen but he wants nothing to do with her. She's one of those woman who can't take rejection . . . or a hint."

The idea of the pretty Jane relentlessly hitting on him is unsettling.

"I'm being honest, Sophie. This is totally out of character for him. Completely. We're all actually quite in shock over it. Truly." Elizabeth tells me earnestly, "I mean, when Eduard said that he walked upon you two kissing—"

My face turns bright red.

"Oh my God. I didn't mean that. I really didn't mean to say that—" Elizabeth is just as mortified as I am.

"We didn't really kiss," I say quietly then look away. "And it's okay. I know how I must look." I want the floor to open and drop me through it. I am that girl who has no shame, and people talk about me. I'm so mortified.

Elizabeth puts a hand on my arm. "Don't say that. I'm not judging you. I would probably do the same in your situation. Clayton is pretty," she searches for the word, "impressive. Don't worry, he's like a brother to me. I'm just saying that it's okay. I could tell he was attracted to you the moment he saw you in the lounge at the airport. Anyone could. And you him. Oh no, the look on your face, I'm just putting my foot in my mouth. I'll stop now."

I actually laugh. I do like her and her candor. "It's okay. Thank you, Elizabeth." I mean seriously? What I am supposed to say?

Thankfully, Elizabeth gives me a moment to myself and my eyes immediately search for Clayton. He's still at the bar and is giving Jane his full attention. Great. I pick up my drink and take a long sip, trying to distract myself and get my buzz back, hoping that will help. Eduard walks back from the bar and sits down. I study his features for the first time. He has a beautiful face in an artistic sort of way. He's got perfect symmetry. I'd love to paint him.

"Clayton just bought the bottle of fifty-year-old Dalmore. Let the party begin!" He seems thrilled by this.

Obviously it is a big deal. I have no idea what Dalmore is but I can't wait to find out and I can't wait for Clayton to make his way back to this table and sit down next to me. I try hard not to look back to where he's standing with the lovely Jane.

"Wanna dance, Sophie?" Erik shouts at me with his eyes narrowed, probably pissed that I keep looking over at Clayton like a loser. He raises a brow. It's clearly a challenge.

"Sure." I'm up for it. At least we won't be the only ones on the dance floor. There are some other people dancing as well, a couple of tall guys who look Slavic and some girls who just look wasted.

Erik comes around the table and grabs my hand and wraps his arm around my waist to escort me to the dance floor.

"I had to save you from the stalker stares you were giving him," he whispers in my ear.

"I'm sorry," I giggle.

"It's okay. I forgive you. Even though I know I've taught you better." I roll my eyes.

"What's Dalmore?" I whisper up at him as we walk to the dance floor.

"Very old Scotch. It's gotta be a least ten g's."

"As in ten thousand dollars?" I say in disbelief. Who spends that much on one bottle of alcohol? The thought is staggering.

"That's what rich is, babe."

I am so out of my league on so many levels that I don't know what to say. I decide then and there that Clayton is too rich for me. Too posh. Too handsome. Too *everything*. I didn't grow up poor or from the wrong side of the tracks but holy hell, the money he throws around is insane. And completely unnerving.

We reach the dance floor and Erik starts busting his moves. The one thing I'm pretty confident about is my ability to dance. I can move. Really shake the hips, dance my ass off, *move*. And when I'm slightly intoxicated, everything gets even better because all my inhibitions disappear. Erik and I have partied with each other enough to know how to work it—and we do.

I try not to think of Clayton or Jane or how rich he is or the fact that he might be watching me and I just dance. Soon, the group of Slavic-looking guys are moving around us, or me, to be exact, forgetting about the girls they were trying to pick up before. I dance with one of the guys because I can. Because I'm single and yes, because a part of me wants to make Clayton feel jealous, if he's even watching. It's terrible, I know. He'll probably ride off into the sunset and marry Jane but this can be my shining moment.

The guy I'm dancing with leans in closely, a bit too close for my liking, and I get a whiff of his alcohol-infused breath. Gross.

"What's your name?" he asks in a thick accent that I think is Russian. From the corner of my eye I watch Orie grab Erik's arm and pulls him away. That's my cue to join them.

Ugh. But since I've used him, I have to be polite. "Sophie." I intentionally don't ask him his name.

"I'm Mikhail," he says.

"Nice to meet you," I respond politely.

"You're really hot, you know. I've had my eye on you since the restaurant."

Huh? Was he even at the restaurant? I didn't look at any of the guys there because all my attention was focused on Clayton.

"Umm, okay." This is awkward. My rash decision to make Clayton jealous has put me in a seriously uncomfortable situation. Why can't a dance ever just be a dance with a straight man? It always has to be or lead to something more.

Okay, it's time to politely end this. I brush my hair away from my face and am about to excuse myself when Mikhail puts his hand on my arm.

"Let me buy you a drink, beautiful."

Before I can say a polite, "no, thank you," I'm pulled away from Mikhail into a rock-hard chest. The arms that I was studying and fantasizing about wrap around my waist, his hands, those gorgeous hands with their long, well-shaped fingers, splay against my belly, causing goose bumps to rise all over my body. And heat. There's that damn heat again.

"The lady *has* a drink." It's the most possessive a man has ever been about me. I'm beaming.

Mikhail holds up his hands in defense. "I'm sorry, man. I didn't know she was taken."

"She is." Clayton's voice is hard. Angry. He's pissed, I can tell.

I think I stop breathing. I am? By him? Does he mean I'm taken by him? Of course he does, you moron! I don't think he appreciated my dancing queen moment at all.

"Fair enough." Mikhail smiles at me. "You can't blame a man for trying." He turns and walks away and I'm left wrapped in Clayton's arms, with the music pumping.

"I don't share, little girl," he whispers into my ear, his voice cold.

Little girl?

"Excuse me?" I turn and try to move out of his vise-like grip but he won't let me. I'm plastered to his body, forced to look up at him as he looms over me.

Bad idea. I can see his anger. His eyes radiate the emotion, turning him into a stunning, cold statue.

"Little girl?" I say.

"I know what you were doing. And that's a child's game." My stomach instantly ties itself into knots. Oh shit.

"I don't know what you're-"

"Lying doesn't become you, Sophie. Your face is innocent of guile."

I think he just complimented me but I can't be sure because he doesn't sound too happy about it. I figure I need to get some distance between us.

"I'd like to go now."

"Perfect," he says as he takes my hand, practically pulling me after him.

"I mean that I'd like to leave alone."

I'm pretty certain I see Clayton rolling his eyes, but I can't be sure because it's so dark in the club. All I know is that he completely ignores my request and drags me after him. He waves goodbye to the table and then nods at the bartender. He just wants his bill.

"My villa." His voice is commanding, leaving no room for argument.

His jaw is tightly clenched and I can still feel the anger oozing off his body. Clayton literally pulls me out of the club. The hot air hits us hard. There's a slight breeze that is nice but does nothing to ward off the impressive heat.

I wonder what Erik and Orie are thinking? They're probably disappointed that I left the club holding Clayton's hand despite their warnings that I should play hard to get. We walk up the steps and are outside within seconds. Clayton walks briskly, completely ignoring me. I dig my feet into the ground. "Hold on a second!"

He stops, doesn't release my hand, and turns to look at me. His face is perfectly composed. But he looks really aloof. All because I danced with some guy?

"What is your problem?" I know my voice has gone up like ten octaves but I really don't care. I'm not the type of woman who allows a guy to order me around, and here's a perfect stranger doing just that. He needs to explain. Like now.

I watch him raise a brow, look me over with that icy glare, and I wonder what I'm getting myself into. He stares at me for a long moment before answering. I know he's doing this to throw me off balance and make me nervous. Law school and my father did teach me a few things about the art of war. And damn, he's really good at it. My father would definitely be impressed.

"I told you, Sophie. I don't share. And I don't do games. And I especially don't do jealousy."

Well shit, he certainly seems jealous to me. Right?

"You could have fooled me."

I can't believe I just said that. Talk about uttering some bold shit. Even Clayton seems surprised by my words. I see it for a split second before his eyes turn cloudy and guarded. I've managed to pull my hand from his and back a bit away from him, hoping to gain some distance from the towering god. The angry, towering god, I might add.

"You're right."

At first I don't think I've heard him correctly because honestly, it's the last thing in the world I'd expect him to admit to me, but he does.

Before I can even have a second to be happy about that revelation, he starts to stalk me. I back away from him until I'm cornered against a wall with nowhere to go. He leans into me, hands on both sides of my head, trapping any possible exit I could make.

"You're absolutely right, Sophie. And it's a first for me. A fucking first. And I've decided I don't like the feeling at all."

I lose my stomach. I feel a rush of excitement move through my body. I can barely breathe. He's never been jealous before? I try not to smile in giddy pleasure.

"So what now?" I whisper. He smiles darkly at my innocent question.

"So now I'm going to find out why the hell I'm so drawn to you. I'm going to see if you taste as good as you look."

I gasp. Holy shit. For the first time in my life, I'm incapable of thought. His lips crush mine with savage seduction as his hand moves through my hair, pulling my face as close to his as possible. His other reaches down to cup my bottom and literally lifts me up off the ground as he grinds his hips into mine and pushes me against the wall.

Oh, God. I feel every inch of him and I lose it. My hands are entangled in his hair, holding him tightly in place. His tongue moves into my mouth with expertise and takes complete ownership, branding me completely as his, and I moan in reaction. His tongue licks and devours my mouth completely. Tasting every part of me. His lips suck mine, and lord, does this man know how to kiss.

I feel his hands move down to the back of my naked thighs, caressing my skin, then reach under my short dress and grasp my butt. He groans in satisfaction as he deepens the kiss. I feel every part of him. It is so sinful but feels so good I can't stop him. I don't want to stop him. I push my hips into his, feeling the proof that he wants me just as badly as I want him, and then suddenly he tears his mouth away from mine and steps back.

"Jesus," he whispers.

I'm panting with need. With want. I have never felt this way in all my life. I want him. I want to go to bed with him. Give him my virginity. On a silver platter, paper plate, I don't care. It's his.

I try to get a grip. *Is it just me?* It can't be. I look at him and watch as he closes his eyes and takes a deep breath in.

"Fuck," he says. Yes, Clayton. I'm thinking the same thing.

It takes me a minute before reality starts to sink in and I realize I've just acted like a wanton whore. I need to get out of here fast. I look for an escape route. Downstairs? Back to the club? God, no. I can't face my friends. Erik will know. I roll my shoulders back and lift my chin. I'm going to walk to my goddamn villa. He can't stop me. What am I so afraid of?

"Well, good night, then." I almost add a "that was fun," but thankfully catch myself from further embarrassment. I proceed to make a wide beeline around him and start walking down the path toward the overwater bungalows. He stops me after I've gone about three feet and grabs my hand.

"I'll take you back." He sounds so serious. My mind races as we walk back, the air between us sexually charged.

"Stop thinking, Sophie." At first I don't know if I've been talking out loud or if he just suspects the obvious. I look over at his strained face. We've hit the long wooden path now, on our way to the end of the ramp of bungalows.

"Please stop thinking. I can feel it," he continues in a commanding voice. He looks over at me, piercing me with his bright blue gaze, and I practically stumble from his words and the general hotness he exudes. My eyes wander to his lips again.

"Fuck!" He swears again, reaches out and grabs me, picks me up and hungrily kisses me. I gladly give in, opening my mouth, giving him my tongue to suck, allowing him to hold my ass—my bare ass, by the way. Yes, I do have a thong on, but that might as well be nothing. He pulls his mouth away from mine only once to say, "Wrap your legs around me."

I do as I'm told and he kisses me again as he walks down the dock. It's the single most erotic moment in my life. Okay, I've never really had another moment like this and it's so great; I don't know what to do with myself. I feel a need so potent that it almost makes me cry out with longing. Someone could walk by and see us at any second. People could be behind us, I don't care. I just want this man.

My hands grip his neck, his shoulders, anything I can touch. I'm wrapped around him like a grapevine and I have no intention of letting go. Ever. We kiss and kiss.

It all seems over too quickly. I'm surprised to find myself pushed up against the door of my villa. How did we get here so fast? My legs are still wrapped around his waist and he's just looking at me, seemingly satisfied that I'm so disoriented. And I'm happy to note that he's breathing just as heavily as I am.

His eyes are dark with desire as he stares into mine.

"You're a goddamn witch." I don't know whether to be insulted or thrilled by his words.

I notice with some shame that his hands are still on my bare bottom. No one has ever done that before! I feel like an alien has taken over my body. I've never acted this way in my life.

I take a shaky breath and unwrap my legs from their death grip around him and my feet slowly reach the ground.

"Listen. I'm behaving totally out of character for me. So I totally understand if you never speak to me again." I don't. But I do. I can't even look him in the eye. I don't even know what I'm saying.

"You do?" I hear his amusement.

"Yes. I mean, what kind of . . ." I pull my card key out of the pocket of my dress and turn away from him, trying desperately to find the slot for the card. I don't even want to finish the sentence. Clayton takes it out of my hand and leans into me from behind. His mouth finds my throat and licks its way up to my ear. If he didn't have a strong grip around my waist, I'd fall to the ground. He slips the key into the slot easily and the door clicks open.

"Listen carefully, Sophie. I have every intention of seeing you tomorrow, the day after, and the day after that. But it will be by my rules. And starting now, you will follow every one of them. Do you understand me?"

His rules? I can feel my breath start to leave me again. What does he mean by that?

"We don't even know each other," I whisper. The familiar uncertainty starts to wash over me.

"It's too late for regrets." Clayton makes me turn around to face him. He lifts my chin up and leans down to place a soft, chaste kiss on my lips. "We're in too deep now."

He kisses me again, but not the kind I want. I guess he can tell because I see the satisfaction on his face.

"I will call you tomorrow."

I nod because I'm incapable of speech and step back inside my room. The door is open and I really don't want him to leave. He leans against the doorjamb.

"You have to shut the door."

"I don't want to." I can't seem to help myself from saying the truth. I don't care. His eyes darken with desire. I know he likes what I just said.

"Sophie. Please. Shut the door." He sounds like a man in pain.

I stare at him and take in his utter beauty. The light from the moon makes him seem to glow. He is the most handsome man I have ever encountered. And he wants me. He kissed me. He's standing here staring at me, looking like he will pounce at any minute. I can't believe it. I'm afraid if I shut the door and let him go he won't come back. And I'll wake up and this will just be the sweetest dream I've ever had in my life.

"I can't." *What if you disappear?*

I hear him swear softly again. Then he steps forward and wraps his arm around my waist, pulling me up against him. His hand runs through my hair again and I lean into it this time, closing my eyes.

"Look at me," he says.

I do as I'm told.

"Christ," he quietly utters.

Whatever he sees in my eyes makes him lean in for another earth-shattering kiss, this time more urgent. I answer by wrapping my arms around him, moving my hands up his back and through his hair. What little control Clayton has evaporates in a second and I know I've won. His lips trail down my neck. I moan in response. He lifts my hands up over my head, interlacing our fingers, and kisses the side of my neck and moves down to my chest. I can feel how bad he wants me and it causes heat, sweet heat, to explode through my body.

I would let this man have his way with me right there out in the open if it weren't for the voices echoing in the distance. I hear them before he does and I pull away quickly, panting madly, scared that we'll get caught by someone. Clayton steps forward to come after me but I put my hand up.

"Someone's coming." My voice is shaky. My legs are wobbly. I can barely stand but my sense of propriety has kicked in. Clayton closes his eyes and puts his hands on his legs.

"Shut the door now, Sophie. Or I'm coming in after you and I don't care who sees."

"Good night, Clayton." I shut the door quickly before I change my mind and lean heavily against it. I know he's still on the other side. I want to open it so badly, but I can't. I need to maintain some sense of decency.

Self-respect.

Modesty.

I throw myself on my bed and close my eyes. It's still hard to breathe normally. I touch my lips softly, they're still swollen from his kisses. I wonder what time he's going to call me in the morning? What if he doesn't call? No, that's not good. Don't think like that. He will. He will. Stop. Stop it, Sophie. *Stop now.*

The phone rings. My heart race goes on overdrive and I think it's going to pop out of my chest. I pick it up after two rings.

"Hello?" I know I sound breathless.

"You shut the door so quickly I didn't get to say good night." If I could fly, I'd be soaring across the sky. A big grin sweeps across my face.

"I'm sorry."

"Don't be. If you hadn't closed the door when you did, you wouldn't be alone right now." My stomach drops at the thought. What's the cool thing to say back to him?

"I'm just as much to blame."

"I don't think so." His voice is low, sexy. "I think I have more experience than you in this department."

Uh-oh. Do I suck at kissing? Do I scream virgin? Ugh.

"There is no doubt that you do." I can't think of anything else to say. It is clearly a fact that he has an incredible amount of experience. I, on the other hand, am massively lacking in this area of expertise. Still, I don't want him to think I'm a total loser.

"I have dated, you know," I add almost defensively.

"Have you?" I think I detect a frostiness enter his tone.

"Well, yeah." Duh. One guy. And we barely touched each other. Just thinking about all the time I wasted with Jerry makes me ill. *The fact that you dated only one guy should make you ill,* my mind screams out at me.

"How many men have you dated?"

Suddenly I feel like this isn't a conversation that will end well. His voice is quiet and serious and I don't understand why, when I bet he can't even count how many women he's been on dates with. And without a doubt, had sex with.

"I asked you a question."

I try to be the adult.

"I think we should end this conversation."

"Tell me." Lord, he sounds angry.

"What's the point?" I stall.

"The point is that I want to know."

"One," I say quietly, "I dated one guy." My honesty is so pathetic. Why can't I make myself sound cool?

"Who was he?"

"Jerry. His name is Jerry and I grew up with him and we dated but we were more like brother and sister. You're right. I'm a virgin. We barely even kissed. Are you happy now?" Talk about giving the man too much information. He didn't ask to hear all that! Why would I just offer it up to him? What is wrong with me?

I think I hear a sigh of relief but it could be my imagination playing games with me.

"The only reason why I know about your innocence is because I happened to hear your friend talk about you."

I'm mortified. Of course he heard. Erik screamed my lack of sexual experience out to the world. Oh my God. He must just think I'm a naïve twit.

"Can we change the topic now?"

"Innocence is a virtue that should be commended. It's a rarity. Especially in this day and age."

Don't I know it, I think sullenly to myself. Before I can answer him he says the one thing that takes all my doubts and fears away.

"And I like it."

Suddenly I'm glowing.

"Goodnight, Sophie. Sweet dreams."

"You, too."

I hang up and close my eyes. As Clayton commands, I have the sweetest dreams.

Chapter Six

AT EXACTLY TEN A.M. I am lying face up on a massage table overlooking the enchanting Indian Ocean with a small Filipino woman staring down at me. This is Noom, the island healer. She's about four foot ten, rail thin, and is wearing baggy white pants and a t-shirt. She has a very pleasant smile that instantly puts me at ease. She's managed to take my mind off the fact that Clayton hadn't called as of the minute I left my villa, which was at exactly nine forty-five. I don't take him as the kind of guy who sleeps in, but who knows? He is on vacation. Of course, my mind goes straight to the dark place of insecurity, which practically swallows me alive.

"You have too much going on in here!" Noom pulls me back to the moment as she points at my head. She delivers this line with a thick accent. She doesn't look too happy about this revelation.

"Well, yes." Doesn't everyone?

She wrinkles her brow and shakes her head at me.

"This is no good. It's too much," she puts her hand on my forehead and closes her eyes. "I can hear your constant chatter. How you no have headache all the time?"

She can hear me? Well, shit. I try to explain myself to her.

"Noom, isn't it normal for your mind to be thinking? Isn't that a good thing?"

"No." She doesn't hesitate in responding as she moves away from me. "That is no peace. Especially when your mind tell you bad thing."

"My mind does not tell me bad thing," I say back to her as I sit up to watch her grab a handful of crystals from a sink. I wonder what she's going to do with them.

"Does your mind tell you you're beautiful?" No.

"Does your mind tell you you're smart?" No.

"Does your mind ever let you have peace?" Well, no. Hmmm, she might be onto something. "How is that healthy for you?"

I try to think of a suitable reply but I can't.

"Have you ever meditated, Sophie?"

I think of the small fortune I've spent on countless yoga classes, trying to find my inner Zen. I took them with Orie, who is awesome at yoga. He tried to help me find my balance but I never really felt that I was at peace, like the other students in the class. When the yoga instructor would ask us to be silent in meditation for ten minutes, I would always mentally prepare my to-do list, which would stress me out, and then I'd wish for the end of the ten minutes so I could get going.

"Of course. I've taken yoga." I choose not to tell Noom this story.

She shakes her head at me.

"No. I asked, have you meditated? Have you sat with *yourself. In complete stillness*. Have you allowed yourself to be? Just be, Sophie?"

I think back to the plane ride from Los Angeles. How long did my stillness last? Thirty, maybe forty-five seconds? If that.

Noom brings me back by taking a deep breath in and then exhaling to show me by example. She points to her stomach.

"Just breathing in. Feeling your life force, your energy from inside."

I think about this and I realize I've never actually spent time with myself just being. Breathing. Closing my eyes. I've never really thought about it before now.

"Give me your left hand." I give it to her and she puts a smoky quartz crystal in my palm. It feels light and cool. "This is to take all the bad thought and energy out of your body. Let the crystal flow through your body and release. Release all the negative." Release? Just how am I supposed to do that?

"Give me your right hand." She places a clear quartz in this palm. "This brings inner peace and light back into your flow. Good chi. It brings positivity."

Well, that's nice. I clasp the crystal in my hand. I need good chi.

"You too young to feel so heavy."

I immediately look down at my stomach, wondering if it is bloated. Noom laughs.

"Heavy in here!" She points at my head, then my middle. "Your core is so heavy. Why? I see no damage in you. All your pain, you have created yourself."

I beg to differ, Noom. I immediately think of my parents.

"Yes, it is true. When you understand that you have all the power in your life to create joy and sorrow, you will be free."

I wonder if that could be true.

"Lie back and close your eyes." Noom places another crystal on my forehead. "This is for your third eye. We will open the window today so you see things more clearly, so you understand the power you have and how you must use it for good."

I like the sound of that.

"And we want to bring out your magic."

"Magic?" I ask. "I don't have any magic." I think I'm going to kill Erik for getting me into this.

Noom slaps my stomach. "Everyone has magic. Why are you so hard on yourself?"

Hell if I know but, "I'm not." I say defensively. It's kind of weird talking to her with my eyes closed and crystals all over my body.

"You have loving family." I snort. Noom pushes my stomach again. "Why you do that?"

Oh, Noom. You have no idea.

"My family does not love me very much right now. I think my mom and dad probably hate me." Wow. I can't believe I just spewed that out. I know I sound childish but it's how I feel.

Noom moves around the table and places her hands on my head. I wonder what she's doing and then I start to feel a strange sensation move through my body.

"Your mother never hate you. She give you life. That is a miracle. You are a part of her." She's quiet for a moment then, "You no have kids right now." I can hear the smile in her voice when she says, "Oh, *you still virgin.*"

I blush. Oh great. Even Noom can tell?

"You are innocent so you don't know." I think of my behavior with Clayton last night. That hardly qualifies as innocent. Noom continues. "But when you do give birth to a baby you will know that you can never hate your child. Your child is love. Your child is you."

Noom starts to move her hands around my body, pushing down on my stomach, my throat, my thighs, then my head again. I feel a slow peace begin to move through my being. I feel extremely light.

"You must release all the toxins from your body. All the negative thought. All the fear. It must go now. Release yourself. Be free."

"How do I do that?" I whisper to her, afraid that I can't.

"Just be." She places her hands on the side of my head and it feels so good. "Be still. One with the moment. With your breath. The now. There is no yesterday. No tomorrow. Only this moment. It is wonderful, no? Listen to the hum of the ocean. The feeling of the crystals, the power they have. This is joy. This now is so special."

It's strange but Noom is right. There is peace in this moment.

"Release everything, Sophie. And be free."

It is the most appealing proposition I've had in a long time. Noom then starts to play the singing bowls I saw underneath the table. The sound is haunting, the vibration so strong that I feel it permeate my body. I let myself go and listen to the music from the bowls and the feeling of the crystals on my body, and I do as Noom says. I release. Before I know it, tears are streaming down my face.

"Let go, Sophie. Be happy. Live for now. It is all we have." Noom's voice reaches me through the vibrations moving in and around my body, like she's chanting a mantra. "There is nothing to be afraid of anymore. Just release."

And I do.

I let go.

An hour and a half later (Noom went overtime free of charge), I'm back in my room looking at the phone to see if there are any messages. There's only one, and it's from Erik and Orie wanting to know how my session went. I decide I will call them later. I release a deep breath because I realize it is okay that Clayton hasn't called me. For now. I feel a sense of Zen from my experience with Noom and I decide I will do what she says and release my fears, or at least try to.

I look out on the ocean. What am I afraid of? Why don't I ever just jump in the water and swim like everyone else? Why would a shark single me out? It's a ridiculous fear I've had all my life for no other reason than I saw a movie when I was younger that put the fear of *Jaws* in me.

How absurd.

I put on my purple bikini and walk out to the edge of the deck. I look down at the water then away, averting my gaze. No, I don't want to look at it. I don't want to psych myself out if I see some fish swimming around. I'm just going to jump. Take the plunge. Release all the negative energy and begin again.

I take a deep breath. It's now or never. I take a few steps back and run. I land in the water, but not before I scream my heart out. Yes, I know. It sounds crazy. But I'm scared to death of sharks. Or at least *I was*, I tell myself. The water is cool and I appreciate how it feels on my skin. I try to block out my fears as I keep my eyes closed and just let myself sink for a minute, and try to bask in the wonder of the sea.

This isn't so bad, I think. If my eyes are closed it's not so scary. Oh God, was that something slimy that just swam by me? Don't think. Don't think. Don't think. I can do this.

And then, before I know it, I'm rudely grabbed by the arm and pulled up to the surface. I'm lucky I don't take in a deep gulp of seawater as I'm hauled roughly through the water, away from my deck and toward the opposite direction. After a moment, we reach the deck and I suck in air, arms flailing, wet hair in my face.

It's him again.

I know his touch. He's got his strong arms wrapped around my naked waist and he literally yanks me up the stairs to his deck until only my calves are in the water. I cough up some water and very dramatically flip my hair away from my eyes. His arms are still around me when I look up at him, and all I see is fury.

"Are you insane?!" he hollers.

"Me?! I jumped in the ocean! I was going for a swim!" I yell back at him. This was my moment of freedom. Of Zen. Of releasing fears. And he just took it away from me!

"Going for a swim? In a school of sharks?!" He's so angry I can feel his body shake with it.

His words wash over me like an ice cold shower. I did what?

"Did you not look in the water before you jumped?!" His voice is as gentle as a lion's roar.

Huh? Well, shit. No.

Oh my God.

A school of sharks? Was that slimy fin touching me a shark? I turn in his arms and stare at a dorsal fin that is poking up out of the water. I can't answer him. Noom told me to release my fears. Well I sure as hell released them. I jumped right out into the water with *Jaws!* Oh my God in heaven.

I promptly faint in his arms.

I wake up some time later in a giant, fluffy bed. I'm disoriented and it takes me a second to recall the moments leading up to my dramatic swoon. Sharks. In the water. With me. I can feel the nausea start to sweep over me again.

"Don't you dare pass out on me again."

How did I not notice him? He's sitting next to me, leaning over, holding a wet towel in his hands. I'm in his bed. His face is etched with worry. Holy hell. I'm in his bed, I think again. He's in his swim trunks and I'm given a healthy view of the wonderful expanse of his tan chest, which is so well sculpted it makes me want to lick my lips. He's got a sprinkle of light gold hair across a chest that would put any fitness model to shame. Lord, have mercy.

That's when I notice that one arm is now on the other side of my waist, lightly brushing my bare stomach in an extremely intimate way and it evokes that familiar warmth within me.

"How are you feeling?"

My mouth is parched for all the wrong reasons.

"Okay."

"Why did you do something so ridiculous?" I cringe at the insult.

"I was releasing my fears." It comes out before I can stop myself.

He frowns, looking perplexed.

"Releasing what fears?"

"Of the ocean." *Keep admitting,* Sophie. "Of sharks. And so I just ran and jumped."

He looks completely dumbfounded.

"You're afraid of sharks?"

"Yes," I mumble. "I was trying to seize the moment and let my fear go." There, that sounds cool, right?

Not so much. I watch as the anger leaves his face and, shoulders shaking, he begins to laugh . . . hard. It's unbelievably hot to watch, even though it is at my expense. I mean, it is funny. Shit, it's more than funny. It's hysterical. I can't wait to share the story with Erik and Orie. Almost.

I smile at him. "A gentleman wouldn't laugh."

"Whatever gave you the impression that I'm a gentleman?" The words are said quietly, a smile remaining on his face as he looks at me tenderly. My body reacts to his affectionate look and I feel a surge of excitement.

His hand inches over slowly, moving lightly over my skin until he rests it fully on my stomach, caressing me all the while. I suck in my breath and watch as his eyes darken.

"You saved my life. That makes you a gentleman." Or a knight in shining armor, I think to myself. Maybe a bit of a mysterious knight.

"When I heard you scream like that I almost had a heart attack. You scared the shit out of me." I love that he was so concerned.

"I ran out and saw you in the middle of a school of sharks and I almost died. I couldn't get to you fast enough. Jesus, Sophie. Don't ever do anything like that again."

Trust you me, I will never do anything like that again, I think to myself.

"I won't."

Clayton looks somewhat mollified by my acquiescence. His fingers starts to trace lines and my skin tingles from his touch.

"You didn't call."

Clayton's eyes meet mine. I wonder if my session with Noom has something to do with my sudden boldness.

"Yes, I did. About thirty times. I waited until ten because I thought you needed your sleep." I'm instantly placated. He didn't forget me.

"I was with Noom."

"Yes, I know," he says. I raise a brow. How would he know that? "I figured if you weren't in your room, you probably booked a spa appointment. So I called and checked."

That was daring of him. And then the most pleasant thought fills me like a dream. He likes me. He cares enough to see where I am.

"Why didn't you leave a message?"

"I don't do messages." Like he doesn't do jealousy. I laugh.

"So what *do* you do?" I ask softly.

He gives me a devilish smile. "Now that's a loaded question."

"I didn't mean—"

"I know you didn't. It's fun teasing you. You're so easy to read. You're unlike anyone I've ever encountered before."

"Is that a good thing or a bad thing?" I ask him shyly.

"Good." He smiles at me. "Very good."

I am flying through the sky again. I'm so glad I jumped in the ocean with the sharks. Look where it led me. I love Noom!

"I want to know you." I watch the shadows move over his face when

I make the statement.

"I'll bore you," he replies.

"Try me."

He's pensive for a long moment, but when he looks at me his gaze is guarded.

"Ask me whatever you'd like."

"And you'll answer?" Somehow, I sense that is an impossibility.

"Depends on whether or not I like the question."

"That's not fair."

"Try me."

"Alright. So tell me everything." Since this has been a day of unexpected daring, why not continue?

His finger traces a path up my stomach toward the valley between my breasts. My eyes close in response. "You have to ask a specific question."

"I can't concentrate when you do that." Clayton leans down and licks the path his finger had traced. I let out a moan.

"What would you like to know?" he whispers as he kisses my stomach and places his cheek against it. "You have beautiful, soft skin, you know."

What was I going to ask him? He's doing this on purpose. I know it and he knows it. I try to remain immune. But it's like he's got this magic spell that makes me incapable of rational thought.

"Who are you?" I finally say.

"Clayton Astor Sinclair." He kisses my stomach, licks a spot, then blows on it.

"Sounds important." I can feel his smile.

"It's just a name."

"It suits you."

"I kind of like it myself," he says teasingly.

Okay, next question Sophie.

"What do you do for a living that you can afford all of this?"

"I'm in the shipping business."

I try to move so I can look at his face while I ask him these questions, but he won't allow it.

"No moving. You're trapped now."

Trust me, I don't mind.

"You own your company." It's a statement. I just say it out loud to confirm what I already know.

"Yes."

"How old are you?" He's so young to have such wealth at his disposal.

"Thirty-four." He looks younger. That's an eleven-year age difference. I didn't quite expect that but then, I kind of like it. It means he's played the field, done his thing, and should kind of know what he wants, right? At least according to Dr. Phil.

"When's your birthday?"

He laughs. "November. Do you think I'm too old for you?" Before I can answer, his hand moves beneath my body and holds my behind. "I'm not."

The sigh that I've been trying to contain comes out at that touch.

"You have a great ass, Sophie. In fact, your whole body is exquisite." Lord, does he know what to say to make a girl swoon. I'm putty in his hands.

"You're trying to distract me again." My eyes open and I look up at him and suck in my breath. His head hovers above me, his hands touching me the most intimately anyone ever has in my life. And yet it feels so natural.

He takes my breath away.

"Don't you want to know me too?" His eyes darken with passion as he moves above me, letting his body settle over mine. Skin against skin. Heat, sizzling heat consumes me. He holds his upper body above mine so he can look down at me but still let me feel the size of him, the difference in our bodies. And the proof that he's just as attracted to me as I am to him.

Holy hell, we'll never fit.

My eyes close in embarrassment at this intimacy. He's so hard against me that it ignites something within me I can't control. I can feel myself getting wet just from him moving up against my bathing suit.

"Open your eyes," he commands.

I hesitate.

"Now."

My eyes open and I stare right up at him. His bright blue gaze is penetrating, daring me to hide. Yet while he wants me to bare my soul to him, I know he still holds back from me. The clouds are there, the layers that have to be carefully peeled away. There's a storm residing in him, something so complicated and dangerous I'm almost scared to touch it.

"I see your innocence," he says.

"Because you know I don't have experience."

"No. It's not about that. There's a softness that radiates from every part of you. A genuine sweetness of your soul. It's all there in your eyes." He touches my face, gently, almost reverently, when he says this.

"Do you know what I see?" My voice is husky with emotion from the praise he just gave me.

"Definitely not innocence."

His words make my heart ache for him.

"I see a handsome, complicated man." I know my words affect him because he actually closes his eyes.

"Open your eyes." I throw his words back at him.

He does, and for a second I see the sadness there before he leans down to consume me. My legs part for him, allowing him to fit between them, his hardness pressing against me is both exciting and terrifying. His hands move into my hair and he kisses me completely, devouring me. My mouth gladly welcomes the assault and I think I've died and gone to heaven from the feeling of pure pleasure I get just by kissing this man. My hands move over his bare shoulders down his back, exploring the perfection that is his body. I feel like I'm touching gold.

Clayton responds to my touch by tearing his mouth away from mine and tracing kisses down my neck, toward my breasts. In a second, my bikini top is pulled down and I have no time to think of embarrassment because his mouth covers my breast and licks and pulls.

"Oh my God." I can feel a pressure start to build and I want to scream in satisfaction.

"You're so innocent," he whispers as he continues to make love to my breasts with his hands and mouth. "So lovely." My hands move into his hair and I grasp his head, never wanting him to stop. His breath is warm against my skin as he continues the sweet torture. He stops for a moment and looks up at me.

"I want you."

I can't breathe. I'm so unnerved by the intensity I hear in his voice that I have to close my eyes against it.

"Sophie. Look at me."

I do.

"I've never wanted anything more."

I believe him.

Something inside tells me to trust him. I know all the signs lead to playing it slow, getting to know him, but I don't care. I know we're both on vacation and we live in two different countries and this could quite possibly become the greatest heartache for me, but there's a part of me that also thinks it could be the greatest joy. I feel like it's right. And if

I'm honest, I have from the moment I first laid eyes on him.

My hand moves of its own accord to caress his cheek, then my finger moves over to brush his lips. I watch his eyes close again.

"I don't know why, but I trust you," I say, and I hear his sharp intake of breath as he rolls off my body and pulls me into his arms. He buries his head in my neck and hair and just breathes in deeply. I'm enveloped by him, held so tightly in his arms that I can barely move, but I love it. I couldn't imagine being in a better place.

I hold him just as fiercely.

And I never want to let go.

Clayton and I are now lying side by side, facing one another. A long while has passed.

"Your accent is funny."

He looks offended by my comment and I hurry to smooth over my faux pas.

"I don't mean it like that. I mean it doesn't quite sound English." A brow goes up.

"It is English. My father is from England; my mother is American. I grew up splitting my time between two worlds and trying to assimilate by blending in. This accent is the result."

"Well, it's really hot," I say, hoping to appease him. From his quick smile, I know that I have.

"Thank you."

Since he brought his parents up, I latch on and ask away. "So your parents are divorced?" As quickly as the words are out, Clayton's demeanor changes. He's on guard again.

"No. They live separate lives. It is a marriage of convenience." He says this indifferently.

I wonder whose convenience, but I wisely choose to keep my mouth shut and just utter, "Oh."

Mad Love

This makes me sad for him. It must have been hard growing up like that. Tossed between two countries. Parents who didn't love each other but were still married. I experienced the exact opposite. I am suddenly so grateful for the overbearing, loving home environment my parents made me suffer through. What if I had grown up like Clayton? I shiver at the thought.

"You don't approve?" Clayton asks softly.

The way he enunciates his words ruffles my feathers. I can hear the snooty tone in his voice. The kind of tone I heard his friends use the night before when they were talking about something that they clearly didn't like. It's obvious that it's an upper-class English way of speaking.

I shrug my shoulders. "No. But to each his own."

"You definitely disapprove." He seems amused by this. He probably thinks I'm so naïve. But, seriously? I voice my opinion.

"I can't help the way I feel. That has to be hard on a child. There are ramifications. Scars that don't easily heal."

"Are you going to quote Sigmund Freud now?" He says teasingly.

I rise to the challenge. "Being entirely honest with oneself is a good exercise."

Clayton smiles. "Didn't he also say that words have magical power? They can either bring the greatest happiness, or deepest despair."

"He did," I say.

"Then choose your words wisely."

The sting I feel from his comment is diminished when he reaches out and brushes my hair away from my cheek. Yes, that's how easy I am around him.

"You're beautiful, Sophie. Tell me about you."

I have a feeling that I'm not quite as interesting.

"But we're not done with you."

"There's plenty of time to get back to me and psychoanalyze my childhood. Now it's your turn."

"I'm an open book," I say nonchalantly.

"I doubt that."

"I really am. It's almost a problem. I wear my heart on my sleeve and I don't know how to hide what I feel. If I do try to pretend, the truth eventually ends up erupting out of me like a volcano. I can't seem to help myself," I confess softly. If Erik were here he could give him a million examples.

"I wish I could be more diplomatic. But I can't control my emotions," I finish.

"I like that. It's so different from what I'm used to," he responds.

Right.

The women he's been around are all like Jane and Elizabeth. Refined, posh, and perfect. Contained. I'm just the opposite. Well, I like to think of myself as somewhat refined. Posh? Not so much. Contained? My dad, Erik, Orie, the list is endless, would laugh in my face if I tried to get away with that adjective to describe myself.

"I can see every thought on your face. It's fascinating," Clayton says as he studies my reactions.

"I don't know how to hide who I am or what I feel."

"I don't want you to."

I feel myself flushing. He looks like he wants to kiss me again.

"You're dangerous," I blurt out.

Clayton's eyes widen at my words but he doesn't deny them. "I am. I'm glad you know it."

He's admitting it. He's actually *warning* me. Oh crap. *Does this mean you're going to break my heart?* I'm suddenly overcome with fear. This is a man who could destroy me. Break me into a million pieces, irrevocably ruin me for a long time.

I sit up quickly and am mortified to find my bikini top still down, my breasts out in plain view. I see the desire flash in his eyes. I blush and stand up, turning away from him so he can't see any more than my bikini-clad bottom.

"Where are you going?"

"I have to meet Erik and Orie. They'll be worried," I lie quickly. I need to get away from him. He's like a drug. And I'm afraid the more time I spend around him, the more addicted I'll become, and then when it's done I won't know how to survive.

"Sophie—" He gets up as well but I practically run out of his room toward the front door of the villa. But when I put my hand on the doorknob and think I'm home free, Clayton places his hand above mine, holding the door shut. Shit, he's fast.

"Sophie. Turn around." Why I turn around is beyond me. Being in such close proximity to Clayton is a hazard to my health. I look up at him and try to act brave.

"I'm not letting you run away."

I'm about to tell him that I'm not running but I can't even bring myself to say the lie. Instead I choose truth.

"I'm scared." Then I'm more blunt. "You scare me."

His hand is still above me, resting on the door, his body leaning in toward mine. I know my words hurt him because I can see it on face.

"I don't want to scare you."

"But you do. How you make me feel. It's disturbing and overwhelming. And it's exciting. All these emotions, all at once, vacillating back and forth. One minute I'm okay and the next I'm scared of how I feel all this so fast. And now I feel like you're warning me. And I don't understand it." I let everything come out. "I'm not like you. I've never felt like this before. It might be my immaturity or inexperience, I don't know. But I don't know how to handle it. And I just need to breathe again. Without you distracting me."

How in holy hell this has become so heavy so suddenly, I have no idea. I just met Clayton and there's so much between us already.

He stares at me hard and I stop breathing again. If he kisses me, I'm done. I know it. He knows it. But he doesn't try. Instead, he turns the doorknob and opens the door for me.

"The last thing I want to do is frighten you." He's back to being aloof again. It's crazy to think that two minutes ago he was being so loving and considerate toward me. I can't let him think that he frightens me in a scary serial-killer way, so I reach out and gently touch his face.

"Don't. *You* don't frighten me."

"Didn't you just say I do?" he asks in a dangerously soft voice. "You told me that I scare you."

"I didn't say it like that."

"Then what exactly do you mean?"

"This is new to me. All of it. I'm experiencing something that I don't fully understand. It's the unknown that scares me. I just . . . I'm trying to rationalize it all in my head and I keep talking myself in circles and—"

He stops me from finishing my sentence by grabbing me and pulling me close to him.

"Stop talking."

I nod okay.

"I'm going to let you go and think about all this. You can analyze it as much as your pretty mind would like. But I already know what the outcome will be. And if you're honest, so do you." His voice is commanding. I know he's not happy with me, or with how I'm running away, so I wisely choose not to speak.

"You can have this afternoon to yourself or with your friends. Whatever you choose. But it's your last without me."

Fuck.

He kisses me hard on the lips then pulls away. I'm disoriented from his kiss and I know that gives him immense satisfaction. I shakily walk away from him and head to my villa, which is painfully close to his. I don't dare turn and look at him because I know he's standing there waiting for me to walk inside.

Seconds later, I'm in my room. I start to breathe again as I fall on my bed. Except I don't feel as free as I thought I would. Clayton is all around me. He's in my mind, and if I close my eyes I can even imagine his touch on my body. There's no escaping him.

Chapter Seven

"Jesus. Fucking. Tits," Erik says dramatically.

After I sat in my room for about five minutes and thought over the events that had transpired, I rushed over to Erik and Orie's villa to tell them the whole story. The two stare at me from the couch in utter shock.

Orie is the first to move and he immediately makes a beeline to the bar and pulls out a bottle of Rosé. I know he's too stunned to even comment.

"I know," is all I can manage to say back.

Orie pours wine and thankfully brings it to us.

"I'm speechless," he says as he hands me a glass. "But I've got to say, I'm happy you took the plunge and jumped in the ocean. That was so brave of you, Sophie."

Erik holds up his hand, demanding silence. "I can't even talk about that part of the story now. It's so fucked, I can't even address it."

I laugh. "I know." We clink glasses from habit.

"Do you think this is Noom's fault?" I dare to ask as I look at the two of them.

"Noom?" Erik looks like he wants to spit up his wine. "Really? Is that the best you can do, Sophie?"

Orie plops down on the lounge chair. "This relationship already feels so heavy."

"I know!" I nod in agreement. "Is this normal?"

"Since when do you do anything normal?" Erik gets up and walks over the lounge chair and scoots in with Orie. I watch them cuddle up to one another. I can't stop my smile.

"But I'm so normal."

Orie laughs in my face. "Girl, sometimes you say the funniest shit."

"What's that supposed to mean?"

"Where should I begin? First, out of left field, you drop out of law school. You break up with a guy you've known all your life, which I don't disagree with, by the way. You convince Erik and me to come all the way across the world with you because you need to 'find yourself' and get away from your family. You insist you need to do it in the Maldives. After twenty-three years of being the biggest prude around, you fall for a guy who literally screams hard-core S-E-X, and you're asking if we think any of this is *normal?*"

When he sums it up that way, I totally see his point. But I still feel the need to defend myself.

"I'm just free-spirited."

Erik and Orie find this vastly amusing.

"Sophie, we love you so much we're not even going to make fun of that ridiculous statement."

"Thanks a lot."

"Let's just get back to the problem at hand," Erik says. "What are you going to do?"

"More importantly, what is she going to wear tonight?" Orie interrupts.

Without even hesitating Erik answers, "White. She's a sacrificial virgin taking her last steps. Innocent. Pure. Spectacular."

"I love it. Long, wavy hair flowing behind her. Totally ethereal."

Are they crazy? They're planning my outfit? The sad part is I can totally picture it in my head as well.

"I saw a gorgeous white dress in the gift shop," Erik says.

They are full-on having a conversation without including me.

"I know which one you're talking about. It was amazing. It would look so good on her, especially if she gets more sun. The golden tan on white, you can never go wrong with that."

"Did it have a *gorgeous* price tag as well?" I cut in, wanting to be included.

"It's our losing-your-virginity, end-of-days gift to you." Erik answers, almost brushing me off as he and Orie start to plan my outfit.

"No way!" I stand up. "Did you guys hear anything I said to you before?"

They look at each other before turning to face me. Erik speaks.

"Sophie, babe, yes, we did. What do you want us to say? You're half in love with him already. I think it's rad. It's incredible. It's fucking awesome. Stop running. From all you've told us, he's fucked up, no doubt. But you picked him. He's your destiny. Your whole life has built up to this moment, tonight. Twenty-three years of virginity has led to this. And God willing it will be one giant orgasm."

"Amen." Orie clinks glasses with Erik. "Hopefully he lives up to all the hype."

I lay back on the lounge chair.

"But he's so rich. And he's so handsome. And he's *English*."

"Those are three favorable marks in my book," Erik says as he stands up and walks over to the iPod. He puts on some cool dance mix he heard while he was in Ibiza.

"And what about what happens after? I mean, is it just a wham bam thank you ma'am type of experience I'm going to have? Is that all I should expect?" I have to ask.

"Did you really just say *wham bam thank you ma'am?*" Erik looks horrified.

I try another cliché. "How about love 'em and leave 'em?"

"Why does it even matter? Aren't you the new spontaneous Sophie who's living for the moment? Why do you want to torture yourself and think about what happens after?"

He has a point.

"You're right. I'll try—" I say.

"You won't try. *You'll do.* Stop worrying. Just be. It will be way easier and less stressful and a million times more enjoyable if you live in the moment," Erik tells me. "Nothing else matters."

I nod in agreement, but I'm not really so sure.

He puts his hands on his hips and faces me. "Since according to Mr. Perfect, this is the last afternoon we have you to ourselves, what should we do?"

"We have to go buy her that dress." Orie says.

"I don't need the dress—"

"Are you kidding me? I know what you packed for yourself. I told you to bring something sexy, but you didn't listen."

"You knew I'd meet a guy?" I roll my eyes.

"Yes. Anyway, you always have to be prepared, Sophie. That's travel packing rule 101. Haven't you learned anything from me all these years?" Erik sounds like he's explaining this to a child.

"We've got it handled," Orie says. "Let's get the dress. Sophie, go to your bungalow and we'll meet you there after and plan the look and the outfit."

"How do you even know it's going to fit me?"

"Does a bear shit in the woods?" Erik says.

I nod, trying my hardest not to laugh at how annoyed he looks.

"Is the pope Catholic?" Erik continues, getting all dramatic on me.

"Yes!" I laugh.

"Am I not the most amazing stylist in the twenty-first century?"

"You are."

"And the hottest." Orie stands up and pulls him close. "Sweetest. Most good-looking man I know."

"I second that," I say loyally, smiling at the way the two of them stare into each other's eyes. Even though they've only been together for a little under two years, I can't remember a time when they weren't a couple. It's like they were made for one another.

Erik met Orie at a party in Los Angeles. At the time, he was in a long-term relationship but had found himself instantly drawn to Orie. He called me on his way home.

"So I met this guy . . ." His voice was giddy, filled with excitement.

"What guy? You have a boyfriend," I reminded him. I loved his ex, even though the two never seemed to go a week without a fight.

"I know, Sophie. But this guy, there's something about him. I felt like I knew him. I've never really experienced anything like it before."

"Maybe you do know him. You are the mayor of West Hollywood," I reminded him, hoping my voice didn't sound full of censure, even though I wasn't very happy about him looking at other people when he was still in a committed relationship.

"No. I would remember. I don't know how to explain it." Erik's voice was soft, so different from his usual confident tone. "I know I'm with Miguel and I love him. I'd never do anything to hurt him, but something kind of called to me. Don't judge me."

"I would never judge you," I told him, because I knew he wouldn't cheat on Miguel.

It was three years before Erik and Orie were both free and clear and could be with each other. They had kept in touch, ran into each other a few times at various events, and, after they finally got together, both of them had told me that they knew their time would come.

It's funny that now I finally know what Erik meant when he said he just felt drawn to Orie. It makes absolute sense to me.

"You guys are making me blush," Erik interrupts my trip down memory lane. Erik blushing is about as possible as a pig flying.

"As if." I laugh.

"I can be shy," Erik says defensively. "It's happened. Once. Twice, maybe."

"I'm not going to respond to that, babe." Orie sounds amused. "I'll let you go on living in your dream world."

Erik pinches his cheek then looks over at me with a serious expression. *Crap, here comes the lecture,* I think.

"Alright, you need to go to your room and stay there. Don't jump in the shark-infested waters outside your bungalow. Don't call him. Don't even move beyond the ten-foot radius of your bed and deck. And for the love of God, shave your legs."

Orie turns up the volume on the iPod and starts dancing around the bungalow in excitement and I can't stop the adrenaline rush that comes over me. The countdown for the evening has just started.

I used the opportunity to get out my sketchpad and pencils and draw my view of the ocean. Landscapes are one of my favorite things to paint. I love to add a bit of my own magic to the beauty that is already there. I become obsessed with getting the color of the water right, the dreamy current. It all has to be perfect. As usual, I quickly lose myself in my work. Time and place seem to disappear when I sketch or paint.

These are the moments when I realize how much I need my art for my sanity and happiness. It's been my passion my whole life. It's also been my secret sanctuary. I get such a feeling of fulfillment that I can't even put it into words. I feel peace when I paint. It's like I was born to do it. If I'm honest with myself, I knew when I enrolled in law school that I would eventually drop out.

I never believed I would last in that cut-throat environment. There was no joy in it for me. Yes, I could get the grades. I understood the law but I was bored and scared—frightened of how it would bring me a kind of existence that would inevitably make me unhappy.

I remember sitting in a Torts class, eyes glazed over, and feeling overwhelmed and desperate. *Is this going to be my life?*, I thought in horror. What if this monotony was what I had to wake up to every day? It was too depressing to consider. It was so completely unappealing to me that I ended my torture then and there. I got up during the professor's coma-inducing lecture and walked out and never looked back.

It was the happiest day of my life.

And this is the part my parents cannot understand. They think passion can be found in any profession. That you can miraculously make yourself love something because it is the responsible thing to do, the right thing to do. But it's simply not true. Passion can't be willed or found. It just is. And I think it works that way in every part of your life, from jobs, to friends, to relationships. The spark has to be there or you'll just be lost. You have to love what you do and who you're with. And want it every day. Otherwise your life will be one, big, empty void and you'll search for happiness and never understand why it keeps escaping you.

The idea of spending my life practicing law was unacceptable. And now more than ever, being with a man just because it's what society or my family tells me to do is appalling. Now more than ever I've felt something different with a complete stranger and I know better now. I can thank Clayton for this miracle. In a single moment, with a single gaze, he showed me what I had been searching for, what I had been missing all my life.

Speaking of Clayton . . .

I blush at the thought of the coming evening.

I'm apparently prepared to jump into bed with a man I just met. *Oh, a nun would jump into bed with Clayton,* I tell myself defensively. I know there's no way in hell that I'm the only woman who would act this way. Anyone would. I think about his kisses and the way his hands feel on my body and desire washes right over me.

Stop, Sophie.

I try to concentrate on the soothing sound of the ocean and not a bed. Anything but a bed. Let me clarify, a bed with Clayton in it. Sigh. I know this is going to be an impossibility.

I'm jolted out of fantasyland by the loud ring of the phone and I'm glad it stops the sinful thoughts in my mind. I run inside from my deck and grab it, thinking that it's Erik and Orie, ready to come over and turn me into Cinderella on her way to the ball.

"Yes, I shaved my legs."

"They felt soft enough to me this afternoon."

Damn.

Why don't I think before I speak? I'm too embarrassed for words. Why do I continue to be such an idiot?

"What else have you been up to?" he says into my silence.

Oh, you know, just fantasizing.

About you.

Lord.

"Um. I've been sketching." I try to sound cool.

"Can I see?" He sounds genuinely interested.

"I don't show anyone my work until I'm done."

"I'm not anyone."

And there goes my heart again—banging against my chest. No, he's not just anyone. He's the man who is dominating all my thoughts. Not letting me concentrate. Just making me think about him in all sorts of scandalous, X-rated ways.

R-rated. Okay, PG-13, but a PG-13 with lots of action.

"Admit it, Sophie," he continues.

I give him what he wants. "I admit it. But I'm a little apprehensive about showing people my work."

"You're shy about a lot of things. And I think you're perfect. I have no doubt that your art is as well. I want to see what you do."

He does know what to say to put me on cloud nine.

"I'll think about it."

"I'll have my way, you know." I don't mind the arrogance I hear in his voice because I know he's probably right, but I'm also wondering if this phrase is his company slogan.

"We'll see," I say.

"I can be very persuasive."

"I have no doubt."

Clayton laughs before he continues, "I took the liberty of getting us all a table together. I hope you don't mind." The funny thing is, I don't really think he'd care if I did mind, because he already did it. But as it happens, I'm happy he's taken the decision out of my hands.

"That sounds great."

"Reservations are for seven. Shall I swing by your place and pick you up?" I smile at his words. It sounds so formal.

I can't believe I have to say no to him, but Erik and Orie are my dates to the party. I tell Clayton and he actually sighs. There's an uncomfortable silence before he says, "You're very frustrating."

"I don't mean to be. I came here with them. They dropped everything to come with me so I wouldn't be alone. All because I said that I needed my friends."

"I know," he finally says after what seems like an eternity. "But I'm not a patient man, Sophie. I can let them escort you down to the beach, if they must. After you arrive, you're all mine."

I like the sound of that.

"And Sophie?"

"Yes?" I say anxiously.

"You and I are having dessert in my villa after." His voice is so sure. "Alone."

Holy.

Shit.

At exactly seven o'clock I'm staring at myself in the full-length mirror, totally amazed at what I see. My loving friends have outdone themselves. The dress, is long, white, and flows whimsically in romantic waves around my body. It fits beautifully, but it's just a little too long. There's a bit of a train that adds to the goddess look that Erik and Orie say they were going for. The material is almost sheer and gives a hint of the outline of my body as it drapes around me. It's strapless, fitted at the top, then cascades to the ground. My tan compliments the dress perfectly. They were so right! I do look a bit like a Greek goddess.

Orie has styled my hair, letting it tumble in loose curls down my back but giving it a beachy, wind-blown look so it doesn't seem like I'm trying too hard, *or so he says*. I opted to put on only a bit of mascara and lip gloss, because my color is perfect from my new tan. I'm so flushed from excitement that I don't need any blush. Erik moves up behind me in the mirror. He's wearing all white as well, as is Orie.

"You look stunning, Sophie. Just stunning." He puts his arm around my shoulder. "I think I'm going to cry."

Orie joins us. "Our girl is all grown up."

I watch as the two of them admire their handiwork. They are obviously very pleased with what they see.

"You guys are too funny. Thank you, thank you, *thank you* for this incredible dress and for making sure everything is perfect. A girl can't ask for two better friends." My voice is hoarse with emotion.

"No, she can't," Erik agrees.

"Honestly, I don't know what I'd do without you," I tell them sincerely.

"Neither do I."

Orie narrows his eyes at Erik. "Must you detract from a sentimental moment? She's trying to be sweet and emotional."

"I'm only agreeing with her," Erik says.

I can see the twinkle in his eyes and I laugh. "Sophie knows how much we love her. She knows how much she means to us."

I'm touched by the emotion I hear in his voice. He is my best friend. Through thick and thin, he's always been there for me. Through all the years we've known each other he's never questioned why I had to see him immediately or the amount of times I cried about my parents or Jerry, which would have driven any other man to drink. He just listened to me. I know I can always count on him. In the chaotic world we live in, this kind of friendship is invaluable.

"You know how much I love you too." I say as the tears well up in my eyes.

"Don't cry and smear your mascara," Orie commands as he pulls me in to give me a kiss.

"I won't," I blink back the water in my eyes.

Erik holds out his hand.

"Shall we?

I gladly take it and follow the guys out of my bungalow. They were totally cool with sharing a table with Clayton and his friends. In fact, Erik promised to do some investigative work and try to get as much information on Clayton as he could, especially after Clayton and I left, which Erik was sure would happen. I didn't tell the guys about Clayton's plans for "dessert" because I didn't want the added pressure that would come with them knowing. I promised myself I would not think about being alone with him, or have any expectations. Who knew what would happen? What if the islanders are right? What if the world ends tonight? At this party? One can never be too sure.

We make our way toward the white sand beach and I'm awestruck by the magical ambience that the hotel staff has created. Candles line the beach and look like shimmering stars on the sand as *Somewhere Over the Rainbow* by Israel Kamakawiwi'ole echoes through the night. God, I love this song. It always strikes a chord with me and brings only happy thoughts to mind. The tables have been set along the water's edge so everyone can experience the allure of the Maldives. It's almost like a fantasy. There are already many people hanging out by the water or seated at their table. We stop on the sand when we're about twenty feet or so away from the tables, just to take it all in.

"It looks like a dream," I whisper.

"Kind of feels like one," Erik answers as he squeezes me tightly. "I don't think I'll ever forget this night."

"Me neither."

"Act cool, Sophie baby. He's staring right at you," Orie whispers softly.

"And from the look he's giving you I think we did a damn good job," Erik says with a smile.

My heart rate accelerates from their words and I immediately search the tables for any sign of him. I zero in on him instantly. Oh, my. Yes, he certainly does like what he sees. His friends are chatting around him but he's ignoring everything they're saying, because his gaze is fixed on me. He's leaning back in a chair just taking me in. I notice, with some embarrassment, that his friends are now all looking at me as well. I try to ignore them and focus on Clayton, who is too handsome for words. He's wearing tan linen pants and a crisp white linen long-sleeved shirt. It's unbuttoned at the top, exposing a part of his chest.

Suddenly he stands and starts to walk toward me.

"The man's got style," Erik says as Clayton reaches us. I'm secretly pleased because I know a compliment from Erik is not easily earned.

"Hi," Erik says politely.

"Erik. Orie." Clayton answers cordially, then reaches out his hand for me. I walk to him without hesitation. "You look lovely, Sophie. Exquisite."

Lord. His mom must have really taught him well. Or maybe his nannies.

"Thank you. You look really beautiful."

Orie coughs, I know, to cover his laughter at my somewhat lame reply. I flush with embarrassment. Well, shit, the words do just seem to tumble out of my mouth. I'm okay with it, though. Shouldn't he get a compliment from me, too?

Clayton pulls me away from my friends and up close to him. I can tell he likes what I said by the way his eyes light up and look over my face caressingly. I smile shyly.

"We'll just go on over and join everyone. Don't mind us," Erik says behind me. I can hear him mutter something about manners to Orie. I smile at Clayton and roll my eyes.

"Did you miss me, Sophie?"

"Yes." The words come out before I can stop myself. Talk about desperado.

"Good." Is that all I get? Clayton smiles at my look, then leans down to kiss me. There's an urgency there that tells me what he failed to say.

"Shall we join our table?"

Our table? I like the sound of that. "Yes, that sounds lovely."

He takes my hand in his and we make our way back to the group. Elizabeth smiles at me warmly, standing to embrace me.

"What a stunning dress! Did you buy it in the gift shop? I feel like I saw it when I went in there yesterday for some suntan lotion."

"Yes. Erik and Orie treated me. I'm very lucky to have such wonderful friends," I tell her. "You look so pretty, Elizabeth. Your dress is incredible. I love the color."

She blushes and waves off my compliment. "I don't look like you. I'm dying over your dress. I wonder if they have my size?"

"It was the last one," Erik tells her as he takes a seat. He and Orie are across the table and a few seats down. He checks out her short green dress in a second says, "Versace?"

Elizabeth nods in excitement. Erik knows how to make a woman obsessed with him.

"I usually don't go for something so loud, but I thought, why not give it a try?"

"It's a great fit for you," he compliments her. "Love the fabric and the color goes perfectly with your blonde hair."

I watch Elizabeth bloom like a flower from Erik's praise. He can make you feel so secure; it is one of his many talents. It's probably why so many Hollywood starlets love to work with him. I've seen him do it with women who are afraid they've lost their youth and women who are overweight. It's his way. How he makes someone feel. Like you're the most special person in the world. And the thing is, he genuinely means it.

I look over at what seems to be an angry Jane and wonder if she always has that pinched grimace on her face. Does she ever smile? How on earth did they all become friends? Elizabeth is so pleasant, so nice. Jane is just a pill. She reminds me of the Debbie Downer character on *Saturday Night Live*.

Luckily, I'm saved from wondering about her any longer because Clayton takes me to the head of the table and pulls out a chair for me on his right. When we sit, he takes my hand again. I know I must be smiling like a loser, but I just don't care. I see that Clayton and his friends have been drinking champagne. Clearly, the party's already started.

"More drinks for the table?" Clayton asks the group politely.

"For sure. I say let's start this end of days party with shots of lemon drops," Orie says. I love him. He must have read my mind.

"Here, here," Eduard agrees.

"Let the games begin," John seconds. My gaze meets Erik's and he raises a brow. I know what he's thinking. And yes, I agree with him; a shot is exactly what I need right now. I am a giant mass of quivering nerves.

"What would you like, Sophie?" Clayton asks me quietly, leaning in.

"I'll just have what the table is having, thank you," I respond politely.

"Not tonight."

I let him see my frown.

"I'm having a shot, Clayton."

He actually has the audacity to smile. I get a nice view of his perfect white teeth and full, sensuous lips. I lose my stomach. I wonder if I'll ever become accustomed to looking at him. Probably not.

"I like the way you say my name." His voice is seductive, his eyes, glued to my lips. *He likes the way I say his name,* I think dreamily.

Hold on, Sophie! He can't be ordering you around.

"You're not going to distract me," I say. I have to set him straight now.

"I was just telling you a fact. I like the way my name sounds when you say it." His eyes move slowly from my lips to my chest then up to meet mine, and it's almost like I can feel his touch.

"I'm still having a shot."

He smiles again.

"Care to bet on it?"

"Excuse me?"

"I won't have you drunk tonight."

"As if . . ." Does he think I'm some sorority girl who doesn't know her own limits?

He interrupts me. "I don't even want to entertain the possibility of it happening tonight. I'm sorry. I want you to remember everything about this evening. From start to finish." He grabs my chin with his fingers and caresses my skin with his thumb. The noise around me dulls. I can't even think anymore. It is just the two of us.

"I'll make sure you're nice and relaxed." He moves his thumb against my lips then leans away from me, leaving me longing for more.

Flushed.

Hot.

Bothered.

Well, shit. Now I definitely need the alcohol.

Chapter Eight

I FEEL LIKE I'M A voyeur peeking into a world that I'm not really a part of, that none of this is really happening, because honestly, how did I end up here? I will myself to stop looking at him and lean back in my chair and try to get as comfortable as I can.

I look over at Erik and Orie. They are my safe, happy place. I resist the urge to reach out and grab a glass of any type of alcoholic beverage that might be on the table and just down it in one sweeping gulp. My nerves are starting to get the best of me. The conversation going on around me dulls as alarm bells go off in my head and the realization hits me. Clayton represents the last hurdle in my life that I have to get over. He's literally a great white shark and I'm about to jump in the ocean with him!

How am I going to eat? Or even sit here for the next few hours and just smile as the anticipation builds inside me, making me more nervous by the second? I'm going to leave my old self behind and try to swim in a sea that he's clearly mastered.

Before I can dwell any longer on this he reaches out and puts a hand on my arm. "Would you like a glass of champagne?"

A glass, or a bottle?

"Yes, please." Make it quick. Forget the glass, I'll just take swigs from the bottle. But instead I say calmly, "A glass would be lovely, thank you."

"I ordered a bottle of Cristal and Krug Clos D'Ambonnay. But I can order another if you have a preference in flavor? I can help you choose?" he asks politely.

If the man buys ten-thousand-dollar bottles of scotch, I'm sure his taste in champagne is just as rich. And completely out of my league. I'm good with a bottle of champagne from Trader Joe's. And P.S., they have really good champagne. Who cares if it's $9.99? It tastes great.

"I'm sure what you ordered will be just fine. But thank you for the kind offer."

"You don't sound very happy with that option. Do you want champagne? Or would you prefer a bottle of red or white?"

I wish I could tell him to bring me one of each.

"I love champagne, Clayton. But thank you."

He stares at me for a beat. Searching. "You look a little pale. Tell me what's wrong."

I hesitate for a second then look around to make sure no one is listening.

"I'm a little nervous." He has to know. He has to feel it on me.

His smiles tenderly.

"Trust me, Sophie. I promise I will take care of you. You'll enjoy everything that happens. We're not going to do anything you don't feel comfortable with." He gives me a sexy smile before adding, "But I think you'll want every part of it."

Really? But I don't know what I want because I've never had it before. So how will I know what I want is really what I want and not just something great I've imagined in my head? I look at him, willing him to answer the questions in my head. And God almighty does he ever with that seductive look of his. The butterflies start again. I stare at his mouth, remembering just how sweet his lips feel.

"Don't look at me like that," he says softly.

"I'm not looking at you in any way."

"You are."

"I'm not."

"Are you arguing with me?"

"Yes."

He laughs.

"You'll soon realize that arguing with me is a useless endeavor. I always win."

"And you always get what you want," I reply tartly. I try not to roll my eyes.

Clayton cocks a brow.

"Yes."

"You sound like an overindulged child."

"Careful."

"Why? Do you bite?" I flirt.

"Only if you ask nicely."

I can feel my cheeks get flushed and I force myself to keep his stare. I know he's trying to shock me and I need to show him that I can hold my own.

"It's doubtful that will ever happen."

"Don't be so sure."

Before I can answer, Erik calls my name.

"Sophie, how are you doing over there?"

I look over at my friend and smile brightly. I know he was watching my face and reading me. God, he's good. I watch as the waiters bring out standing ice buckets and place them around the table. They quickly begin pouring drinks for everyone. I look over at Clayton and shake my head. The man certainly knows how to spend his money. But right now, a drink is exactly what I need and I've never been more grateful.

"I'm doing well."

"Have you had a chance to look at the menu?" Erik asks.

"Not yet."

"There's so much to choose from, I'm getting a headache just thinking about it all," he tells me as he flips through the pages.

"I've actually already ordered for the table," Clayton says and we all look at him. "I ordered some of everything. I thought we should try it all."

"Gluttony is a deadly sin, Clayton," Elizabeth says with a smile.

"If you believe in that sort of thing."

"Blasphemous bastard," John says, laughing. Clayton's sharp gaze flickers over him in disapproval and one simple glance makes John look instantly contrite.

"Apologies."

Clayton acknowledges his words with a slight nod. An awkward silence follows before Elizabeth saves the day.

She lifts her champagne glass and looks around the table, smiling at everyone.

"If this were my last night on earth, I can't imagine being in a more perfect place."

I like her even more.

"Well said, Elizabeth." Eduard lifts his glass. I watch her blush under his friendly gaze.

Interesting.

"Then enjoy," Clayton says.

"Who was it who said to live every day as if it were your last?" Eduard asks.

"Lots of people. Us. This table. Right fucking now. Let's do it," Erik answers him as he stands with his glass. "It's time to live a little, people."

The table cheers at his words. He looks straight at me.

"Sophie Walker. Thank you for coming into my life eight years ago. I love the hell out of you. You made me and Orie, the love of my life, come to this paradise with you . . ." His voice is emotional and it takes him a moment to get his breath. Yes, I'm touched, but my stomach drops thinking he's going to add the dreaded line "to find yourself."

The bastard would do it. He'd think it was hilarious. Oh shit.

After a dramatic pause, he lifts his head and meets my gaze dead on.

"Now we're sitting with new friends, sharing new experiences. Who knows where this ride will take us?"

Everyone but Jane seems to love what Erik says. They all toast and clink glasses, then take the shots that have been placed in front of them.

I mouth an "I love you" to Erik and Orie. I count my lucky stars that I'm so blessed to have such amazing friends.

"So let's think about this for a moment. What if tonight is the last night on earth?" Eduard asks us as he leans in.

"Well, if it is, I am happy to be spending it with old friends," John chimes in as he lifts his glass, "and new." He nods to me, Orie, and Erik, before continuing, "Cheers to everyone. May this *not* be the last night on earth, but if it is, I hope we are all pissed out of our minds when the end comes!"

Then they all lift their shot glasses. I'm beginning to sense the pattern for the night. I'm sure that everyone at the table is going to blitzed in about a half an hour. I hope I fall into that category, regardless of Clayton's wishes.

"Let's say this night will be just the beginning," Orie says to the group.

"I like that," Eduard laughs. "That's a very enlightened way to think."

"Well, what do you expect? The end sounds so fucking morbid," Erik says.

"Can we just drink now, for the love of God? And quit this heavy conversation? It's so depressing," Jane says in annoyance. She looks around the table and notices that I'm still holding my champagne flute.

"Are you not a shot girl, Sophie?"

"Sometimes."

"Then lift your glass. It's rude not to drink what your host has offered." I hear the biting tone in her voice.

"Sophie doesn't like to do shots," Clayton returns with a polite smile.

"And how would you know, Clayton? You've known her for a little over a day. Leave the girl alone and let her have some fun. Must you be so stiff all the time?" Jane's voice is cold, challenging.

I'm embarrassed by what she's said and I'm suddenly annoyed with myself for letting someone I really don't know dictate what I'm going to drink. What the hell is wrong with me? I'm supposed to be turning a new leaf, becoming a more assertive version of myself.

"You're right, Jane." I absolutely agree with her, because she *is* right. I've never allowed anyone to tell me what to do, so why am I starting now?

I pick up the small shot glass.

"Cheers." I smile widely at Jane and down the drink. I hear impressed whistles around me. I'm pretty sure Clayton isn't one of those cheering me on.

Damn, it's strong. I try not to cringe and to act like a professional, but it's hard. I carefully look to my left and notice that Clayton has also downed his quickly. Bravely, my gaze meets his and I instantly regret it. He's very pissed. It radiates off his body.

Mad Love

"Did you enjoy that?" he asks me icily.

"I did." I stand my ground. I'm not going to let this man tell me what I can and cannot do.

He seems annoyed by my answer. I watch the emotions play across his face, then I watch his demeanor turn completely indifferent.

"I'm glad. Would you like another?" Oh boy. This doesn't sound so good. A part of me wants to say yes and to hell with him and his bossy ways, because he's obviously very controlling and that needs to be dealt with, but the logical part of me knows that if I do I'm going down a road of no return. And I might not like the consequences.

"I'm alright, but thank you for asking," I answer in a voice that is as indifferent as his. "I'll just stick to champagne. It's wonderful, by the way."

His blue eyes capture mine.

"A wise decision, Sophie."

My heart drops.

There's a threatening tone in his voice again. I feel queasy.

"Don't do that."

"Do what?" I pretend I don't know what he's talking about.

"Look away from me like you're trying to hide from me."

I look and am happy to see that the rest of the group is immersed in their own conversations and paying no attention to us.

"Look. Whatever world you come from, I don't. Women don't just follow orders or blindly listen to everything a man says." I tell him.

I can feel the warmth of the alcohol rush through my veins, the buzz slowly creeping over me. And I know from experience that after the general feeling of buzz comes drunk, and that is the last place I want to be.

"I'm an American, you know."

Clayton is suddenly amused.

Did I just say that? *Yes,* you idiot, *you did.*

"I gathered you were. Did you suspect I didn't know?"

His lips twitch with mirth and I know he's trying hard not to laugh.

"I'm just saying."

Clayton loses it and starts laughing. The others look over curiously, but then resume their own conversations when they realize he is not going to share what he finds so funny.

"Are you finished?" I ask him, totally annoyed.

"Not quite, baby." Oh. I like that endearment.

"Well, let me know when you are," I tell him as I pick up my glass of champagne and take another sip.

"Do you think your father would approve of you allowing anger to dictate your actions?"

"What does my father have to do with this?"

"He's an attorney. A litigator. Containing one's emotions is an essential part of his craft. You never show your enemy weakness, or your hand. Isn't that the motto *American* trial attorneys live and die by?"

Crap. He has a point. I did react to Jane's goading me, but it was as much the implication that I was allowing Clayton to control me as it was about her.

"Your cheeks turn red when you're angry, you know," Clayton says before I answer. "It is a spectacular shade. It compliments your natural color perfectly." His eyes assess my face, a look so smoldering that it makes me want to jump straight into the ocean.

My heart races.

"Don't distract me."

"Come close to me," is his answer to that. "Lean in. I want to tell you something." His gaze is scorching, and, like a moth to a flame, I bend to him. He takes my chin and turns my head so he can whisper in my ear.

I get all hot and bothered.

"I want you."

Shit.

"I want to feel your skin against mine," he continues. "I want to take your dress off and then run my hands through your hair, see the way it falls down your back, how it brushes against your body. And then after I take my time memorizing every part of you, I want to taste you. Start at your lips and make my way down." He turns my face so I'm forced to meet his passion-filled eyes.

I'm pretty sure my mouth is hanging open.

"Are you game?"

I'm surprised I can nod.

"You still look worried."

"A bit." I can't lie.

"About which part?"

Not you. Not how you make me feel. Not how you make my body come alive. All that's the good part.

"What comes after." There. I said it. It is out in the open now. If he wants to run, that's fine. Erik would kill me if he heard what I just said. I'm supposed to just be in the moment and not wonder about anything else.

He moves a finger along my lower lip. "Don't be."

Easy for him to say.

Before he can respond to the look that's written all over my face, I see Noom standing at our table. She's wearing the baggy white pants and linen shirt again and looks like she just came from a session.

"Sophie!" she says in a happy voice. Lord, the woman does exude this Zen that is enviable.

"Noom." I stand and hug her petite frame. She pulls away and holds my hands, taking a step back to look at me in an approving way.

"You are glowing tonight," she says kindly.

I blush under her knowing gaze, acutely aware that Clayton is listening to our conversation.

"You're too kind, Noom. It's just the island weather." I motion toward the beach and the ambience of the party, trying to change the topic. "This is all so incredible."

"Yes, it is. I am happy you truly appreciate this gift. The gods will reward you for this, Sophie."

Lord Almighty, Noom says the damndest things.

"The gods?" I ask softly.

"Yes. A little bit of God lives in all of us. Even you. When you see true beauty and appreciate it, the universe rewards you."

"You see light in everything, Noom."

"Because I choose to. Once you do, the whole world will be a wonderful place. What you wish, will be."

Imagine that. It seems too good to be true.

"It is true. Don't doubt it, my friend," she tells me with a wise smile.

Clayton stands up and puts a possessive arm around my waist, then reaches out to take Noom's hand.

"Noom. It is always a pleasure."

I watch Noom's eyes turn from twinkly to guarded. It's a look I haven't seen on her face before.

"Mr. Clayton," she says back politely.

"I met Noom last year," Clayton tells me.

"Yes," Noom says.

"Fortunately, I didn't decide to jump into an ocean filled with sharks after my session with her," Clayton teases.

"Sophie?" Noom doesn't understand.

"I seized the moment," I say, blowing it off. Clayton's hand moves up to the back of my head and brushes it softly. I lean into his touch.

Mad Love

Hold on a second.

"You saw Noom?" I ask curiously.

"Yes."

I'm sure I look shocked. It seems completely out of character. "I'm surprised."

"How could I resist the resident Maldivian healer? Noom is said to be the best," he explains as he smiles cordially at her.

"Everyone has their own reason for seeking comfort, Sophie," Noom tells me quietly. I don't think Clayton appreciates her comment and I can feel his muscles tense around me.

There's an awkward silence as Noom looks from Clayton to me and I wonder what she's thinking. Or better yet, what she felt when she put her crystals on his body.

"Sophie, I want to introduce you to another healer who is here right now," she says as she points to the other side of the small u-shaped beach, where there are more tables. "I think you'll like him."

I don't want to leave Clayton's embrace, but I feel like I owe Noom for my current situation.

"I would love to meet him." Clayton doesn't look too thrilled with my announcement. "I'll be right back," I tell him and squeeze his hand in reassurance.

Noom nods a polite goodbye to Clayton and then we walk away.

"You really swam with sharks?" she asks as we walk.

Well, I wouldn't really call it swimming, I think to myself. More like sinking and holding my breath. But Noom doesn't need to know that.

"Yes."

"I'm proud of you, Sophie. That takes a brave soul."

"Thank you. But I wasn't so brave afterward when I fainted," I admit to her.

Noom laughs.

"Fear is good. Fear makes us human. It makes us know our mortality and our worth. Don't be embarrassed by that. You should be happy with yourself for facing your demons."

"The sharks, you mean?"

"Your demons, Sophie. The sharks only represent them."

I'm quiet as I absorb Noom's words. What am I afraid of if not sharks? When did I become afraid, and why? I guess Noom is right and that I should be happy that I actually took a plunge into the sea. I just faced one of the biggest fears I've ever had in my life. Maybe it's a metaphor for me facing my life head on from now on.

"You know that tonight is very important," Noom tells me.

"I know. It's the end of days."

"No. It is a day that we can realize our true potential. That is why it is so special. It is a soul ascension. You see that it is a full moon tonight."

How could I miss it? The moon looks so close it's like you can almost touch it.

"We believe the moon is very powerful. Every cycle brings depth into our lives. There is a beauty in the change that the moon brings. It helps us remember the cycle of life, of birth, and death. And then again, the rebirth. With every full moon we are shown that it is possible for us to become our true potential. So this evening is about celebrating that."

Her words hit me hard and for the first time I look up at the giant, white, beaming orb that is lighting up the night. It really is a spectacular sight. I don't think I'll ever look at the moon the same way again.

"That's a wonderful thing to say, Noom."

"Truth always is."

Noom finds the table she is looking for and motions to a man with peppered gray hair. He's in his late fifties, of medium height, wearing glasses, and his look is intense. There's something about him that calls to you. Makes you want to rush into his embrace and cry your eyes out.

I wonder if I'm having island fever.

"Dan, I want you to meet Sophie." Dan stands and puts out the cigarette he was smoking. He reaches out his hand and pulls me into his embrace.

"Nice to meet you, Sophie."

"You as well."

"Noom tells me that we must have a session together," he says.

I look over at Noom, a woman I've known since this morning and yet I feel so close to. It seems to be a recurring theme for me in the Maldives.

"She did?"

"Yes. She said you are very special."

"I am?" I can't keep the shock out of my voice.

Dan laughs. "Why are you so surprised to hear it?"

I shrug. "Well, Noom and I just met, and I've never considered myself as special. Crazy, yes. Special, no."

He smiles at me warmly. "I like your sense of humor. It is refreshing."

"I'm sure you encounter people like me all the time," I answer with a smile.

"Actually, no," Dan responds.

I wonder if that is a good or bad thing. I try to be optimistic and think it's good.

"Would you like to schedule a healing with me? It's different than what Noom does."

"How does your healing differ from Noom's?"

"Don't be afraid, Sophie," Noom says. "It is a once in a lifetime experience. Dan is the one who changed my life and made me see my calling as a crystal healer. We are very lucky to have him here right now. He surprised us all."

So if I see Dan, will I stay in the Maldives and become a crystal healer as well? I don't think my parents would be too happy about that. I'm thinking for them it would be worse than me wanting to be an artist. I think Dan can see the uncertainty in my eyes.

"I promise I will only give you truth," Dan says to me. It all sounds mysterious to me, but whether it's the general weather and sense of relaxation that this place gives me, I agree to it.

"Great. Then I will call your room tomorrow to schedule an appointment."

"Thank you. I look forward to our session." I turn to Noom. "I should get back to my friends now."

"Yes. I'm sorry for taking you from your party." Noom's smile wavers for a second. "How do you know Mr. Clayton?"

Oh boy. I was kind of wondering when she was going to ask me.

"I just met him."

"He is very familiar to you." I blush and look away. Noom rushes to assure me. "No, I don't say that in a bad way. It must be a soul connection. Things that happen so fast usually are."

Soul connection? I wonder what Clayton would think if I said that to him?

I try to blow her comments off. "We're just getting to know each other."

Noom seems to struggle a bit with what she wants to say but then goes for it.

"He is different than you."

Is he ever, Noom. Let me count the ways.

"I know."

"Forgive me, Sophie. But you are innocent—" Noom blushes.

If the sand would swallow me whole, I'd be the happiest person on earth. I really hope she doesn't bring up my—

"I felt your inexperience."

Holy shit. She went there.

The part that's amazing is that I'm actually standing here allowing her to say these really personal things to me. A woman I don't even know. I search for the most polite way to say that it really isn't any of her concern, but she keeps going.

"But maybe you are the food he needs."

I look at her, puzzled.

"For his soul, Sophie." Noom suddenly smiles and pulls me in for a big hug. "Enjoy your evening. I see it. You are the sustenance he's been searching for."

She leaves me standing there staring after her in complete shock.

What the hell is wrong with his soul?

I see a sudden flash of the distance that came into his eyes earlier today at his villa. And I've already seen it several times. Yes, there's definitely something going on in there. But then, don't we all have the same types of issues? Don't we all have our very own demons? I sure as heck do. I decide not to obsess about her comments because the riddle will most certainly not be solved tonight, and I head back to our table.

As I make my way across the beach, my eyes meet Clayton's. I get the feeling he's been watching me the whole time. I can't seem to break his gaze as I head over to him. Once I'm close, he stands up to pull out my chair for me. For all his, "I'm not a gentleman" comments, he sure acts like one.

"So tell me about that man."

He never does jealousy, right?

"His name is Dan," I tell him as he sits back down at the head of the table.

"Did you book a session with him?"

"Yes, for tomorrow. Or at least he's going to call me tomorrow."

"Tomorrow might not work for you," he tells me with a secret smile.

Really?

"Why?" I ask.

Before he can answer, Erik interrupts.

"Why didn't you introduce me to Noom, Sophie?" Erik shouts out to me from across the table.

"We wanted to meet her," Orie chimes in loudly.

The table is now on another round of yummy-looking cocktails. I pick up my boring champagne and take a sip. I suddenly feel like Clayton and I are the old farts at a table full of fun teens.

"Sorry, I totally forgot. I'll try to find her later on and bring her over to you guys."

"Who was she anyway?" Jane asks with a hint of disdain. If looks could speak, hers would definitely say, *"Why are we talking about the hired help?"* God, does she need a reality check.

"A crystal energy healer." Erik tells her, totally unfazed by her attitude. Or if he is, he hides it well.

Jane laughs in amusement. She looks so condescending. "Oh, my God. You don't believe in all that rubbish, do you?"

"Why not?" Orie asks in a bitchy tone. I take another sip of my champagne and get ready for good old Jane to make a nasty comment. I've already come to the conclusion that it is inevitable with her.

"It is completely ridiculous."

"Have you ever had a session with a crystal energy healer?" Orie asks her seriously. I know that he has a severe disdain for negative people in general. I almost feel sorry for her.

"No," Jane snorts. "I would never think of seeing a charlatan."

"Isn't that a bit unfair? Don't you think you should at least try something before you form an opinion?" he responds.

"I don't have to experience her healing to know that it's a load of bull, intended to prey on weak-minded individuals." Jane smiles coolly at Orie as she picks up her drink and takes a sip. The bitch's claws are out and I'm boiling now. I don't appreciate her insinuation.

"Well, I, for one, believe," Elizabeth interjects with a quick smile, clearly trying to avoid an argument. She looks at me curiously. "How was your session, Sophie? Tell us about it. Maybe Jane will understand if you explain it to her."

All eyes turn to me. Everyone except Jane seems pretty interested in Noom.

"It was nice," is all I can think to say, all I want to reveal.

"Come on, give us some more details, please," Eduard demands as he leans in curiously.

Clayton reaches out, takes my hand, and squeezes it.

"Sophie doesn't have to share a private experience with a table of people she barely knows." He literally speaks my mind. I smile at him gratefully. I think I love him at this moment.

"Why not? If she believes in the airy fairy she should stand by it," Jane returns rather bitchily. "Unless she's afraid of what we might think."

Oh no, she didn't.

In an instant I sit up taller in my chair and smile coldly at Jane. She doesn't know me at all. I've spent enough time watching my father chew people up for breakfast and spit them out for dinner, and I picked up a thing or two along the way.

"What is it you'd like to know, Jane?" I ask, in an overly inquisitive, sarcastic tone.

Erik and Orie smile in anticipation. If Erik could rub his hands together, he would. They've witnessed scenes like this go down a few times.

"More details than 'it was nice.' That's a safe comment. But then maybe you like to play it safe."

The silence at the table is deafening. She's just launched an attack against me. Every single person sitting here knows it and I'm actually glad she did, because now I get to put this bitchy Debbie Downer in her place.

"Jane—" Elizabeth tries to warn her. She gives Jane a look and I wonder again how in hell these two women are even friends. But Elizabeth doesn't need to defend me—I'm perfectly capable of doing it myself.

I hold my hand up and smile politely at her.

"It's alright, Elizabeth. I've got this."

I turn my attention to Jane.

"Are you sure you're ready to hear the truth?" The warning in my voice is unmistakable.

"Yes. I am ready to hear what *you* think is the truth, Sophie."

If we were in a boxing ring, the starting bell would have just rung. I lean in comfortably on the table, totally relaxed, careful to keep my tone cool, calm, completely unemotional. I could hear my dad's voice in my head: *To win any argument, one must remain unattached, almost bored, and above all, amused by one's opponent.*

"The truth is, it was an incredible experience. Mind blowing. I've had Ayurvedic and stone massages, acupuncture, Chi Nei Tsang, if you even know what that is, but this is in a league of its own. I felt energy around my body when she did her healing. We're all made of energy, so it isn't a leap of faith to believe in this. That's not "airy fairy." That's science. And if you care to know whether I'd do it again, the answer is yes. Would I recommend the experience? Yes. Absolutely." (And now for the chew.) "Especially for someone who is very narrow minded and desperately needs to grow spiritually, intellectually, and emotionally."

I take a moment to smile at her and I'm happy to note that she looks stunned. "You know, since you asked."

The table is dead silent.

I watch as Jane's face turns bright red. I immediately feel guilty for my attack, but good Lord, does it feel good to have shut this lady up.

"I guess that sums it up," Clayton interjects with a smile.

"I'm so in, girl. I need to see her." The tone in Orie's voice is one of pride. I know he and Erik just enjoyed that. They love to see what happens when my hackles are up.

"I'm definitely going to book a session with her, too," Eduard agrees in excitement. "I like the sound of her."

"Me, too," Elizabeth chimes in. She smiles shyly at Eduard and then looks away.

Hmmm. Was that a look of longing I saw in her eyes? I look over at Eduard and notice that he is completely oblivious. Not shocking, since he's a man, but still. Elizabeth is incredibly beautiful and sweet. I'm surprised he hasn't pursued her. They all travel together. That tends to help spark a romantic fuse. What's wrong with him? How can he not notice this woman?

My train of thought is distracted by the arrival of a hundred different appetizers to our table. The food varies from Indian samosas, to sashimi and sushi, to Thai chicken skewers. You name it and it seems to be on our table. This man, I've come to understand, doesn't mess around. About anything.

"You weren't kidding when you said you ordered everything." I say to Clayton.

"Well, the theme is a world market of food so I thought we should try something from every corner of the world," Clayton says. "What can I get for you?"

"I'll help myself, thank you," I tell him and then watch as he ignores me and literally piles food on my plate. I laugh. "Why did you even ask?"

"I thought I'd be polite," he tells me with a smile. Everyone pounces on the food.

"That was quite a chastisement," he says so quietly and nonchalantly that it takes me a second to realize that he's talking about Jane.

"She kind of deserved it," I defend myself, hoping that he doesn't take her side.

"She more than deserved it." Clayton helps himself to food then turns to smile at me. "You're very good at that. It's no wonder your father is upset that you quit law school."

Did I tell him that? I guess I must have, because how else would he know? But I don't remember telling him. Funny. In any case, I'm happy he doesn't disapprove.

"I guess."

He remains quiet and the awkward moment with Jane suddenly seems like it never happened. Everyone is talking and enjoying one another. Eduard and John start to tell childhood stories of when the boys went on trips together on holiday breaks and have the table laughing in no time. I'm secretly thrilled to get to know as much about Clayton as possible.

"The best trip was to Klosters in Switzerland. Do you remember, Clayton?" Eduard asks him with a devilish smile.

"I recall some moments," Clayton returns evenly. He gives his friend a look.

John interrupts in hysterical laughter. "You recall?" He's clearly had one too many. "You recall? My god man, you were thrown out of the Walserhof on your ass. And a very naked ass, I might add. Don't you remember?"

Eduard and John can't stop laughing and Elizabeth and Jane join in. Obviously this is a story they all know well.

"The first Sinclair thrown out of the Walserhof!"

John can't seem to get a grip. I look at Clayton, who's leaning back in his chair staring in amusement at his friends.

"We gotta hear this story," Erik demands. "This is not fair. You can't be the only ones laughing."

"I want to know why you were naked," Orie adds.

I couldn't agree more.

Eduard holds up his hand and looks around at the table, signaling everyone to quiet down.

"We always took yearly ski trips. Since Clayton was back and forth from Singapore and we didn't get to see him often, we really looked forward to these trips."

Back and forth from Singapore? Okay, so one of his parents must have lived there.

"Were your parents with you?" Erik asks.

They all look horrified at the thought.

"What kind of trip would that be?" John asks, with a roll of his eyes. "Can you imagine?"

Erik shrugs his shoulders. "Actually, I can. I travel with my family all the time. They're cool as shit."

"Trust me. If you met the people who gave birth to us, you'd understand my comment," John mutters darkly and takes another sip of his drink.

I look over at Clayton, who's staring down at the table pensively. I hope he didn't have it as bad as these guys. What are you thinking, Sophie? He probably did. Birds of a feather tend to flock together.

"Let's not put a damper on our conversation, John. No one wants to get depressed. Besides, you pay the family therapist to listen to your problems," Eduard lectures his friend.

Family therapist? My life is beginning to look like a Pixar movie in comparison.

"So we arrived at Klosters, John and I, and Clayton was already there," Eduard goes on.

Clayton looks over at me and shrugs his shoulders as if to apologize for his friends.

"We soon find out he'd arrived a day early. Turns out that our good old boy was having a bit of a dalliance with Sir John Pemberton's wife," Eduard says.

"The wolf was only nineteen at the time and Pemberton's wife was in her late twenties," John blurts out, finding this vastly amusing.

"Old Pemberton always did like them young," Eduard chimes in as he throws back his drink.

Clayton's friends chuckle as they remember what they think is a funny anecdote. But I can't keep the consternation off my face. He seduced a married woman. They call him *wolf*. And his friends think this tale is amusing? What is going on here?

"The wolf?" I say and look at Clayton.

"A name I was called in my younger years."

"Hungry like the wolf..." John belts out the old Duran Duran song. Elizabeth nails him in the ribs with her elbow and gives him a dirty look. He still doesn't seem to get it. And now, of course, sour Jane looks positively radiant.

Uh oh. Does this make me the next victim of the hungry wolf?

"I was nineteen," Clayton explains, undaunted.

"In case you haven't noticed, dear Sophie, Clayton has unusually bright blue eyes, just like a wolf. They always lured them in," Eduard says. By "them" I know he means women.

I mean, let's be real, I was lured in by them, too!

"Well, finish the story," Orie tells Eduard as he motions for him to go on.

"How do you mean?"

"There's got to be more to this then him being called wolf and sleeping with a married woman."

I almost spit out my drink. Leave it to Orie.

"I think we've heard enough," Clayton warns his friend. Oh no, we haven't, I think, and say, "No. I'd like to hear the rest of it too." I wear a fake smile. "He stopped at the best part."

I pick up my drink and down its contents. I look around the table and smile sweetly at Jane. This evening is definitely getting interesting.

I lift my hand and motion for the waiter, who rushes over to me.

"I'd like a pomegranate martini. With Grey Goose please." I look around at the table. "Anyone else want anything?"

"That sounds delicious; I'll have one as well," Erik says loyally.

Orie raises a hand with a smile. "I'm in."

I don't dare look over at Clayton. I know he's probably annoyed I'm now having hard alcohol when he wanted me to stick to champagne or wine to prevent me from getting drunk. But you know what? I don't care. His nickname is *the wolf!* Hearing that his predatory skills with women are akin to a deadly hunter in the animal kingdom is pretty full on. And scary.

John, who is beyond drunk, continues to sing "Hungry Like the Wolf." Elizabeth looks at me in horror and mouths, *"I'm so sorry!"*

It's like a bad romantic comedy. Except it's my real life.

Elizabeth tries to save face. "I think we all know how Clayton ended up being thrown out of the hotel naked."

"Well yes, *we* do. But they don't. And it's the best story. They haven't heard the funny part yet," Jane says. *Now* she's the life of the party.

Eduard looks at Clayton, who I've avoided looking at, and has the sense to seem a bit scared.

"I think that's enough rehashing of the past for tonight," Clayton warns him again.

But John shouts out, "Pemberton found the wolf in bed with his wife and Clayton had the nerve to tell the old man that she seduced him and that he didn't know she was married!" John laughs. "Security came in and escorted him out because management were scared of Pemberton. He demanded they march the wolf buck-naked through the lobby and out the front door! He didn't even let the poor guy put a cravat on. Lucky for him, our car pulled up at the same time!"

And how is this even remotely funny? Honestly? But the rest of them seem to think it is the most hilarious thing they've ever heard.

"I *didn't* know she was married," Clayton says in a tone that would make any man cringe. Unfortunately for John, he's too sloshed to hear the ominous threat.

"We never believed that, you know. You kept saying it, but of course you knew!" John continues in a drunken stupor.

Erik reaches out and pats him on the back, hoping to jolt him back to earth. "You're going to be in real deep shit if you continue on, my friend." Erik's got a smile on his face but we all know how true his words are.

"Bah! Clayton knows we're taking the piss out of him," John waves Erik off. "There's more!"

Chapter Nine

"I THINK WE'VE ALL HEARD enough, Johnny," Clayton tells his friend as he stands up and extends his hand for mine. "May I have this dance?"

I smile awkwardly because I know everyone is staring at us. And I don't want to seem annoyed, which I kind of am, even though I have absolutely no right to be. But I'm also dumbfounded because his friends are so strange. Why do they think this is an appropriate story to tell in front of me? And every detail of the story? Did I need to know all this?

"Of course," I say and stand up, refuse his hand out of principle, and make the excuse of picking my dress up off the sand. Clayton waits patiently while I step away from the table, then takes my hand firmly in his. He won't let me get away. We walk toward the music.

The band is playing a soft reggae tune as we join the other couples on the dance floor.

"I was just a child, Sophie," he says as he pulls me into his arms. I keep my eyes on his neck as I put my hands on his chest. The familiar feeling washes over me as I savor his touch. The pulsating energy that seems to course through my veins makes me forget time and place. I can't even keep it together for a second, even though I just heard a wicked story about his womanizing ways. What's wrong with me?

"Look at me," he says.

"I'd rather not right now," I tell him honestly. "I'm trying to digest all that."

"Are you upset with me?" He sounds incredulous. I lift my gaze to his.

"The wolf?" I'm pretty sure my face looks appalled and I don't try to keep the disdain out of my voice. "Really?"

At least he has the decency to look a bit embarrassed.

"I'm not going to apologize for my youth." He stares at me and I have to agree with John and the however many other women he's been with, that yes, he does have the most burning gaze I've ever encountered.

"That was a different time in my life. And I'm sorry if it upset you . . ."

"It doesn't upset me, Clayton. It scares me," I abruptly answer.

"Get over it. It is an old story and you'll probably hear more of them in the future. Everything that happened then made me who I am today."

"Did you know she was married?"

"No."

I stare into his eyes, hoping I'll see the truth. And it's there. He lets me inside for a second and I nod in acceptance. I feel the tension leave his body and he smiles at me in relief. He leans down and puts his forehead against mine.

"You know what they say about wolves?"

"What's that?" I ask softly.

"That they mate for life." I lose my stomach, a combination of his words and his embrace.

"Do they?" I say calmly.

"Yes, they do." He kisses me softly then pulls away.

"We're leaving now." Yet again, it's not a question; it's a command. His eyes are blazing with passion and I'm satisfied to see that he looks as unnerved by our intense chemistry as I am.

"I want to be alone with you," he continues. I wish I had a fan to cool myself down. He takes my hand and gives me a look so incredibly intense that it makes my body burn.

"Are you ready?" he asks.

Am I ready? We both know what is going to happen. There's no hiding from it. I look up at him. The stars in the sky frame his head and shoulders like a painting. I know this night is going to change my life forever. In addition to the obvious, something more profound is going to happen. I've read so many books about destiny and defining moments that I know I'm living that experience now. I push any thoughts that could ruin this moment out of my mind and I just be, as Erik advised me.

"I am ready," I finally answer.

He gives me a sexy smile and leads me back to the table, where we quickly say our goodbyes to everyone. Clayton doesn't let me linger around Erik or Orie. I wave at my friends and follow him. When he continues right past the deck that leads to our villas, I give him a puzzled look.

"Where are we going?"

"It's a surprise."

I feel an anxious twinge, but I stay quiet and follow him. You could literally cut the air with a knife, our sexual tension is so palpable. I want him to kiss me again, make me feel alive and take away my fears of what lies ahead. Clayton takes a turn down a tree-lined path toward the main docks.

In the blink of an eye I'm picked up, pushed against a palm tree, and Clayton's mouth is on mine. He takes savage control, and I'm more than happy to let him. I move my hands through his hair and pull him in. His tongue curls against mine and I gladly take it, sucking in all that he will give me. I can feel him hard against my body and I love that he wants me as badly as I want him. I moan when his mouth leaves mine to trace kisses down my neck.

"You are a witch," he whispers.

"So you keep telling me," I pant.

Clayton abruptly pulls away from me and pulls me further along the path. "I'm not going to let my desire get in the way of what I've planned."

Shit. Why not? As we walk, he says, "I'm going to ask you an uncomfortable question."

I'm instantly on edge. "Okay."

"Are you on the pill?"

My face heats up instantly.

"Some women do take birth control even though they're not sexually active," he explains, as if I'm five years old and don't know how the reproductive process works. Could this be any more mortifying?

"Thank you, Clayton, but you can assume that I know about the birds and the bees."

"That's not what I asked." He's says with a smile. I know he knows I'm humiliated by this conversation, but that I also understand why this is a perfectly logical question for him to ask.

"I'm on the pill." Lord, is this uncomfortable.

"How long?"

Really? What is he, my gynecologist?

"Are you serious?"

"I want to know." I wonder why he cares.

"About three months," I say, annoyed. "And do you want to know why?" I ask the last part sarcastically.

"Yes, that was my next question."

Is he for real?

"I was stressed out and my body was out of whack!" I practically yell at him. "Are you happy now?"

He stares at me for a long minute.

"What? " I ask.

"I'm not happy your body showed a reaction to stress."

Lord almighty. I'm so annoyed, I blurt out, "What about you?"

"Men don't take birth control, Sophie."

I can hear the laughter in his voice. He takes a step toward me, slowly, watching me as he speaks. He knows the effect he has. He knows how he makes me feel. He knows the power he wields, the wolf that he is.

"But if you're asking me if I used protection in the past, then yes."

He's staring down at me, his hand brushing my face as he speaks. "Always."

His fingers move to my lips, touching them softly.

"I've never had sex without a condom." Those intense eyes of his seem to bore into me, daring me to move or speak. "I've never felt a woman without protection."

I need water.

"And in case you're wondering if I'm healthy, yes, I am."

Actually, I want to know if it's possible for the sand to open up and suck me through it so I can be done with this mortifying conversation and never have to look at you in the face again.

"Don't be shy. This is a very adult conversation to have. It's only natural, considering what's going to happen between us."

My pulse races. I try to get a grip and take deep breaths. He reaches out, takes my hand again, and caresses my palm softly.

"Let's go, baby."

Baby.

I love the way he says baby. It's so sexy. I choose not to say another word as we continue on. He leads me to the main dock of the hotel, where our seaplane landed.

"What are we doing here?" I ask.

"You'll see."

We reach the end of the dock, where a small motorboat, captained by Bikram, waits. There's champagne on ice with two glasses on a small table and a bowl of fresh strawberries and cream next to a cushioned seat. It is *so* romantic.

"Welcome, Miss Walker. Mr. Sinclair."

"Hi, Bikram," I say warmly as he helps me into the boat. Clayton follows and picks up a life jacket to put on me.

"Seriously?" I don't want to ruin the effect of the dress, given the romantic boat ride we are about to take.

"Yes. I don't want to worry," he says as he buckles me up. I can't believe that it was only a day ago that he did this before. The day I met him. And now look where I am? Where I'm going. What's about to happen. It feels like a million years ago. It's unreal that so much can happen in such a short time.

I try to stay cool.

Clayton, who, of course, is not wearing a life jacket, pours us each a glass of champagne, hands me a strawberry with cream, and lifts his glass for a toast.

"It is only the beginning."

We clink glasses and take a sip of our drinks as Bikram slowly pulls the boat away. Clayton moves close to me on the small seat and pulls me in to his body, the life jacket making it kind of awkward, but it's still nice to cuddle up to him. I lean back and look up at the moon and stars and I think I must be the happiest woman alive. The night is magical. I couldn't ask for anything more.

"Are we doing a cruise around the island?" I ask him as Bikram speeds up and the motor roars.

"No."

"Then what?"

"Patience," Clayton tells me with a smile. He sets his champagne glass down on the table. "I think you'll like what I have in store for you." He leans down and kisses me chastely on the lips. I'm disappointed when he pulls away. His eyes darken with desire and he leans in again, kissing me more seductively, then licking my lip.

"You make me forget myself," he whispers. My smile is immediate. "You think it's amusing?"

"No. I just thought I was the only one who lost control."

He holds my face with one hand. "Rest assured, you're not alone in this predicament."

I lean into his touch then turn my face and kiss his palm. I know he likes this show of affection because he pulls me tight against his body.

"How far are we, Bikram?" he shouts out.

"Not long, Mr. Sinclair. Ten minutes."

Clayton takes a long sip of his drink. I'm so happy that he's as affected as I am. I lean back into his arms and enjoy the rest of the ride. I want to memorize everything about this moment so I can replay it over and over in my head for the rest of my life.

When the boat nears a dock lit by tiki torches, I see that our destination is a small island that appears to be deserted. Bikram maneuvers the boat up to the dock.

"Thank you, Bikram," Clayton says. "Is everything I requested inside?"

"Yes, sir." Bikram holds a bag in his hands. "I will need your shoes. I will give them back to you when I pick you up."

"Why?" I ask curiously as I slip out of my heels, not that I have any problem with it. I watch as Clayton does the same.

"No shoes on the island. It is about complete relaxation," Bikram explains. It sounds positively decadent and I like it already.

Clayton helps me out of the boat, takes off my life jacket, and hands it to Bikram, along with a tip.

"We'll see you in two days," Clayton says.

Bikram smiles in appreciation then nods to both of us.

"Yes, sir. Enjoy yourselves."

Wait. *What?*

Two days!

Clayton and I watch Bikram speed away. There is no turning back now. I can't very well swim back to the hotel. I don't even know where we are. Not completely true. We are somewhere in the Indian Ocean. My iPhone might be able to find my location. When Bikram is a speck in the distance, I'm acutely aware of how incredibly silent the night is. How close the stars are. We are literally in the middle of nowhere.

"Is there anyone else on this island?" I ask Clayton, even though I already know the answer.

"No."

Oh. My heart starts pitter-pattering again.

He looks down at me. "I let Erik and Orie know, don't worry."

"Clothes?"

"Taken care of. Along with your personal toiletries."

Who went in my room and gathered my stuff? I don't ask him. I look around in wonder. *He rented an island for me.*

"Let me show you where we are staying."

I'm only capable of nodding and plastering a smile on my face. I

Mad Love

don't miss the emphasis he puts on the "we." A wave of nausea sweeps over me and I try to talk myself out of throwing up. When I was growing up my parents always told me never to talk to strangers, and here I am, about to sleep with one. The irony is not lost on me.

Grow up, Sophie! Just grow up, my mind yells at me. Let's just look at the facts; you're a twenty-three-year-old virgin, the most gorgeous man in the world has generously offered to rid you of this dilemma, and he rented an island to do it on! An island!

Who rents an island?

He knew he was going to get lucky tonight. He didn't have to do all this! But Lord, it is incredibly chivalrous and caring of him, or a bit insane . . . I'm not quite sure which. I follow him down the long dock and onto a tiki-torch-lit sandy path. I'm guessing he's been here before because he knows exactly where he's going. We're both quiet, just holding hands and enjoying the night.

And then we come upon it. Where we are sleeping.

And I lose the ability to breathe.

It is a large, straw-roofed villa that is kind of like where you'd imagine Robinson Crusoe lived. Twinkly lights illuminate the walkway up to the residence and large candles frame the entrance. Clayton motions for me to go first and I slowly make my way up the stairs. I open the doors and what I see takes my breath away.

There are candles everywhere. A plush, L-shaped white couch curls around a long coffee table, looking out on the ocean. All the sliding doors are open, letting in a gentle breeze. To the right is the kitchen, which has every appliance you could desire and which, I imagine, is fully stocked, because Clayton doesn't seem to forget any detail. The deck has a long table and chairs to eat and enjoy the spectacular view, and wraps around the entire villa. Stairs lead down to the sandy beach. I can't wait to explore it in the daylight. To the left is the master bedroom, and I take a moment before I step inside. White, long-stemmed roses and huge white candles are everywhere. There is a retractable roof, which is currently open. The view from the bed is unreal; it's almost like you can reach out and touch the stars.

Oh starry night.

I'm sure I look beyond impressed.

"Clayton, I don't know what to say. I feel like I'm in a dream." I turn around to find him.

He's a good distance from me, standing by the bedroom door, casually leaning against the frame. He's watching my every reaction.

"I'm glad you like it."

"Like is hardly the word," I say with a smile. "*Absolutely love* would be a much better description."

I shyly look away from him, trying to distract myself from what's about to happen by looking around the room.

"Have you stayed here before?" I asked tentatively, dreading his response but wanting to know.

"No. I was told about it."

I feel relieved that he didn't come here with whatever woman he brought with him on his last trip. Crap, why even go down that road? *Not tonight, Sophie,* I tell myself. Tonight you're not going to think about anything that can ruin this.

I tremble in anticipation of what is to come.

Chapter Ten

WE STARE AT EACH OTHER in silence for what seems like an eternity. The electricity between us crackles like a fire. I watch as he slowly unfolds his arms, lifts his hand, and starts to unbutton his linen shirt, his eyes never leaving mine.

Oh. My. God.

I think I might hyperventilate. I watch the last button come undone and I'm given a clear view of his bronzed chest as his shirt drapes open. If you saw a picture of him right now, you'd think you were looking at a photo in a sexy Gucci ad.

Lord, have mercy.

My legs are glued to the ground. No way I can move. He looks like a dream, like the guy you had fantasies about as a young girl. And he's here. Standing in front of me. Wanting *me*. He moves away from the door and slowly makes his way to me.

Like a wolf, stalking its prey.

My breath quickens nervously. I wonder if he can hear it. I feel flush all over my body, as if he's already touching me, making me want him. An eternity later, he reaches me, stands inches away, and just watches me with that look. God, when he's this close, I realize just how tall he is, how powerful. He's just so wonderfully delicious to look at.

"Take my shirt off," he says.

Lord.

Carpe diem, I tell myself. I lift my shaky hands up to his chest and just place them there for a minute, trying to get a grip on myself, hoping he can't feel them trembling. I hear him suck in his breath as my hands begin to trace a path down his chest, over his muscled stomach. His body is chiseled like stone. He's like a walking piece of art.

I become bolder and step closer to him, moving my hands through the light sprinkle of golden hair, then push the soft material of his shirt off his shoulders, letting my hands follow the path it takes as it falls to the ground. My fingers roam over his muscled arms and I wonder how many times a week he works out. He's barely breathing. I look up at him and see the fire in his eyes.

Oh my. He wants me.

I take a shaky step backward and stare.

"You're perfect," I tell him as I stare into his bright gaze.

If possible, his eyes darken even more. He slowly looks my body over, from the top of my head to the tips of my toes. As his eyes linger on my lips and chest, I can almost feel him touch me in those places, our connection is that strong. I try to be as confident as he is and look him over too, and I see the proof of his desire. I wonder again if we'll fit. We have to, right? It's basic anatomy.

I don't think about that much longer because he takes a step closer to me. He reaches out to play with the material of my long dress. He rolls the fabric between his fingers, and then traces a line over my breast, my heart, my throat, and then my lips, where I know he can feel my rapid breath.

His hand moves to my hair, and he begins to move my shoulder as he walks behind me. It's unnerving not to see him, just to feel him there. I gasp when his hands touch my back, brushing my hair forward over the dress. I shiver in anticipation. I know what he's going to do.

He finds the zipper and slowly pulls it down. My dress falls open and I instinctively reach out and hold it up, keeping it from slipping to the ground. The design of the dress didn't allow me to wear a bra. My backside is completely exposed to him. The only thing I'm wearing is a crème lace thong. I give a silent prayer of thanks that I've always cared about the look and feel of my lingerie, even though no one but me has ever seen it.

I hear his sharp intake of breath, and then I feel him lean forward and kiss my back. His hands move around to the front of my body, over my hands, which have a death grip on the dress. He slowly unclasps my fingers.

"Let it go, Sophie," he whispers seductively in my ear.

Fear of the unknown has me holding on like the dress is my lifeline. But I have to let go. It takes me a second, but then I do. It falls to the ground, and now I'm almost completely exposed. His hands move down my waist and reach my thong. He tugs at the waistband then very gently pulls it down, his skin rubbing against my body. He moves back up and wraps his arms around me from behind, pulling me in close to him. I can feel how hard he is against me. I'm so thankful he's still wearing his pants. He leans down and kisses my neck.

"Do you have any idea how beautiful you are?"

Am I?

The way he's looked at me has made me feel sexy and alive, but I can't even think to answer as he licks his way down my neck to my shoulder blade, his hands still, allowing me to become comfortable with my own nakedness and his proximity to it. Then he moves around and picks me up in his arms, cradling me against his chest.

I don't have time to be embarrassed about my breasts or any other part of my body being exposed because before I know it I'm on the bed and his body is on top of mine. He leans up on his elbows to look down at me. Lord. I'm completely naked underneath him.

I state the obvious. "Your pants are still on." It's the only thing I can think to say.

He smiles. "I know. I don't want to scare you."

"I think we're past that point."

He laughs at my words.

"I guess we are." He leans down and kisses me softly on the lips. I trace the hard lines of his back, tracing the hard lines of his body. It's hard to keep my wits about me with him so close.

"I've never wanted anything more in my life," Clayton whispers before he leans down and kisses me again. His kiss is hot, hungry, his tongue ravishing every crevice of my mouth. This is unlike any of our other kisses, because this time I can taste the full force of his passion. And it rocks me to my core.

He pulls away and begins to kiss my breast. His tongue licks my nipple and sucks while his hand cups my other breast. I arch up to him, moaning in pleasure. Each sensation is so new to me that I savor every second.

"Oh my God." The whisper comes out. He pulls up and looks down at me. I can hear his deep breaths. My eyes flutter open and find his. The look he gives me is one of pure ownership. Pure possession. As if I belong to him.

"Has anyone ever touched you like this, Sophie?"

"No."

"What about this?" His finger touches my hardened nipple.

I shake my head and close my eyes, trying to hide the intense reaction I'm having to his touch.

"Open your eyes." I take a shaky breath and look up at him.

"Yes or no?" he asks me again.

I can barely even remember what it was he asked.

"No."

Clayton's hand moves in between my thighs. "And this?" I instinctively try to close my legs against him. He won't allow it. His hand moves between my legs. I know I'm wet with need.

"Look at me, Sophie," he commands. I do as I'm told. "Answer the question."

"No, Clayton," I whisper softly. I gasp as he slips a finger inside me. It is such a strange feeling; I don't know how to react to it. I grab hold of his hand and try to push him out, even though it feels so good.

Clayton reacts swiftly. Keeping his fingers firmly in place he covers my body which his chest, his mouth finding mine, his tongue moving deeply in my mouth. His fingers begin to move in and out slowly and the feeling that comes over me is so intense that I forget my embarrassment. His thumb touches me softly and I feel like I'm on the precipice of exploding. My hips move with his hand, against it, wanting more, needing more. I don't even know what I want, but I know he can give it to me.

"You're so hot for me. I love the way your body responds to me," he says as he pulls his mouth from mine and licks his way down to my breast again. The feeling of his hands in the most private part of my body is so overwhelming, that I feel myself coming to pieces.

"Clayton!" I scream out as I explode over and over again. My body shakes as I reach climax. It is the most intense feeling I've ever had. I tremble, and all I can think is, *Holy shit*. This is what I've been missing? Clayton moves away from me quickly and takes off his pants. In a moment, his body is over mine again and I can feel every part of him. I can feel him against me, touching me. I can barely think; I'm still reeling from the orgasm. But his naked body against mine is making me fill with desire again.

"Sophie, I want you to look at me."

"Okay," It's hard to open my eyes because I'm lost in a vortex of desire. I just want. I hold his shoulders as his hand moves in between my legs again, touching me and making me crazy with longing, and then he slowly eases inside me. I feel an unbelievable tightness as he pushes farther into me. He groans in pleasure and I keep my eyes on him, desperately trying not to close them.

"God, you feel so good," he whispers. I'm glad. But I'm still trying to get used to the feeling of him inside me. It's so different, but good.

Just when I think I'm okay with my body feeling so full, he pushes all the way in and I can't stop the scream that rips out of me. *The pain! Holy shit. He's so damn big!*

He leans into me, kissing away the tears that I can't help, but not before I catch a glimpse of the immense satisfaction on his face. I try to move away from him, but he holds me still.

"Shhh, baby. Give it a second. It will feel good, I promise. I will give you satisfaction."

How is this supposed to feel good? I have to tell him what I'm thinking.

"You're too big. We don't fit." He licks away one of my tears and chuckles. I can feel his smile against my face.

"We were made to fit, baby." I suck in my breath at those words.

And before I can respond he kisses me softly, like I'm the most precious thing in the world to him. My fingers move over his warm skin and I kiss him back just as tenderly.

"You're so exquisite. Your skin is like silk. Your body is paradise.

And it's all mine," he whispers against my mouth before kissing me again, his tongue sweeping into my mouth. I feel the now-familiar heat move through my body. The thought of being all his, the feel of him, it all starts to make my body sing again. The liquid fire races through me.

Clayton is wrong. He's the witch. He seduces me with one look; one touch and I'm lost. His hand moves in between our bodies, where we are joined together, and I feel such intense gratification from this touch that I instinctively lift myself to him and move them slowly, with him deep inside, letting me find my way. And then I forget time, space, who I am, and I just . . . feel.

It is all the encouragement Clayton needs before he grabs my hips, takes control, and starts to move in deeper, slowly, then out. The sensation is so, so incredible, I can't think. He moves in again and I meet him. Oh my God. I never want him to stop.

I wrap my legs around his waist and hold him tightly as I try to take more of him inside. Is it possible? He moves faster, burying his face in my neck, kissing me, licking me. Moaning in pleasure. I hold on to his shoulders, his sinewy arms, and then I feel the build toward climax start again. His fingers grip my ass as he pounds into me harder. And harder. Oh my God. It feels so good.

"Come for me again, Sophie."

And as if my body was made to obey him, the vortex of bliss begins again. He thrusts in harder and I meet him, wanting to reach the euphoria he wants to give me. I'm frantic with desire as I pull him in deeper, the wave of satisfaction coming for me so hard and fast that I think I'll die from the exquisite feeling. He pushes further and I reach the peak and explode, climaxing again and again.

It is obviously unlike anything I've ever experienced in my life before. And this time, I scream out his name as the euphoria rocks through my body. He finds his release at that moment, his eyes on me, then buries his head against my neck as he comes inside me, thrusting in and out, prolonging my release, filling me with ecstasy. The last coherent thought I have before falling asleep is that I can't wait to do it again.

The sun shines brightly in the room, waking me from my perfect slumber. For a minute, I forget where I am. Then I look down and see the tanned, muscled arm wrapped around my waist like a vine. Oh shit. Memories of the night before wash over me. I can feel a blush steal up my body as I think of how shamelessly I behaved. Sleeping with a man, giving myself so completely to him, who would have thought it was possible? That I would be this person? Sophie. Virgin. Walker.

He nuzzles my neck as his arm tightens around my waist, pulling me closer to his chest. I feel his hard-on against my back and in a second I'm warm all over as I think of how much pleasure I felt with him inside me. I wonder if it's always this good. Do all couples experience this kind of bliss? Before I can think about that for a minute longer, Clayton pulls me on my back and leans over me, smiling.

"I can feel you think, you know," he tells me. I get butterflies in my stomach as I take in his gorgeous appearance. His hair is mussed from sleep, he has a bit of stubble, and his eyes have that sexy, slumberous look. Good God, he even looks divine in the morning. I wonder if I look a fright. I hope not.

He studies my face for a moment, and then his hand moves to my forehead and pushes my frown down. Mr. Sinclair seems to be in a playful mood.

"Regrets?"

Is he serious? What more could a girl ask for? I've heard horror stories over the years about girls losing their virginity. He made it the most perfect experience of my life.

"None," I answer honestly.

"Then what are you thinking?"

I blush.

"Tell me, Sophie."

I can't meet his gaze.

"Just that, you know, you look really good when you wake up," tumbles out of me.

He doesn't answer right away, so I look up at him. Oh my. His eyes are heavy with desire and he looks like he wants to attack me. Ahhh, the wolf is back. I kind of like it. Okay, I *really* like it.

His hand moves up and cups my breast, massaging it softly, rolling my nipple through his fingers, his touch possessive and confident.

"You're very sexy, you know. You have this innocence about you, even now. Like a beautiful angel . . . even though I've seen the other side of you." My stomach drops at his words. "And I haven't even begun to play."

"Play?" I can't help but ask softly.

"I'm going to make love to you every which way possible. And then I'm going to show you how to pleasure me. I have so much to teach you, Sophie. Bliss you can't imagine."

Oh my God. The way he talks. Who says things like this? I can feel myself getting wet just from his words. Heat and longing course through my veins at the thought of him having his way with me. Yes, he can. I'm all his. I can't wait to get started. As if he's tuned in to my body, his hand moves down and his fingers slip inside me, cupping me at the same time. My hips arch up for more. His smile of satisfaction is telling.

"You're wet for me already. I like that. Because I've been up half the night wanting to be so far inside you. And I've been thinking about how you're only mine."

I want him again. I want to know how to make him as crazy as he makes me. But I can't even find the words.

He spreads my legs and settles between them. My eyes close as I feel him start to enter me. There is a moment of discomfort as my body adjusts to his size and then I forget about that because all I want is for him to be deep inside me. He grabs my hair and twists it in his hand, pulling my face up to his so he can kiss me. It's open mouth, carnal, his tongue devouring mine roughly, making me so hungry for him that I pull him in.

He thrusts into me. Hard. Filling me up, and God, do I love it. My thighs move up and grip him tightly as I silently begging him to just have me every which way. He rolls onto his back, pulling me on top of him. I groan in satisfaction from the feeling of having all of him inside me. So deep, God, just so deep. He doesn't move, so I can accustom myself to the feeling of him, both hands still, holding my ass.

My eyes can barely stay open as I look down at him, reveling in the feeling of having him like this. I'm lost in a tsunami of feeling. My lips part, my head tilts back as I grip him, thinking I'll die if he were to disappear.

"Christ." Through my passion-filled haze, I look down at him. The look on his face makes me feel crazy with desire. Those eyes, aglow with hunger, eat me alive, like I'm the sexiest thing he's ever seen. His lips are parted and I can hear him hiss with satisfaction as he looks from my breasts to my face. It's at that moment that I realize how much I turn him on. It's the most powerful feeling I've ever had, knowing that this man wants me so much. I arch my back and let my hands move lightly across his skin, teasing him, testing this newfound power that I have.

Clayton knows my game and quickly proves who is teacher and who is student. His hand rubs against me, sending a vibration of unadulterated ecstasy through my body. The feeling is painfully exquisite.

"Do you like that?"

Shamelessly, I whimper in response.

He touches me again, slowly, masterfully. I almost come undone by the tantalizing bliss.

"Now I want you to move, baby." His voice is harsh with desire. I rock forward, then back. Shit. It feels good.

"Again," he commands, and this time he lifts my ass up and down. My head falls back from the intense, mind-blowing feeling. And then I follow his lead and start to rock forward and back, moving my hips on my own, taking more and more of him inside me, loving the feeling of being in control and the pleasure, sweet Lord, the pleasure of having him. Within moments, I can feel the build inside.

"Clayton," I whisper, groan actually, feeling my climax about to wash over me. His answer is to roll me over on the bed and push so deep inside of me that I think I'm going to die of euphoria. And God, it would be a happy death.

"Is this what you want?" His voice is raw with need as he thrusts into me even harder.

"Yes." He increases the rhythm, pumping me harder, and before I know it, I feel the explosion move through my body. I call out his name, squeezing him tightly, feeling as though I will die without him inside me, and then he climaxes, plunging even deeper, pushing against me.

We both lie there for a moment, panting breathlessly, trying to regain control. I can't stop trembling.

"Jesus," I hear him swear against my ear.

He pulls out of me slowly and I wince in pain, proof that I am definitely not a virgin anymore.

"Are you okay?"

I blush.

"Yes, thank you. I'm just a little sore," I admit.

A look of satisfaction appears on his face again.

"I'm glad."

He gets out of bed, perfectly comfortable with his nudity, and looks down at me. I'm instantly mortified and close my eyes. I mean, he's naked, for the love of God! Clayton laughs right in my face.

"Are you shy now?"

"I'm not used to—" Well shit. I'm not used to any of this!

"I know. It's just fun to tease you, Sophie. It's so easy to get a reaction out of you. Are you going to open your eyes now?"

Do I have to?

I pull the sheet up around my breasts and look at him. "I'm glad I'm such a source of amusement."

"You're perfect."

He leans down quickly and places a chaste kiss on my lips.

"Afraid to look?"

"Hardly," I tell him, and to prove the point I let my eyes move over his muscled body. My mouth goes dry. It's not right, not normal, how damn near unreal his body is. Or how large he is. Shit. Did all that fit inside me?

"It's all yours, baby."

With those final words, he turns around and heads to the bathroom. I'm given a healthy view of his well-shaped ass and I resist the urge to pinch myself.

All mine, I think.

For now, at least.

Chapter Eleven

THE NOISE OF THE shower brings me back to reality and I finally have a second to take it all in. I'm not a virgin anymore. I can't believe I've had sex . . . and with an enigmatic, smart, alluring stranger, but a stranger nonetheless. Damn; I wish I could call Erik and Orie or text them—something! They must be dying. I can't even begin to imagine the kind of stories they're concocting in their heads. None of which could possibly come close to reality.

I gingerly move out of bed, wrapping the sheet around my body to cover my nudity, and I'm happy to see that the discomfort isn't as bad as I thought it would be. I look back on the bed and see the small drops of blood on the sheets, more evidence that I'm no longer a virgin. Right there, plain as day for everyone to see. And by everyone, I mean him.

I look around for a clean set of sheets, hoping I will find something before he gets out of the shower. My search takes me to the giant armoire in the living area. The view holds me captive for a moment. In the light of day, it is bewitching. We have a large deck that sits on the white sand beach. It is a cloudless day and the sea is so calm it looks like glass. I actually can't wait to get in and do some snorkeling. Knee deep, of course.

I open the armoire and am happy to find many sets of clean sheets. The resort is obviously well prepared, and I am so thankful for it. I hurry back to the bedroom and almost trip over myself when I see Clayton standing there with a white towel wrapped around his narrow waist. His golden skin is a mouth-watering contrast to the towel, his broad chest still glistens with drops of water, and it's all I can do to keep my mouth from popping open in utter lust.

He brushes his wet hair away from his forehead, looks toward the bed, then back at me. My flush of embarrassment is instant.

"Let me take that."

I think my toes even blush.

"I've got it," I croak out.

"Sophie, I'll take care of it. Take a shower, relax." He walks toward me. I step back, holding the sheets in front of me like a shield.

"I've got this." *It's my blood!* I shout to myself. *My* innocence, lost on the bed!

"No." He reaches me, shiny with water and so damn handsome that I'm practically limp, and takes the sheets from me. "Take your time, sweetheart. Let me do this." Oh. There's another endearment. Sweetheart. God, I love hearing it.

"I'm responsible for that anyway," he adds.

My eyes close and I lean against the wall, wishing I could just spontaneously combust. I rush past him into the bathroom and shut the door. Once safely inside, I let out a sigh of relief. Lord almighty, my wires get crossed when I'm around him.

I let the sheet fall to the ground and turn to look at myself in the mirror. I don't look any different.

I'm happy to see that my toiletry bag is sitting on top of the counter. I brush my teeth quickly then grab my shampoo and conditioner and turn on the shower, which could fit ten people. It has multiple showerheads sticking out in every direction, to hit you in every which way possible. And the luxury doesn't stop there. There's also an entire dressing room in here, with floor-to-ceiling windows that face the ocean. The bathroom is the size of my bungalow! It's really quite unbelievable. I can't even imagine what this place costs.

As Clayton suggests, I take my time in the shower and think about the night before.

His hands. His mouth. His skin. God. I see quick, erotic images of him and in a second I find myself wanting him again. Is it possible? Maybe I'm some sort of sex-deprived person? Well, that shoe certainly fits. Hmmmm. Finally, I force myself to turn the water off and get out. I wrap a large, white, fluffy towel around my body and look around for my bag. It's neatly placed in the closet of the dressing room. All my belongings have been unpacked, placed in drawers or hanging in the wardrobe. My things are on one side, Clayton's are on the other.

I've never shared a closet before. With anyone. I lived at home when I went to college and after I graduated I moved out and rented a one-bedroom apartment in Westwood on my own. It's so strange to see your personal things next to a man's. It is so very intimate. I find I like it. I hurry and change into a dark blue bikini and throw a matching summer tank dress over it. I walk back into the bathroom and brush my tangled hair. I decide to leave it wet because I know we're going to go in the ocean, lie in the sun, and who knows what else, but there is definitely no need for me to blow-dry it.

I open my make-up bag, look at myself in the mirror, and pick up my powder brush. I guess I should at least try and be a vixen, even though I have no idea how. I wish Erik and Orie could magically appear and do a once-over on me. Since I know this is not going to happen, I'm left to my own devices. I definitely don't want to look like I'm trying too hard.

The door opens.

It startles me even though I know it's Clayton. He's wearing his black swim trunks. No shirt. All that glorious chest there for my perusal. My mouth waters. I wonder if I will ever get used to it. We make eye contact in the mirror.

"You don't need any of that. Your face is beautiful naturally." I beg to differ, but I wisely choose not to say anything. And honestly, I am happy that he thinks so.

He comes up behind me and pulls me up against him and I melt. His naked skin burns against mine and I tingle all over from the feeling.

"I was getting worried about you in here." He nuzzles my neck. His warm skin sends a jolt of electricity up and down my spine.

"You told me to take my time," I remind him.

"I know. But I find myself getting anxious when you're not around."

Laughter escapes me and I raise a teasing brow.

"For the entire two days that you've known me?"

Clayton has the decency to look offended.

"You don't believe me?"

"No." *Foot in mouth,* Sophie. "I mean, yes."

Lord.

"I can assure you that I am not a liar. That is a trait I abhor and will not accept in family, friend, or lover." When he says lover, he looks down at my lips and I watch as his eyes take on that familiar glow. Yes, I guess I am his lover now.

Clayton's eyes meet mine in the mirror.

"I wanted to be near you from the moment I set eyes on you in the waiting area in Male."

His words take my breath away. And then there's the look in his eyes. *That damn look.* And if there was any other doubt in my mind I'd only have to remind myself of all his actions. Yes. It all leads to one glaring truth, Sophie. He likes you. Clearly. But what I don't understand is *why?* Why does he feel this way about me? What makes me so special? This is a guy who can have anyone in the world. Obviously, money is no object for him, he has the right pedigree, and he happens to be too good looking for words. So why me?

I try to convince myself to stop going down the ugly, self-doubting path. I know how quickly I'm capable of turning all this into something very loathsome when it has been just the opposite. As if he can sense it in me, Clayton quickly turns me in his arms and grasps my chin, forcing me to look up at him. He looks so serious.

"What's going on in there?"

I know he is referring to the storms he sees. The insecurities, the incidents in my life that left me scarred and thinking that I wasn't good enough. It is so pathetic that I still think about the rejection I experienced in school. But I do. I was never asked out by the popular guys, in fact, *no one* ever asked me out. No guy I ever secretly had a crush on even gave me the time of day. Watching perfect-looking girls in high school get everything they want was a real confidence destroyer. So I turned that feeling of insecurity into my own kind of armor. Maybe that's why I never let Jerry in, or any man for that matter. Or maybe I was just waiting for the right one. The one staring at me in the mirror right now.

I don't answer him.

"I'm serious, Sophie. I can feel your mind going to all sorts of places, and I can tell they're not good. We're going to have to change that about you."

"Are you clairvoyant or something?" I ask him in amusement,

brushing off his comment.

"Maybe. Who knows? But I can just feel you."

I know, I think to myself. *I can feel you, too. All around me. Deliciously warm and inviting.* And I can read your moods as well. I wonder what this means. I'm sure Noom would tell me that we have some sort of psychic connection.

Funny, but the thought doesn't seem so crazy to me now.

"Do you believe me?" His look is serious.

I take a moment.

"I do," I tell him honestly. "I believe you. But I just . . . I just don't understand why."

Could I sound any more pathetic? Probably not. But I don't dwell on it because I watch as Clayton frowns at me.

"Were you bullied as a child?" He suddenly asks.

Oh my God he thinks I need therapy.

"No! I just, you know—"

"No, I do not know."

I don't think he's going to let me out of this awkward conversation so I just continue on in my honest way. The only way I know how to be.

"I wasn't popular in school and so maybe there's a part of that I carry around with me." I shrug as if it's no big deal.

He pulls me close tenderly.

"They were fools," he whispers. "But I'm happy for it because now I have you."

I'm glad he's so happy for it. But I don't know if I can say the same, especially if I'm reliving it right now.

"So now it's your turn," I tell him.

"I just," he searches for the words then continues on as my mind races in a thousand different directions, "I just felt like I knew you when I saw you. It sounds crazy, but I knew you. I hadn't even seen your eyes, but I knew what color they would be. I knew your body, your hands, I knew every part of you."

I'm speechless. It is the most romantic thing anyone has ever said to me in my life, and it might be totally naïve, but I understand what he means. I get it. When he walked in the waiting room, I felt his energy before I even saw him. I was just drawn to him.

I'm in deep shit now because if I'm honest with myself, I know I'm already half in love with him.

"Sophie?"

"Yes?" I reply.

"Who do you think moved your villa?" He gives me a soft smile.

Wait.

What?

"You changed our villa?" I know he can hear the surprise in my voice.

He doesn't seem the least bit embarrassed by this confession.

"Yes."

"I don't understand." Why would he move us? *Was this all a ploy?* Within three seconds I'm robbed of my security. I hold my breath in anticipation. I turn in his arms and try to read his face, but he gives me nothing.

"You know why," he says softly. "I book the villa I'm in and the four bungalows adjoining mine so I'm not disturbed. When I first set eyes on you, I knew I wanted you next to me. I had to know you."

Hold on a second. There are many things in his statement that need to be addressed.

"You don't like people?" I ask first.

He laughs, clearly amused. "I enjoy my privacy. I have it so rarely that I guard every private moment I get."

Okay. That's fine. Sounds totally normal. I can understand this. Now onto the other point. Is this what happens when he meets a woman he thinks he wants?

I pray I'm wrong.

"Do you always do this sort of thing when you meet someone you want to know?" I regret asking instantly because I think I'll die if he tells me yes, that it is a common Clayton Astor Sinclair practice.

His face is instantly cloaked in detachment. He's gone from looking like a considerate, caring lover to a block of ice.

"I don't know if that comment even deserves an answer."

It doesn't take a brain surgeon to tell he's pissed. And on top of being angry, he's offended. What he undoubtedly thinks is a romantic gesture, I've turned into a tactic.

But I don't care. I want to know. I deserve to know.

"It really does."

"My answer won't change anything."

"The only thing it doesn't change is one glaring, obvious thing." The blush creeps up my cheeks when I mention my virginity, or lack thereof. I wonder when I won't have this reaction anymore.

I am happy that I'm being so assertive. Score one for Sophie Walker. And let me tell you, this is practically a first. On the other hand, Clayton is not happy.

"You're still mine."

God. There he goes with the Neanderthal comments again. The ones that make my toes curl and get me hot and bothered, when they should probably do just the opposite.

I gently move out of his embrace, giving myself a few steps of ground to muster some courage and get a grip on my desire. I put on my best USC Law School, litigating, bad-ass face. And I tell him the truth.

"I don't belong to any man, Clayton. Least of all a guy I've known for a couple of days."

The atmosphere in the room goes from bad to worse. Picture ominous black clouds spewing thunder and lightning. My heart beats rapidly in my chest as I watch the tsunami get closer to the shore.

"Would you like to take back what you just said, Sophie?" he asks in a dangerously soft voice.

Now he's *warning me*.

Crap.

Yes, as a matter of fact, I do want to take that back, I shout to myself, panicked by the look in his eyes. But shit. I can't back down. I just can't. For some perverse reason I have asked for this. I hope he can't tell that I'm a little bit afraid. Okay, wary. No. Afraid. Definitely afraid.

"No, Clayton," I enunciate his name the same way he did mine. "I don't want to take that back. I belong to no man."

It takes all my willpower to hold still and act like I don't care. The last thing I want is to shake like a leaf and ruin my newfound courage. I turn to the mirror and pick a lip gloss from my toiletry bag and carefully dab some on. I can feel him behind me just seething. I wonder if there's another exit to the bathroom beside the one he's kind of standing in front of.

Is he a fast runner? Probably. I'm pretty sure that he excels at everything.

"There's no other way out," he says.

My eyes dart to his in the mirror. How did he know?

He smiles coolly. "You're easy to read, baby."

Oh shit.

"Just remember that you asked for this."

Before I can even ask what it is that he thinks I asked for, he pulls me around in his arms and his lips meet mine in savage ferocity. I welcome the assault on my mouth as my hands move to his head and pull his face closer to mine. Our tongues clash and I'm immensely satisfied when I hear him moan with desire. And that sound brings me back to reality.

Hold on a second! I need to remain aloof. What am I thinking? I can't just cave in to him! I move my face away from his, trying to get a grip on my raging hormones. This behavior is not normal! I have to take a stand now or else I'll lose all credibility.

I try to picture myself in my Torts class in law school. That's a good one. Boring. Dreadfully painful. Okay, I got this.

I hear Clayton chuckle as if he knows my game. He lifts me up on top of the marble sink, clearly not deterred. He pulls me in close toward him, so that I'm forced to practically straddle him and starts to kiss my neck. I try to remain uninterested. Remind myself that I can't tolerate this kind of behavior. I tell a guy I don't belong to him and he goes caveman on me?

But it's hard to remain cold. It's *so* hard.

Hard to pretend that his touch doesn't affect me when I'm so inexperienced that I can't help but have it feel so thrilling. And damn him, he knows this! It takes him only a few minutes before I've melted and my lips start to respond to his, my hands move up to grip his arms, my legs go from limp to gripping him tight. And just when he has this response from me, he grabs my bikini bottom and pulls it off, pushes me back so my head brushes up against the mirror and before I know what is happening, he grabs my ass and pulls me up to his mouth. With the skill of a master, his mouth and tongue drive me to the edge. Sweet. Holy. Shit.

His tongue. Inside me. Deep. Licking. Sucking. I think I'm going to explode from the sheer ecstasy. I can't even grip his head and pull him up to me, because I have to hold on to the counter for dear life.

And every damn time I come close to finding release, he pulls back, like he knows I'm about to come. He licks, he pulls, he blows, knowing exactly how far to push me before easing back. The grip he has on my ass is so tight I can't even wiggle away from the blissful torture.

Oh my God.

"Clayton," I whimper in need.

Suddenly he is making love to me softly, slowly. Erotically. I push myself up to him, trying to get more, but he won't give it to me. He takes one hand and slowly moves against me as he licks and sucks. I want to scream. Fuck! What is he doing? I look down and see him there, in the most intimate part of my body, and I'm so turned on it *hurts*. I want him inside me. Filling me. Just so deep inside. Holy shit.

"Please!" I beg him to give me what I want. But he'll have none of that. Instead he grabs my body and turns me around so I can look at him in the mirror. One of his hands holds my hair back, the other is wrapped around me, moving against me, grazing me, then stopping. I can barely stand it. I'm dying with need.

With want.

With lust. I close my eyes and try not to think about how good he feels inside me, how he fills me, how it's just so damn perfect.

"Look at me," he says, his voice raw with passion.

I can't, I'm so mortified by it all. By my need. By my inability to maintain control. By my lack of shame.

He pulls my hair back tighter, gripping my head so hard that I'm forced to look at him.

"How bad do you want me, Sophie?"

I'm going to die if you don't fuck me, Clayton, I think to myself. Please. But I don't give him what he wants.

Somehow he's loosened his swim trunks and is moving his hips against mine. I want to scream. I'm so swollen with want that I've lost the ability to think. I try to push up against him, forcing him inside, to give me the release I need.

I close my eyes again and Clayton pulls my head back again, forcing them open.

"*I want you to keep your eyes open.*" His voice is rough, his eyes glowing with something more than passion. He's the wolf now and his need to conquer and subdue is written all over his face.

And yet, in my passion-induced haze, I know this is torture for him as well. I can see how bad he wants me, but he's trying to teach me some type of fucked up lesson. At this point, I don't even know what it is anymore.

In a distant part of my mind, I can hear myself say with longing.

"Clayton, please!"

He pushes me down on the counter and leans on me, barely grazing, just circling, as he whispers in my ears.

"Who do you belong to?" he demands to know as his fingers thrust inside me. The ecstasy is so staggering that if he wasn't holding on to me, I would fall off onto the floor.

"Who?" His licks my neck as his mouth moves up my throat.

"You!" I cry out, desperate for him.

"Say it. All," he orders. I hear the passion in his voice. The need.

"Go ahead and scream it, baby. No one can hear you. Only me."

God.

I hate him.

I love him.

I hate him.

I love him.

"I belong to you, Clayton." My voice is raw with hunger. "Are you happy? I belong to you! *You asshole!*"

I'm practically sobbing now with need. It is so humiliating that I had to add the last bit for my own self-worth. I swear I can feel him smile, and yet he still wants more.

"That's good, love. You're learning. We're almost there."

I cry out in frustration. Jesus! What else?

"You're mine, Sophie," he says through gritted teeth as he pulls up against me, his hands on my breasts, on my stomach, moving all over my body. I'm delirious with fucking want.

"Say it."

"I'm yours," I pant out, because I am. He knows it. I know it. Fuck. The entire W Spa and Resort knows it. "I'm yours, Clayton. I want you!" I scream at him in a feverish frenzy. I've lost all inhibition, all sense of decorum. This is me. Sophie Walker. Wild. Uncensored. Bare. And I don't give a flying shit anymore.

"Are you happy? I'm yours and I want you so bad—"

Thankfully I don't have to finish the sentence because he thrusts deep inside me, giving me exactly what I want, until again and again I reach sweet release.

My legs are wrapped around his waist and he's leaning over me on the counter, still deep inside. I've orgasmed I don't know how many times. I'm completely satiated. Happy, even though he's clearly got some major issues, but hell, I'm so content, I could sit here all day.

"You make me forget myself," he says.

I can feel his body tense when he says those words. It's apparent that he doesn't like admitting this to me.

"Let's just say the feeling is mutual," I grumble.

He pulls out of me suddenly. And I feel the loss.

"Let's shower."

Clayton is again as cold as a block of ice. I let him grab my hand and pull me into the giant shower. I even let him wash my body, and it literally takes all my willpower not to get turned on again by him and his magic hands.

I rinse off as I watch him rub the soap quickly over his body. He's been quiet the entire time, just staring at me, watching, observing. Doing that goddamn thinking thing he does. I try to act cool too, and gracefully get out of the shower. I pick up a plush towel and start to dry off. I want to give myself one minute without him. One minute just to think normally. To be Sophie.

Smart Sophie.

Innocent Sophie.

Virgin Sophie.

Shit. The last adjective is obviously not even a possibility to entertain. I'm definitely no virgin anymore. I discreetly look over at Clayton. His eyes are down and I can tell he's stewing. He still hasn't said one word and I'm suddenly deathly afraid. Let's be real. This is a guy who is used to models, to the most beautiful women in the world throwing themselves at him. They know how to act. They know the game. They've had experience. And here I am an innocent who was totally played by a master. I keep drying myself with the towel while I think.

"Are you trying to rub your skin off?"

Damn him. He's been watching me have my internal dialogue. I hope my lips weren't moving, as they sometimes do when I'm silently yelling at myself. Erik and Orie were kind enough to point that out to me one time.

"I'm just drying myself off," I reply aloofly.

He gives me a cocky smile.

Yeah, yeah. He knows I'm full of shit.

"Are you happy now, Clayton?" I blurt the words out before I can help myself.

Shit. Why did I just ask him that question? *Because you want to know,* my mind annoyingly tells me. You're like a newborn puppy looking for a pat of affection. Any affection. Even just a light tap.

And let's be real, he should be happy. He got his way. And I know

I'm screwed. I'm the one who entered this weird, strange union with no experience and now have to suffer whatever consequence it brings.

"You sound like you're reprimanding me." His brow is raised.

He moves a hand through his wet hair as he looks at me. I wrap my towel around my body. I wonder if my skin looks as good.

"Get that look off your face," I tell him. "I've had enough of the Clayton Astor Sinclair rules of punishment for the day."

"Clearly you haven't."

Okay. Maybe not, but there's no way in hell I'd ever admit that. I turn and face him. Hands on hips, jaw jutting out. Before I have a chance to say anything, he adds, "I'm going to try and be patient with you, Sophie."

Ha!

"*That* was an example of your patience?" I can't keep the incredulous tone out of my voice. I hope he is seriously joking.

We stare at one another for a long, silent moment. I force myself to keep his gaze and not be the usual shy Sophie and look away. It's hard, though. Especially when my opponent is a man who is clearly stronger than I am. More experienced. Hotter. Smarter. And yes, so rich that I can't even comprehend it. His wealth is so staggering and overwhelming that you are just enveloped in it.

The rational part of my brain knows that my thoughts make no sense, but here's the thing, he was born into this world, and no matter how privileged I thought I was growing up, Clayton is on a whole other level. So maybe I feel like his wealth also gives him carte blanche, a green light to speed off in his Bugatti when the rest of the world is stuck at a red light in a Honda.

"Believe it or not, but yes. This is the most patient I've ever been."

It takes me a moment to come back to earth from my inner dialogue. When his comment registers in my head, I realize that I am in trouble now.

"I see red when you say my full name, by the way." This is a warning. Obviously. You'd have to be a complete idiot not to get it. This pisses me off too.

"Do you?"

"Yes."

"Well, you'll have to forgive me. I don't have the family manual. Maybe there's one I can download and read through quickly so I'll know the 'dos' and 'don'ts.'" I want to pat myself on the back for this rebuttal. I think it's a good one.

Not Mr. Clayton Astor Sinclair, who cocks his head to the side and slowly smiles. Instead of feeling warm as I usually do when I see that sexy look, I suddenly feel like I'm in some dangerous waters. I wonder what his next move is going to be? What is he thinking? In an instant, I'm flooded with a wave of uncertainties. Am I just a fun diversion during his stay here in the Maldives? An American girl who's the antithesis of the women he's grown up with?

The dark path down the Sophie Walker insecurity lane is never fun. It's kind of like my own personal *Nightmare on Elm Street*. You never know what hideous image is waiting around the corner.

On cue, a dark thought enters my mind.

Is he Henry VIII and am I his Anne Boleyn? Amusing, witty, but ultimately unable to keep his attention?

Headless, in the end?

Shit.

"What the bloody hell are you thinking?"

My gaze meets his and I try my hardest to mask my feelings, hoping that I don't look as insecure as I feel.

"Nothing," I say nonchalantly as I pick up my navy blue sundress, which is crumpled on the floor, and hold it up against my towel.

He walks over to me and lifts my chin. I can't look at him. I don't want him to see this part of me.

"Sophie."

I focus on his chin.

"Look at me."

I realize I'm acting a tad childish and I know from firsthand experience that it's pointless to resist him, so I meet his bright blue gaze.

"What's going on in there?" He looks almost concerned.

"I told you—"

"You lie."

It's infuriating that he can read me so easily. I guess I don't have much of a game face. But still. There is no way I will tell him the turmoil I'm going through. The roller coaster of emotions that I'm experiencing. Some things are better left unsaid. My dad taught me that; he drilled it into my head. So I do know how to remain silent.

The frustration is written all over Clayton's face.

"Talk to me."

"Why?"

"Because I want to know everything you're thinking."

I almost laugh. Is he serious? "Trust me, you don't. And honestly, what does it matter? If I say what I feel, you see red. I'm a quick learner." I kind of huff out the last few words.

"Are you angry?" He seems surprised.

"Maybe. Actually, I'm a bit bothered by what I'm gathering is your uncompromising personality, quite honestly."

"I like that," Clayton smiles.

"You like anger?" My stomach sinks at the thought.

"I told you. I like honesty. I like real. I don't want a proper response from you. I want the Sophie Walker response, whatever that is.

Happiness. Sadness. Anger. Joy. I want it all."

"What about when I just said I don't belong to you?" I ask him. "Do you want all of that too?"

Clayton gives me a sheepish smile as he shrugs his shoulders.

"That might be pushing it."

"So we're back to me telling you everything you *want* to hear."

"No. If I wanted to hear the proper and forced thing I wouldn't be here. I'd be back at my villa with my friends, listening to Jane talk about absolutely fucking nothing."

My bitchy smile is instantaneous. Clayton looks amused.

"Don't care for Jane, do you?"

"I haven't even thought about her." *Self-obsessed snob that she is,* my mind mutters silently.

"I know a lot of variations of Jane. Most of the women in my social circle are like her. She is actually tame in comparison to them."

Jane's tame? Just what kind of people does he allow in his social circle? If they're all like her, all he's ever known, what's he doing with me?

"Am I just a novelty?" I finally ask.

I hate that I allowed myself to blurt that question out to him, but as I live and breathe, I know myself. At one point or another it would have found its way out of me. In my defense, it is an honest concern. I wanted to know if I was just a new toy for him. Something different they can all tell stories about when they get back home. His smile quickly disappears and I see that this particular Sophie Walker response may really annoy the shit out of him. I bet he already regrets telling me to be completely honest and straightforward with him.

"For a smart woman, you asked a piss poor choice of a question."

"I don't think so. I think it's completely fair."

He's more than irritated now.

"You're really asking for it, aren't you?" He shakes his head at me, his voice almost scolding as he drops his towel. And I can't help it. My mouth drops open.

Good God Almighty. Clayton Sinclair is a sight to behold.

I take a step back and get some oxygen into my lungs. He raises a brow, aware of how much he unnerves me, the bastard.

I find courage in the white towel that's wrapped around my body and squeeze the hell out of it as I say, "Just what do you think I'm asking for? A minute ago you said you wanted my honesty. Now you don't? You're going to have to make up your mind."

He pauses for a minute, walks slowly to me, and stops when he's a breath away. He uses his sex appeal like a gladiator uses his sword.

"This is going to be fun."

He leans down and grabs his swim trunks, slips them on, and smiles at me. I'm sure he can hear my heart beat a mile a minute. I hate that he can throw me off so easily.

"What is?" Shit. Why did I even ask?

"All of it. Especially taming you." He brushes my cheek when he says that last part and I feel the goose bumps move over my body.

"Jane is tame." I remind him.

"Yes. But you're not nor will you ever be Jane. Or her version of tame."

I'm happy that he knows this. But I feel compelled to explain a few things to him.

"Here's the thing, I've never been a submissive person. I don't take orders very well. And I hate being told what to do. In fact, I have an aversion to it. My mom and dad can vouch for that. I'm trying to understand why the exact opposite is the case when it comes to you. I've been dancing to the beat of your drum from the minute I've met you and it's totally out of character for me."

"I'm not your mother and father. You like it when I tell you what to do because it's new and exciting and because you're attracted to me. And because you like the idea of a man taking control." The words are said so enticingly, his smile so sexy, so impossibly arrogant, that I almost believe him.

"Don't be so sure."

"Sophie." He puts his thumb on my lips "I look forward to proving you wrong. It's who I am. You'll understand one day."

I don't think so, but I choose to keep my mouth shut.

His fingertips find my lips. My mouth opens automatically and he leans down, and kisses me.

"It's the world I come from, baby. We get what we want and we don't take no for an answer."

Chapter Twelve

"WHAT ARE WE DOING?" I ask him when I finish brushing my hair.

"I've prepared us some breakfast, which is very cold by now, but it will have to do."

"You cook?" I say, shocked. I catch a glimpse of him rolling his eyes in the mirror before he leads me out of the bathroom and through the living area onto the deck.

"You can't expect me to answer that."

Well, excuse me, but hell . . . I really am surprised that he cooks! I assume he has a full staff of people back home, who wait on him hand and foot. I wonder if he has a butler who dresses him, like in Downton Abbey?

Probably. Jeez. What a life.

A moment later, I forget everything because I see that Clayton's set the most elegant table—seriously, it's something Martha Stewart would put together. He covered the table with large palm leaves and bright red tropical flowers. Two white plates sit opposite each other, with a red flower in the center of each dish, and the appropriate forks and knives are where they belong, along with two, tall, bubbly, mimosas. In the center is a delicious-looking omelet, along with fried potatoes, tomatoes, and bacon. As if that's not enough, there are also two coconut bowls filled with fresh-cut fruit. It's almost too pretty to eat.

And so completely different from what I had expected from him. Immediately, I think of Don Miguel Ruiz again: *Never make assumptions*. I silently cringe. Obviously, I need to read the book again.

"Thank you for doing all of this." I don't even try to keep the awe out of my voice. "This spread looks like Collin Callender meets Martha Stewart."

"I only know Martha." He says this quietly, like he's embarrassed to admit it.

"You *know* Martha, huh? Is she, like, on speed dial?" I ask teasingly.

"Actually, she's a good friend of my mother's."

Oh.

Right.

Of course she is.

"I've surprised you again."

I shrug nonchalantly, like it's no big deal. I mean, let's face it, I do live in the celebrity capital of the world. I wonder if I should tell him that Ben Affleck supposedly lives nine streets away from my parents. Nah, maybe not.

"I'm from LA, Clayton. I see celebrities all the time." Not true, but what he doesn't know won't hurt him.

"That's right. How could I forget?" He sees right through me.

A moment later, he sits down opposite me and puts a generous portion on my plate and says, "Eat."

I take a taste. Even though it is cold, it's really good.

"This is delicious, thank you."

"You're very welcome, baby," Clayton says.

Baby. He is pretty damn sweet. And hot—I actually think he's getting more good looking the better I get to know him. I instinctively take his hand and kiss it softly.

"You're amazing. Thank you for this. Actually, for everything. From start to finish this is the most romantic experience of my life."

He seems startled by my compliment and I can tell from the faint blush, not so comfortable with it.

"Get used to it," he says.

Is he serious?? I take the serving spoon and dish some omelet and sides on his plate and realize I'm *starving*. I really didn't eat much last night because we left after the appetizers.

Clayton lifts his mimosa.

"Bon appetit."

We clink glasses then start to eat. I notice how proper he is. His manners were probably drilled into him at some posh boarding school. There's something to be said for English etiquette.

I picture him as a child, dressed in a little boarding-school jacket, solemnly studying a book in the corner. He was probably a quick learner and a perfect student. Just the mental image brings a smile to my face. It also raises a ton of questions.

"Are you an only child?"

There's a smile on his face as he finishes a bite of food. He picks up his aviator sunglasses from the table and slips them on as he watches me. My God. Does he realize he could have been a model? I bet the girls fought over him all the time.

"I have two younger brothers."

Whoa. Really? I'm surprised. Clayton totally gives off an only child vibe. He seems like a loner.

I wonder if his brothers look like him. If they do, the women back home must have been beside themselves wanting to hang out with the Sinclair men.

"How old are they?" I move the eggs around on my plate as I wait for him to answer. I figure I'm going to have to *pull* everything out of him. He's not going to offer any information for free.

"William is twenty-five and Michael is twenty-nine, turning thirty next month."

"Are you guys close?"

"Yes."

"Do you work together?"

From his chuckle, I gather he finds my comment vastly amusing.

"Definitely not. William is working at my uncle's law firm. And Michael is off saving the world. Or at least trying to."

"I like him already."

"Do you?" Clayton asks softly, eyes narrowing. I try hard not to roll my eyes.

"I like anyone who tries to make the planet a better place. Unfortunately, not that many people are willing to dedicate their lives to it. I think it's noble."

Clayton is silent. I can't tell what he's thinking, especially now that he has the sunglasses on. So I'm surprised a minute later when he opens up about his brother.

"Michael is quite the do-gooder. He infuriates my parents no end, but continues doing what he loves. He's in Costa Rica right now, trying to save the bottlenose dolphins." He takes a sip of his mimosa. "Before that, he was in the Congo, and prior to that, Vanuatu."

"Why does that make your parents angry? They should be so proud of him." Even my own grumpy, hard-to-please dad would be happy if I was off saving animals instead of wanting to be an artist.

"As a Sinclair, you have two choices. Attorney or family business. And by attorney, I mean become one in order to assist the family business."

"The family business is shipping."

"Yes."

"So you work for your father?"

Clayton's bark of laughter tells me that's a giant "no."

"My father didn't give me any money when I got out of school. He thought I should work for it. So I started my own shipping company with money I made myself investing in hedge funds, I thought I'd give him some healthy competition. Michael and William have had it much easier than I did."

"I'm sure you don't mind reminding them of that, as only an older brother would." I can't resist.

"Of course." He smiles widely. "Every time I have the opportunity."

"And your dad?"

"Relentless, aren't you?" He shakes his head. "Now, I'm actually my father's biggest competitor."

"That must make for an interesting Christmas dinner."

He cocks a brow. "You have no idea."

"So why didn't you just work with him?"

"Because my father is from the old guard, the kind who believes in a conservative way of doing things. I'm of the new age, you might say, much more fearless about taking risks. And what I call fearless, my father would call reckless."

"How did your father take it?"

"He didn't speak to me for two years. My grandfather, his father, forced a reconciliation by feigning a life-threatening illness." A soft smile appears on his face when he mentions his grandfather, and it's wonderful to see. There is genuine affection there.

But let's be real.

This is a little strange. Why would he want to compete with his father? He's his father, not his enemy, for God's sake. This is not normal.

Mental note to self, Clayton Sinclair has some serious daddy issues.

"Your grandfather sounds like my kind of guy."

"The finest of gentlemen."

It's hard not to hear the hero worship in his tone.

"So he's still alive?" I ask carefully.

"Yes. And as tyrannical as ever. But softer in his old age." The smile is still on his face. It's the longest I've seen it there.

"And obviously loved."

"Without a doubt."

I study his face again, reveling in the softness and love that is there for his grandfather. If he could love that way, it would be a dream come true—but I can't allow myself to entertain that dangerous idea for one second. I'd just be setting myself up for heartbreak.

I quickly fire more questions, intentionally trying to distract myself from dwelling on emotional thoughts that could lead to sudden Sophie depression, or SSD, as I call it.

"I assume this is a century-old family business?"

"Yes. Both my father and I are in oil, deep water drilling, and maritime transportation," Clayton interrupts. "I'm contemplating investing in rigs and tankers, but I haven't decided if I want to take on the challenge just now."

No wonder money is no object to him—he's not only made what I can only fathom is an obscene amount of money on his own, but he comes from serious blue-blood, old-school, ancient-lineage, family money too.

Sinclair.

Or is it *St. Clair?*

As in the St. Clair family hypothesized to be of the Merovingian bloodline?

I can feel Clayton watching my reaction and it takes all my willpower to pretend that this is the type of conversation I'm used to having all the time. I go on.

"So are you more successful than your dad?"

"As I said, I am not afraid to take risks and my father is. He refuses to gamble, whereas I have achieved the success I have from listening to my gut, which he believes is foolish."

"Well, he must be proud of you, even though you're the competition."

"Secretly, perhaps," he says quietly. "But he'll take that to his grave."

"Oh."

We're both quiet for a moment. I know Clayton is thinking of his father and I hope I didn't somehow ruin the day for us by bringing up a sore subject. I give him a big smile and pour us both some coffee.

"Do you and your brothers see each other often?"

He picks up a mango slice and takes a bite.

"We made a pact that we would never let more than a month go by without seeing one another."

"I like that."

"It works out pretty nicely. It's just enough time apart for us to want to get together, and briefly enough that we don't kill each other."

"You're lucky. I grew up alone with two overbearing parents."

"Did your parents want more children?" he asks curiously.

"My mom was a dancer and had all sorts of issues. When she carried me, it was very difficult on her body. A year after I was born, she had a cancer scare and opted to have a hysterectomy, just as a preventative measure," I tell him quietly, "so that was it. No more kids. Just me. So they kind of obsess over every little thing."

"Understandable."

True. But try telling a seventeen-year-old that. Or making an eighth grader understand why she is the only one in her class who can't go to D.C. for the graduation trip, the only kid out of a class of one hundred-fifty. The only thing that makes that memory acceptable is the fact that I met Erik during that week in school alone. He was three years older, a junior in high school, and was serving detention in our library.

He had the horrific job of inputting the library card catalog into the computers that had been donated to the school. And I had to spend eight hours a day there with him because even my teachers were away. Now we both like to say that it was destiny.

Even at that age, Erik was hot as hell and always dressed to kill. He reminded me of a blond version of A. J. McLean of the Backstreet Boyz. His hair was spiked and he had dyed the tips black. He wore black shades in the library, which I thought was cool but intimidating as well.

I remember the day we met like it was yesterday. I slowly approached the table that was furthest away from any possible human activity as I did not want to be looked at in pity by seventh graders. That table happened to be close to Erik, who was busy ignoring the world. I unzipped my bag and pulled out my history book. I tried to concentrate on the text, when all I could think was that the best history lesson would have been to actually see Washington firsthand.

"Could you die?" Erik said to me as he leaned back in his chair, completely surrounded by cards filled with Dewey Decimal numbers.

"Totally." It was the only word I could mumble out. I didn't know what to say. He was a cool high schooler, I was a loser eighth grader. I tried not to smile as the last thing I wanted was for him to get a good view of my metal braces.

"It's just wrong." He went on in that dramatic voice that would become so endearing to me later in life. He motioned around the table. I thought he was pointing at all the catalog cards. I pitied him.

"I can't believe they're making you input all those cards. That really sucks." I shook my head at the horror of it all, completely sympathetic.

"This? Who gives a shit about this," he said, waving off his detention assignment. "I'm talking about your parents not letting you go on the class trip." I could feel my face light up in bright, red flames.

"How do you know?" I asked him.

"Everyone knows, babe. The librarians are even talking about it. They think your parents are pretty lame and they feel sorry for you. Unfortunately, they have no pull so their pity is kind of a waste."

I was so horrified that I was the topic of conversation by even the adults in school that I wanted to cry, a ritual habit back then.

"But who gives a shit about D.C. anyway? Politicians are so stiff. Most of them have the worst style ever. I used to dig Clinton's look but he lost me when he let Lewinsky suck him off. I mean, you're the president, for God's sake. Be like Kennedy, fuck someone famous, like Marilyn Monroe."

The tears I was about to shed dried instantly. I was so in shock I couldn't speak. But I was also in awe. He took away the sting of not being allowed to go to D.C. In that moment, he became my new hero.

I smiled broadly.

"Oh shit," Erik blurted out, completely appalled over my braces. "That's full-on. I didn't even know metal was still an option. Or that anyone would ever willingly choose it. That's fucked up."

My hands moved up to cover my mouth.

"My parents wouldn't let me get the clear ones. They think they're toxic or something." I was mortified.

"Motherfucker. You're parents are ruthless, man. They're, like, extreme." Erik was clearly appalled.

"Yeah." I didn't know what else to say.

I looked down at my book sadly, thinking Erik would label me a "loser" and start ignoring me.

"But I guess there's nothing else for you to do but take it in the ass from them. They're in the driver's seat for now." I'm sure my mouth was hanging open; I'd never met anyone that spoke this way . . . especially about parents.

I watched as he started analyzing me, completely checking me out in that way of his.

"You've got beautiful features. Great eyes and lips. Perfect nose, thank God; nose jobs are brutal. But I can totally see it—once you get out of this weird, hormonal stage, you're going to be a knockout." His words gave me hope.

Then he got up and walked over to me, extending his hand.

"Erik."

"Sophie. Sophie Walker."

"Great name. Are you French?"

And we've been friends since then. I actually still get a shiver every time I think of the Dewey Decimal System, because somehow Erik suckered me into helping him with his detention assignment. I had nightmares about numbers for a long time.

"Where were you just now?" Clayton pulls me out of my reverie.

I smile apologetically.

"I was just thinking that if my parents hadn't been so overprotective, I never would have met Erik."

"And so you give credence to the ancient belief that everything happens for a reason."

"I guess so."

Right? I mean, look at me now? In the Maldives, of all places! A location I personally picked because I saw a picture on the Internet and thought, what the hell, let's go. And now I've been intimate and am sitting across from a man I would never have met in LA. There's got to be something to it.

"Are you complaining because you received too much love and attention from your parents?" It's his turn to question me.

"No! Not at all."

Am I?

"It's not like that. I just . . ." I let my voice trail off for a second as I think about what I want to convey. The babying? Their need to know everything? The million calls a day? The fights over boyfriends? Education? Clothing? Everything? My parents took "nosy" to a whole new level. There were times when I felt so suffocated by them, so completely smothered that I just couldn't wait to escape.

I don't want to sound ungrateful because it's not like I didn't hear the way his friends spoke of their own parents. God, they *hated* them! From what I gathered, Clayton comes from a world where children are neglected, even thought of as a nuisance, and sent away at every chance.

Ignored.

Mine was just so *different*. Sure, we had problems, no family is perfect, but these people have serious ones that have been there for generations.

"Just what?" he asks.

"Sometimes they make me claustrophobic, that's all."

A light bulb goes off; I see a pattern. I run across the world to escape being controlled by my parents, right into the arms of a man who makes my dad look like a rookie when it comes to control. I've literally jumped out of the frying pan and into the fire. Thank you, Sigmund Freud.

Obviously, I'm nuts. Clinically. Insane. Put me in a straightjacket—seriously. I don't think Noom's got a crystal to fix this shit. I'm so screwed.

Clayton interrupts my internal plea to be committed with, "You're an only child. They're protective. Can you blame them?" He leans back in his chair, watching me.

"No, I can't blame them. They just took it too far. They never let me fall, you know? And sometimes you have to fall in order to learn how to walk."

"People tend to guard rare stones with their life." I feel my body light up from the comparison.

"Yeah, but they practically stuck me in an armored car with full-time Secret Service surveillance." I joke. "It's just a lot."

"I'd guard you too."

You would?

So maybe this is what I'm drawn to here—the feeling of being protected. I let my mind drift and I wonder what it would be like to be under his constant protection, with him worrying about me, calling me to check in, and taking care of me because I was everything—because I was his life. I could get carried away in this fantasy. I can't meet his intense stare, so I look away.

I'd give anything to know what he was thinking right now.

We both fall quiet as we savor the rest of our breakfast. I'm immersed in memories of my past and I'm certain Clayton's been thinking about his childhood as well. I stand and begin clearing off the table. This is starting to feel so . . . comfortable.

He leans back in his chair, exposing a nice portion of his perfect, washboard abs, and silently watches as I stack the dishes. I try not to be self-conscious. Act cool, Sophie.

"You're very poised for someone your age."

No sooner does the comment roll off his lips then I drop a fork on the deck, my neck and face flushing red as it clangs and bangs for what seems like an impossible amount of time. We both immediately burst out laughing, the tension of the moment melting away with our giggles. Once I regain my composure, I turn to him.

"Thank you, Mr. Sinclair," I say politely, then completely straight-faced, "I take that as a compliment, given your old age and wisdom."

"Old age?" he warns as he slowly rises. He removes his sunglasses and pins me with his heated gaze.

I hold my ground and smile sweetly, then set the dishes on the table.

"If the shoe—" but before I can get the last word out, he lunges around the table at me.

I shriek with laughter and a tad bit of fear. I've never enjoyed being chased, and I turn to make a mad dash back into the house. I've gone about three feet before I'm hauled back into his arms and lifted off the ground. I'm gasping from laughter when his lips capture mine in the most earth-shattering kiss. In an instant, I'm completely lost in my lust. His hands pull my body into his so he can grind against me, and I sigh my pleasure into his mouth.

My fingers once again become tangled in his thick hair as I pull his face closer to mine, just wanting more of his kiss, his tongue. I can't get close enough to him. He moves his mouth away from mine and I groan in response. His tongue and lips trace a sweet trail down my neck as his hands squeeze my ass tighter, and instantly I can feel his erection pressing against me. His skillful fingers reach under my dress to untie the strings on my bikini.

He carries me to a large lounge chair and lowers me gently. In a second he's removed my dress and bikini top and I'm naked, my breasts pressed tightly against his heaving chest as he lays on top of me. I'm now throbbing with desire.

His hands move down my stomach and his fingers slip into me.

"You're so wet for me, baby," he whispers against my mouth as I take his fingers deeper inside.

"I want to fuck you, Sophie."

Yes, please, my mind tells him, as I move my hands down his chest and slowly touch his cock. His body goes completely still as I feel him for the first time.

"Touch me, baby."

I want to. I want to please him and drive him as crazy as he drives me. I grab hold of his shaft, feeling him, wrapping my hand around it. I squeeze him tight, knowing that he likes this from his groan of approval. I become bolder and move my hand up and down the length of him. His body trembles in desire, and it turns me on even more to know that he wants my touch.

"Look at me, Clayton." I throw his own words back at him and watch as he opens his bright eyes.

"I want to taste you."

I don't wait for his approval. I push him on his back on the lounge chair and hover above him, shockingly comfortable in my own nakedness. His eyes move over the length of my body.

"God, you're so incredible, Sophie."

He makes me feel like I am. I'm no longer the shy Sophie I've been for twenty-three years, but instead a bold version of myself, intent on driving him mad. I slowly lower my body on top of his, carefully brushing the tips of my breasts against his skin and a sweet surge of ecstasy moves through my body. His hands move up to my hair and hold my head as I slowly kiss and lick my way down the length of his body.

"Sophie." He whispers my name in a tortured whisper, his need driving me on.

I look up at him and my eyes meet his heavy-lidded gaze. I taste the tip of him and watch in satisfaction as he closes his eyes and moves his head up, the veins in his neck pulsing from the way he's clenching his jaw. I put my mouth over his tip and slowly lower it down, sucking as I do. I feel him grab hold of my hair tighter and I know that I'm doing just the right thing. I take him deeper in my mouth, sucking harder, and move up and down, the same way he moves inside of me.

"Christ, Sophie!"

I like the way he tastes and feels, and I especially love the power I have over him. My mouth takes more of him in, all while I suck and lick, giving him a taste of the sweet torture he has bestowed upon me. His hips move up to my mouth, wanting me to take more of him. I oblige, hell-bent on driving him over the edge. I forget time and space, completely turned on by his response and his need for me.

He grabs hold of my naked waist, and pulls me up on top of him. His mouth finds mine, and I kiss him savagely with my fevered need. He hauls my waist down and quickly plunges deep, deep inside me.

"Oh, my God," I say in pleasure as he pushes even further.

He's a beast in this moment, lost, completely lost in a vortex of desire. His hand twists around my hair, his tongue moves deep in my throat, and I welcome the sweet assault.

"You've bewitched me," is his raw answer as he pulls his mouth away from mine and turns me on my back, so he can fuck me harder, deeper than before.

His hands grab my bottom and lifts me so I can take more of him in. His fiery mouth moves to my ear, licking, teasing, making me wild.

"Does this feel old, baby?" His voice is wild as he pulls out and thrusts so deep inside again that I think I am going to die from the pleasure of it all. He moves again, harder, faster, and I pull him closer to me, wanting every piece of him around me, in me, devouring me.

He slows the tempo, teasing me, knowing how close I am to an orgasm, just to prove his point.

"Clayton, please!" I beg him.

"Tell me," he pants to me. "Is it old?"

My hands move to his ass and I try to pull him in deeper, fully, like he was before. But he won't budge. His experience gives him diabolical control.

"No." I know I sound desperate, but I don't care. He's made me into this person, made me want him so badly it hurts and now he has to give me what I need. Now.

"No? Tell me, baby," he says again softly, methodically, as he slowly sinks back inside me, and I can't hold back the moan that escapes me.

"You're not old," I tell him as I grab his face. I look up at him, see the desire he has for me, and I lift my hips up, intentionally pulling more of him in. His eyes are glazed with passion, with naked need, and it makes me feel so powerful.

I pull his mouth down to mine and suck on his lower lip, the way I did his cock, and I feel his body tense with desire and I become braver.

"You're so hot," I whisper to him. "You make me feel alive. But you have to know this. You have to know . . ." Before I can finish my rambling, he thrusts so deeply in that we both rock back from the force of it.

He gives me exactly what I need and I answer by wrapping my legs around his waist and pulling him closer, telling him in this way how much my body needs his. We both find our climax at the same time. I mumble incoherently against his neck and he shouts out my name.

Our hearts beat so hard against each other that it's almost like they are one.

Minutes later, when I can breathe again, I caress his back and hair, completely in awe over my transformation. Instead of feeling guilt or shame, I feel only bliss, and am so completely at peace. Instead of questioning why and how this happened to me of all people, I think that maybe, as Clayton said about my chance meeting of Erik, I was destined to meet him as well.

He shifts and pulls up away from me so he can look down at what

I'm sure is my thoroughly ravished face. He looks content.

"You're going to kill me if we keep this up."

I roll my eyes. "You started it with your little chase."

"You didn't seem too bothered by it," he says with a tender smile.

"Should I be?" I ask, even though I know what the answer is.

"Never."

The word is spoken so solemnly that it takes my breath away. He kisses me softly on the lips and moves away from me. I miss his warm body instantly. He puts his swim trunks on, then gets up and picks up my discarded bikini and dress from around the deck.

I cover my breasts with my hands when he makes his way back to me.

"You make me lose all control," he tells me as he smiles tenderly at me.

I can't respond because I'm suddenly a little embarrassed to be lying on the chaise naked while he's standing above me. I quickly put on my sundress for modesty's sake, then take the hand he offers to help me stand. He pulls me close to him and smooths out my hair, which I'm sure is completely frizzy by now. Then he holds my face in his palms and pulls it up to his mouth and kisses me hard. I sigh against his lips.

I love you.

What? Who said that? *You did,* you moron. *To yourself. No way can I be in love with him,* I answer myself as I open my eyes and look up at his handsome face. It's just a sex thing. He's made a woman out of me. He's romanced me, unlike anything I've ever dreamed of. He's shown me what true happiness is. But no, *I know where this is going.* I am falling in love with him.

"What's wrong?" he asks as he moves his thumb against my lips. I shake my head at him.

"Nothing."

Clayton looks at me for a long while, then leans down to kiss me again.

"I have to make a few business calls to Singapore. Is that alright with you?"

I nod quickly, not mentioning that according to Bikram, it's supposed to be a no-work zone. "No problem," I reassure him. "I'll just clean up then lie in the sun. There are some books in the villa, I'll grab one of those."

And then when you're inside behind closed doors, I'll silently obsess about my mental state. Who falls in love with a man on vacation? A man who lives across the world? A man who can have anyone he wants? Who does that?

Me. Sophie Walker.

"You sure you'll be okay?" he asks again. "I won't be long, I'm just in the middle of a deal and I need to make sure that everything is going as planned. I promised I'd discuss some final points with my attorney," he explains, hoping that I won't be upset that he has to leave me alone. I'm touched that he's so worried about me.

"Clayton, please. Business is business. Don't worry. I'm totally fine. I'm a big girl, I'm used to entertaining myself. I'm an only child," I remind him, hoping that I've placated him.

"Thank you," he says.

"I got it." I take his hand and kiss his palm. "And honestly, it doesn't matter if you are. I want you to take care of your work. It's important to you."

He briefly closes his eyes then stares at me, his gaze as sizzling as the sun.

"I like you, Sophie. A lot."

My heart stops. Waves of emotion rush over me. I try not to get excited by how his words make me feel, or what they mean.

He doesn't give me the opportunity to reciprocate the sentiment. "You are one of a kind, Miss Walker. A gem. I'm glad your parents guarded you so preciously for me."

My eyes close and I try my hardest not to embarrass myself with tears. *Guarded you so preciously for me.* I'm too sentimental to let something so profound go without being affected by it. "When I'm done, I'm going to take you deep water snorkeling, and you're not going to be able to say no."

Yeah, right.

"Thanks, but I'll just watch you from the beach. I'll wave, I promise. And I'll be on the lookout for sharks."

His laugh is so sure, so confident. He winks at me and says, "No watching for you anymore, baby. From now on, you're going to start living life."

Then he turns and walks inside the villa. *You have no idea how I've started living life, Clayton,* I think to myself.

I tie my bikini bottoms back into place and pull my hair up into a tight knot, then make my way to the table and finish clearing it. I busy myself with washing and putting them away inside. Clayton's husky voice carries into the kitchen, and from the sound of things I don't think the conversation is going well. I realize how bad I want to know about his business, just his life in general. I wish he would offer information instead of me having to beg for it.

When his voice raises a notch, I step back outside to give him complete privacy.

My gaze settles on the ocean. It's really spectacular, like something out of a dream. It's so calm. So still. It's hard to believe that this little piece of paradise out here in the Indian Ocean is even on our planet. It's not accessible to everyone, but it's here, ready to welcome whoever comes.

A sense of euphoria comes over me that I can't really explain. This is the most beautiful place on earth, the most awe-inspiring country I've ever been. I say a silent prayer of gratitude. I know how lucky I am to be here and I thank the universe profusely for working its magic and bringing me here, at this time, with this man.

Noom's words come to mind and I wonder if I should give it a go, if I should try to meditate now? It would be good, right? Carpe diem. Seize the day seems to be the theme of my trip. Clayton's inside on a call that is probably going to take longer than he thought. I could sit out here and read or obsess about my feelings, about the words he used . . . I like you, Sophie. But that won't be good for me, I know. Very quickly, I could take those words and picture him proposing, dream up a dress, a venue, even the color of the wedding invites. No, that is definitely not a good idea.

Even though I've never been able to do it—maybe because I was emotionally and physically blocked—I decide to follow Noom's advice. I find a towel and walk to the edge of the deck, sit down, and assume the seated meditation position I learned in yoga class.

When I took yoga with Orie the physical part was easy for me to pick up with practice, but every time the teacher said, "Clear your mind, think of your breath, and picture light entering your body," I was hopeless. She'd always start with the Om . . . the dreaded Om, as I called it. I was incapable of being still. Of just being in the now. My mind would always wander, as it is doing now. Crap. I try to clear it. I take a deep breath. I listen to my heartbeat. To the water.

I wonder what Clayton's talking about? I wonder if the call is going well? Does he ever call his family to check in? Oh my God, Sophie! *Stop!* Stop thinking, for the love of God! Just meditate. Meditate.

What's so hard about clearing your mind? Any monkey can do it. Okay, here I go. Deep breath, Sophie. Take a deep, deep breath. And . .

. I wonder what Erik and Orie are doing? Oh my God, what I wouldn't do to call them right now, talk to them about my night with Clayton, my morning with Clayton, his sexual domination of me, my complete enjoyment of every part of it. Is it strange that I enjoyed myself so much?

What does that say about me? I mean, this could be how everyone feels, right? I have no clue. It's not my area of expertise. That's why I need to talk to Erik and Orie. I wonder if everyone has an orgasm the first time. If I could search for it on the Internet I would know and then I could read message boards, see what people say and . . . Oh my God. Here I go again. Shit. Sophie.

You're pathetic.

Chapter Thirteen

Gotye's soft voice echoes across the silent deck, thankfully interrupting all my crazy thoughts. "Somebody That I Used to Know" is one of my favorite songs. His voice is so sexy, and just hearing the beat always makes my imagination go to a sexy, romantic world. I turn from my yoga pose and find Clayton standing by the sliding doors of the villa, his hands on his hips, his gaze burning with an intensity that I've come to know oh so well, as he watches me. I wonder if he's a bit of a voyeur. He is always staring. Pensive, almost, taking it all in. I could be right. I smile self-consciously and wave. I hope he wasn't standing there observing my pathetic attempt at yoga, because if he was he must have laughed his ass off.

He makes his way to me. He's got great calves, I think as I admire his physique. Great, masculine calves. Let's be real, everything about his body is perfect, from the strength in his hands, to his wide chest, to his smooth skin and perfectly chiseled features. I wonder what his parents look like. They must be such a good-looking couple to have had a son who looks like him. And his brothers are probably just as perfect looking.

"How was your call?" I ask him.

"Disappointing."

"Do you want to talk about it?"

He shakes his head. I didn't think so, but I thought I would ask anyway. I wish he would tell me, but I respect his privacy and I don't want to overstep my bounds with him. Not that I should have any, but still . . . I know firsthand from dealing with my father that the last thing he wanted when he was super stressed was to rehash a crappy conversation or a shitty day. He preferred to be distracted, eat food, have a glass a wine, or just watch mindless television.

My mom and I always did our best to make sure he was comfortable because we knew the amount of pressure he put on himself. We never wanted to add to it. It's actually one of the few things we agreed on. There was an unspoken rule in our house about my dad. When he came home, and most especially if he looked weary from a difficult day at work, the two women in the house would do whatever we could to lift his spirits, give him relief from all the strain, and be the part in his day that was a joy instead of a burden. It's something I learned from her that I will take with me into my own marriage.

"So what would you like to do?" I ask as I rise from my makeshift yoga mat.

"Snorkel in the deep ocean with you."

I laugh and shake my head.

"Something else?" I raise a brow and look at his lips, hoping to make him forget the idea of snorkeling. Seducing him is good, that will at least keep us out of the water until I can think up something else for us to do.

"I always want to do that. But not now. After, yes. Maybe in the water." He takes my hand and pulls me close. "Definitely in the water." His voice is seductive and low as he stares at my mouth.

Hmmm. I like the sound of that, but still, I'm not going in the water, no matter how hot he or the thought of a sexual rendezvous is.

"I'll distract you, I promise. You won't know where you are," he promises me with a sexy smile. He lets go of my hand and goes back inside the villa. A second later he's back with snorkels and fins in his hand, two sets of each. Ha! As if I'm actually going to follow him into the deep sea? Is he crazy? Clearly he doesn't know how stubborn I am.

"You're not going to win this one, Clayton," I warn him, holding my hands up.

"Just come with me," he orders, then goes down the stairs of the deck to the beach. I follow slowly, because I know if I don't he will carry me out, but I know it's going to get really ugly if he thinks I'm going to go out far into the ocean, and by that I mean more than knee-deep.

He stops at the water's edge and drops the equipment. It's almost comical, because there are literally no waves, a baby could play in this water and be totally fine. It's the calmest possible sea for someone frightened of high tide, sharks, and giant octopus. I still don't care. I walk in to my ankles and actually enjoy the warmth of the water. I turn and smile at him.

"This is nice."

He crosses his arms and chuckles I know he's amused by me and is probably wondering how he can trick me into the water. But I'm on high alert now. I'm not going in there and having a meltdown in front of him; I shiver at the thought. My mind drifts as I notice his arms flex. I lazily admire his biceps and sigh.

"That's not good enough, baby. You're not standing there all day," he finally says.

"I'm perfectly fine just dunking my feet in the water, promise. Take your time out there. I'll just be here and watch, catch some rays," I tell him as I peel off my sundress and turn to give him a healthy view of the ass he claims to loves.

I catch a glimpse of his mouth dropping open before my back is completely to him.

"Christ, Sophie," he mutters.

I slowly turn to face him and can't resist giving him a once over.

"Yes, Clayton?" I ask and his eyes eat me alive.

"Your body is perfect." I watch as he checks me out.

So not perfect, I think, *but I won't argue with you. Whatever drugs you're on that make you see me in that way are just fine, in my opinion.*

"Thank you, sir. But I think you and I both know that your body is the one that's mouthwateringly, deliciously, incredible." Where in the hell did that come from? How did I even come up with something like that? Did I read it in a book? I wonder.

"You're trying to distract me," he says huskily.

"Is it working?"

"Maybe," he tells me as he takes a step toward me, slowly stalking me. He's got full on wolf eyes and I smile in anticipation.

"Have you ever seen the movie *From Here to Eternity?*" I ask him as I think about the two of us replaying the famous beach scene in my head, where they kiss passionately on the sand.

"Of course."

"Wanna role-play?" I flirt outrageously.

I let him pull me up against his body and instantly move my arms up his chest. I kiss his skin softly, lick his nipple, and sigh with contentment when he groans and lifts me up and kisses me full on the lips. I wrap my legs around his waist as he kisses me deeply. He pulls back and cups my face in his large hands.

"I don't need to play. I just want you."

God. I pull his face to mine and kiss him with all the passion I have. Our lips meet and before I know it I'm clinging to him, mindlessly lost in the moment. I could really kiss him for days, I dreamily think to myself. My desire for him is all consuming. I tighten my legs around his waist, trying to show him how bad I want him as well.

My *From Here to Eternity* fantasy is rudely snatched from me as I realize we're waist deep in the water. How the hell did this happen? My eyes flip open in panic and I try to push away from Clayton and walk like a bat out of hell back to the safety zone, but Clayton won't let go of me. His grip is tight and I know it's useless to fight him.

"I don't think so, baby." His voice is so sure. Fucker. He knows I'm no match for his strength.

Since I know I'm safe in his arms, my legs hold him close like my life depends on it. And PS, it literally does. I can hear him laugh against my ear, but I won't look at him because my arms have a death grip around his neck and my eyes are dead shut. I try to calm myself down, I know I'm acting like a complete and utter idiot, but it's hard.

"Sophie. Let up. You're practically choking me. Do you want me to drown?" Yeah, right. Him drown? As if. He tries to loosen my hold, but to hell with that. He asked for it. He deceived me!

"Do you think I would ever let anything happen to you, baby?" he whispers softly in my ear. "Do you think I would ever put you in any type of danger? If I thought for one minute that there was something in this water that could harm you in any way, I would never let you step foot in it." His hand rubs my head softly, massaging my neck to soothe me as he continues. "You can do this. We can do this together, sweetheart."

Sweetheart? Yes, that's how easy I am. Oh my God. I love his hands on my body, I love how he is trying to ease my fears. I love his soft voice whispering to me. I just . . . Fuck. I just love him.

And I trust him to take care of me.

I take in a deep breath and slowly let my grip slacken. I realize how much I hate this fear of mine, this weakness. We have so many great beaches in California and I never went in the ocean once. Not once. I watched. Observed my friends living. All while I was on the sidelines envying their freedom. How many times had Erik begged me to get in? Promised me that he would take care of me, hold my hand? I could never do it.

Maybe I was waiting for Clayton, the man who told me he would not let me watch from the sidelines anymore.

"Look at me, Sophie. Just look in my eyes," he says encouragingly, as if he's talking to a three-year-old child who's just learning how to swim. It would be funny if it weren't so embarrassing.

I slowly pull away from his body, try to be brave, and I hate that I can feel the tremble in my body, the weakness. But I do open my eyes and meet his tender gaze.

It is almost my undoing.

"Embrace the moment, baby. You can do it. I will always keep you safe." He isn't lying, or playing games. He is letting me know that he won't let me go. He won't let my fear overcome me and cause me to have heart palpitations. He won't allow it.

"You've got this. I know you do."

I was mortified by this fear of mine, by Clayton seeing this weakness, but suddenly I feel the exact opposite.

I feel safe.

"What happens if we see a shark?" I ask.

He smiles at me. "Then we see a shark."

"What if it tries to attack us?"

"Then we'll attack back."

I laugh at the absurdity of that statement.

"Don't you want to look around? See the beauty of the ocean around you?" he asks me as he looks out on the wide expanse of water. I can picture what it looks like in my head, I think to myself. I've got a great imagination.

My gaze doesn't leave his as I shake my head. "Not particularly."

"You're going to have to."

"Why?" Isn't this enough?

"So we can conquer this fear of yours together."

My eyes close at his words. Crap. Why does he have to be so perfect? Say the perfect things? It's not right. It makes me want to cry.

"Are you ready, baby?"

"I guess. If *you* say so, then I must be, right?" I can't keep the sarcasm out of my voice.

He gives me a sexy smile.

"You can stay wrapped around me, I like that part, but I want to watch your gorgeous face experience everything," he cajoles me.

He's relentless, isn't he? I open my eyes and smile at him, hoping I don't look as pathetic as I feel. My gaze slowly leaves his and I carefully start to turn my head. I notice that he's moved farther into the ocean, so far that the water is now practically up to our shoulders. If I let go of him I'm going to have to tread water because he's so damn tall. Suddenly, Erik's absurd idea of being "stretched" doesn't sound so bad. Alright, it's now or never.

And then I face my fear with him and look out on the ocean.

The water shimmers from the sun's rays like a dazzling prism. It's so clear that I can see the small fish swimming around us. The colors are extraordinary, bright yellows, purples, and greens, against a canvas of aquamarine. They move about on their daily business, ignoring us, accustomed to people in their habitat. But the sound of the water is what transfixes me. It's like a gentle lull, so tranquil, it gives me a sense of peace just from its calmness. I close my eyes and a crazy stillness comes over me.

I feel one with the water.

And somehow I know that I'll be fine, and that no big, bad shark will come and get me. I stay like that for a while, leaning back and letting my arms just float around me, my ears in the ocean, listening to the sound of now. I feel him gently pull my legs away from his waist and I know what he's doing and I'm okay with it. He lets me loose and I allow myself just to float and be, eyes closed, sun shining brightly on me, and it's marvelous. I don't know how long I stay like this, how long he hovers around me making sure I'm okay, ready and willing to help me in case I have a panic attack. But it's in this moment that I have the first utterly still moment of my life. I hear nothing. Think nothing. I just am. Feeling. Breathing. My life. And it is one of the most unimaginable moments I've ever had. And I owe it to Clayton. He convinced me that I could do it. That I could face my greatest fear.

When I'm ready to move up out of my floating position, I find him a few feet away. The smile he gives me makes my toes curl.

"How was it?"

I nod happily as I swim toward him, but I notice how far we are from the shore.

"It was alright." But my smile betrays me.

He pulls me into his embrace and I wrap my arms and legs around him again.

"Now that's more like it," he whispers in my ear. "I didn't know how much more I could take of you floating like that with your delectable body there for me to view."

"*Delectable body?* Are you for real?" I ask him with a smile. Who talks like this? No one from Los Angeles, that's for damn sure. Most of the guys I've ever received compliments from have told me that I have a "hot bod." He grabs hold of my ass and pushes me down so our bodies are plastered against each other.

Oh yes. He is very real. And for the time being, he's all mine.

"Does that answer your question?" he asks curiously.

I run my fingers over his shoulders then up his hair.

"I don't know. I still can't really tell," is how sex-starved Sophie answers the question.

His eyes blaze with passion and he lowers his head to take my mouth.

"Allow me to show you how real I am, Miss Walker."

As promised, he keeps his word.

It's night and Clayton and I are cuddled together in bed. His arms are wrapped around mine, holding me close as if I might disappear if he let me go. As if.

We spent the rest of the day swimming, snorkeling and making love. And yes, we did play out the scene *From Here to Eternity* and I'd bet that it was a way better version than what I saw in the film, and much more X-rated, of course.

We never tired of each other and I never tired of asking him question after question about his life, his family, anything I could glean from him. He asked me about Erik, my family, and my dreams. By the time we crawled into bed, we were both exhausted, too tired to make love again, but content just to hold each other.

I turn my head up so I can look at him, and I smile at the boyish look he has in sleep. So peaceful. Innocent, actually. I know better, but still, it's nice to see him like this. I move my hand and caress his cheek, wondering what I'll do when it comes time for us to say goodbye. I'm in the exact place emotionally that I didn't want to be. In love. Lust. Overwhelmed. Needing him with a hunger and urgency I never believed was possible.

And I know, somehow I know, that without him, I will be lost.

Chapter Fourteen

BIKRAM DRIVES US in a golf cart to our bungalows. Clayton and I have both been very quiet since he arrived on *our* island to pick us up. Yes, it is now officially "our island." *I still can't believe* how sad I was to leave. It was so nice having Clayton all to myself, just getting to be with him, eat with him, talk to him, and if you can believe, *snorkel* with him? He managed to get me out in the ocean again and we explored the sea together. He held my hand the whole time, and even pointed out interesting-looking fish for me to look at. Now, we're back to "reality," joining our friends again.

He didn't talk to me about staying with him in his villa back at the resort, so I'm assuming we're parting ways, each off to our own place. I'm sad that we're not going to be staying together, even though I know it's probably for the best; this way I won't become even more attached to him than I already am, which is an obscene amount. Since the first night on our island I began to do an official countdown of when I'd be leaving the Maldives. Officially, we have only one week left together.

Clayton told me last night that he booked his villa for an extra week, so he'll be staying on after I go. The thought of him here without me is depressing. *You have seven more days,* Sophie. *Calm down,* I keep telling myself. I don't want to think about the end of the trip before I've even lived it. I know it's not the right way of looking at things, the way Noom would approve of, so every single time the thought creeps into my head, I stop it by forcing myself to live in the now. To be honest, I'm surprising myself by becoming better and better at that.

Practice, as they say, makes perfect.

Bikram turns down the long wooden ramp toward the overwater villas. I am excited about seeing Erik and Orie and catching up. I genuinely missed them, but now after spending so much sacred time with Clayton, I don't know how much I'm willing to share. Suddenly I don't want to give all the details or repeat intimate conversations, because I feel like they should completely and utterly belong to us alone. They'll stay locked inside for now. If there ever is a time when I tell, then so be it.

I'm surprised when the golf cart goes past my bungalow and pulls up to Clayton's villa. I would have thought that he'd go to mine first, which would be the polite thing to do.

When the cart stops, Clayton jumps out and starts to help Bikram with the few bags. I am a little taken aback at how quickly he's left me. I thought he'd stay, hold my hand some more, kiss me, then tell me to drop my things off and walk over to his place. I'm glad I have sunglasses on to cover my shock. Clayton puts his hands on the top of the cart and leans in, smiling at me softly. He looks so damn sexy in his aviator shades. The only problem is that I can't tell what he's thinking with them on. I give him a bright smile, hoping that he can't tell how sad I suddenly am to have to be apart from him.

"Are you happy we're back?" he asks me tenderly.

"Yes, I missed Erik and Orie," I reply quickly, trying to be cool.

But I want to bury my face in my hands and cry my eyes out. I don't know why I'm such a wimp, but I am.

He stares at me for a second longer, then looks over at Bikram. I pretend to study my manicure, biting my lip so my mouth doesn't start trembling in sadness. This is the kind of moment that can lead to Sophie Walker tears, or the floodgates from hell, as Erik lovingly calls them. Clayton taps the top of the golf cart.

"Well, I don't want to keep you any longer, Bikram. Thanks for all you've done."

Does this mean I'm coming in? Or that I'm supposed to walk over to my villa? I can't tell. I can't assume. I can't do a damn thing because I don't know what the rules are in this game. Clayton leans back into the cart and stares at me for a long moment. I realize I have to look up at him and pretend apathy. I know men hate sniveling, weak women, and that's the last way I want him to think of me. I need to act calm even though I feel the exact opposite.

"Well, thanks so much for everything," I tell him. Crap. That sounded so fucked up, I know. But what else is there for me to say?

"What is that supposed to mean?" His voice has a certain bite to it.

Uh, I don't know Clayton, you tell me, I think to myself. You're the one who hopped out of the cart and just assumed that I know what the plan is! I mean, what is a woman supposed to think or feel about this?

Of course, the only thing I'm brave enough to say to him is, "It means that I'll talk to you later."

Right? Isn't that what he wants? I start to collect my small items and get ready to step off the cart.

I watch as he turns to look at Bikram, who is suspiciously backing further and further away from us. I'm sure he feels the awkwardness of the moment and would prefer to be as far away as possible. Clayton takes a second before he speaks. I'm guessing that he wants to make sure Bikram is a good distance away. He turns then to me and takes his sunglasses off.

Oh shit. He's fucking mad! And why is he mad? I'm the one who should be angry! I'm the one who's being rejected on such a massive level!

"You need to walk to the villa, Sophie."

"What?"

A muscle in his cheek twitches. Once. Twice. I've never seen him like this before. What the hell is his problem?

"Get off the goddamn cart," he hisses at me in a low voice as he extends his hand, "or I will carry you off it kicking and screaming and you will only have yourself to blame."

Screw him! Clenching the beach bag I borrowed from the island villa as a memory, okay, *took so I can keep,* with every intention of asking how much it is at the resort, I scoot out of the cart, intentionally on the opposite side of Clayton. If anything, he looks even more furious. I pity poor Bikram and the scene that he is no doubt about to witness.

Since now I'm so pissed that I can't even see straight, I don't hold back. With hands on my hips, I face Clayton across the cart, just as angry as him, and I pull my sunglasses off just so he can see for himself.

"You know what?" My voice shakes with fury. I watch as he seethes from my words, probably barely holding on to a shred of self-control, but who gives a shit? He needs to hear this! "You are not a gentleman. You warned me that you weren't . . . and you were right. I cannot believe I've been gallivanting around with you—against my better judgment, I might add!—living in some kind of . . . I don't know . . . perfect, sparkling fairy tale, completely oblivious to the fact—or maybe just not wanting to admit to myself—that you were going to do exactly, precisely what you are doing right now. Just dumping me. Love 'em and leave 'em, right? I should have fucking known! Well, fuck you Mr. Richie Rich and your fifteen thousand dollar a night villa! I might have thought I was falling in . . . well, you

know . . . but I was wrong! Good. Bye!" I'm shouting now. Every single word is belted out so loud that I'm sure people in nearby villas can hear.

Oh wait, what am I thinking? He doesn't *let* people stay close to him because he has to be all by himself so he can have his goddamn privacy! *Who does that?* Clayton looks like he's been struck by lightning he's so shocked, his mouth agape, probably incapable of believing I have the audacity to speak to him this way.

And then I watch the shock disappear and in its place comes an icy fury. Instead of continuing on with my stinging insults, I opt to turn and walk briskly, *very briskly,* I might add, back to my villa as Clayton suggested. Bikram's back is to me and I'm thankful that at least I had the good sense to put my room key card into my bag. I can deal with my stuff later.

I reach my villa safely. Clayton obviously could not catch up to me, or didn't want to humiliate himself in front of Bikram, who knows? But suddenly I feel like I want to throw something and cry. Seconds later, I hear the cart whizz by and know Bikram probably ran like hell. I can't blame him for wanting to get out of here. I did too.

Clayton is such an ass! I grab my key and plunge it into the lock.

"Motherfucker!" I shout when it turns red. Access denied! I plunge it in again and the same red light flashes again. This is *so* not happening! I try again slowly, gently, hoping that being calm will somehow make the key magically work and the door open, so I can slam it shut and throw myself on my bed and cry the tears that are threatening to spill. I close my eyes before sticking it in the lock again and hold my breath.

Fuck!

"Your key no longer works."

Shit. He's right behind me. Mother fucking shit. I keep my back to him, standing as tall and proud as I can, refusing to turn and look up at him, knowing if I do, I might lose my temper again and it won't be pretty.

"I'll just go and get another."

"I'm afraid that's not possible," he threatens. "The room is now booked."

"Oh really?!" I say as I swing around, ready to go to crazy town, not that I'm not already there, but still.

I wish I never turned around.

Before I can even think of what to say, he grabs me around the waist, throws me over his shoulder, and smacks my ass so hard I cry out in pain.

"Not a goddamn word from you, Sophie! Do you hear me? Not another goddamn word!" he practically roars as he walks back to his villa. A twinge of fear courses through my body, but I quickly brush it aside.

The door is open and he strides inside, slams it shut, and continues walking with me over his shoulder through the large bungalow and into the bedroom. Really? He's gotta be kidding me. Does he actually think I'm going to have sex with him now after he was such an asshole? No way. No way in hell. His hand comes up to cup my ass, rubbing the place where he gave it a stinging slap moments before, and I feel my traitorous body instantly respond to his touch. Why? Why does he have to turn me on like this?

"Put me down!" I practically shriek as I pound my fist into his back.

"Gladly." He grabs my waist and tosses me on the bed. I bounce. Twice. Shit.

He looms above me, his face revealing the extent of his rage. I sit up, because I have every intention of walking the hell out of the villa, but he stops me cold.

"I wouldn't do that if I were you."

I stay still when I hear the warning in his voice. But I snap at him, "And why's that?"

Clayton's smile is slow, sure, but completely void of any of the tenderness that I've become so accustomed to seeing.

"Because I'm so fucking bloody pissed at you, Sophie, I won't be held accountable for my actions," he practically shouts.

My eyes widen as I digest his words and the tone he just used. But in a second, I get my gumption back and I sit taller on the bed, but wisely choose not to move.

"You're pissed at *me,* Clayton? What about *me* being pissed at you?" I huff at him as I cross my arms. There. Take that buddy.

Clayton closes his eyes, probably to get a grip on his emotions.

"And what the fuck do you have to be pissed at me for?" he explodes as his blue eyes blaze out of his stunning face. "How could you behave like that in front of the hotel staff?"

Mount St. Clayton has erupted.

Oh no, he didn't.

"*Hotel staff?* His name is Bikram, Clayton. He's a human being just like you, even if he hasn't been blessed with your extraordinary wealth." I give back as good as him, then instantly wish that I could take it back. Crap. Crap. Crap. I didn't mean it like that. I inch away from him on the bed as I watch his face turn a different shade of red. His anger seems to radiate off his body.

"This is your fucking fault, Sophie."

What is? Before I can even scream back at him, he quickly leans onto the middle of the bed and grabs me by the ankle and yanks my body down toward him. Like a master who knows his craft, he slowly moves his body over mine, pushing his hips into me, causing heat to surge through my being from pure, unadulterated lust. His hand slowly moves up my leg, leaving a track of goose bumps and longing in its wake.

Shit! I know what he's doing. I know what's about to come for me. He showed me this side of him before. He wants me begging. His method of punishment. Simple.

Erotic torture.

Wanting. Needing. Dying from need. *That's* his poison. Torture them until they beg for more and have to give you exactly what you want to hear. *Fuck that shit!*

I twist and turn, fighting him, not wanting him to touch too much of my body, or we both know that I'll be lost.

"No!" I try to twist away from his hold, but he's too damn strong for me, and I know that there is no escaping his touch. Even if I wanted to: My faithless body is already starting to react to him, it's already starting to need him. He knows where to touch, how to get me wanting within seconds.

"Please, Clayton," I plead with him when his fingers move against me to softly caress. A shiver of excitement runs through my body.

"Please don't do this to me. Not again."

His hand stills and he leans over me, his face inches from mine. I look up at him and see the raw anger unmasked. It's intimidating as hell, especially the way he just looks down at me with those wolf eyes.

"You thought I was going to let you go?!"

What?

"Weren't you?" I close my eyes and try to articulate my thoughts coherently. "I didn't know your intention. I thought you were leaving me. We hadn't talked about what would happen after we left the island. Where I would stay—"

"Christ!" He closes his eyes and takes a deep breath, hopefully controlling that anger of his before he looks at me again.

His head falls to my chest. "For someone so smart, it is incredibly appalling to see how superbly obtuse you are. I had your belongings moved to my villa. Do you actually think I would let you go back to your room without me? Do you actually think I would spend one night without you?" He says those last words to my face. *Yelling* in my face, to be exact.

I'm in shock. I don't know what to say. He wasn't going to abandon me. He wasn't trying to dump me on Bikram, or make me walk back to my villa alone. Why couldn't I tell? Why didn't I just look around and notice that my bags were probably taken off the cart with his? Mother fucker! I'm a moron!

I close my eyes over my stupidity. Ugh. The things I said! Yikes. The theme of my life should be "How to lose a guy in thirty minutes of completely idiotic behavior!" He's silent, probably waiting for me to apologize, which he so deserves, but I'm so ashamed by my behavior, I don't know where to begin. Even though I should be happy now, I suddenly feel like crying again because I showed him such a shitty side of my personality.

I open my eyes and they are glistening a bit. I'm trying to hold the tears back, but it's hard. My hands clasp his angry face and I beg silently, touching his skin, his cheeks, beg him to forgive me and not hold this crazy moment against me. I ruined the last part of our romantic trip. And I hate myself for it.

"I'm so sorry." The words are said softly. "Please forgive me. I thought—" My voice trembles.

I know he can hear it, I know he knows I'm on the precipice of losing control, that I just showed him how massively insecure I can really be. His look is still guarded, but not as angry, and then I can't help it, I just cry. My hands cover my face, loathe to have him see me this way, wanting to just dive into the ocean—with sharks, so that they can take me out of my misery.

"Sophie." I hear the tenderness in his voice as he pulls me into his arms and lets me cry. He holds me tight and kisses me on top of my head as I try to get a grip on the dam that's just broken. "Why don't you see how amazing you are?"

I shrug against his chest. "I don't know." I sound pathetic, I know, but I can't help it.

I know he probably wants to laugh, which is better then wanting to be furious at me.

"Christ, baby. Haven't you heard anything I've said to you? Don't you believe me when I tell you how much I want you? How much I want to be with you?" He is angry again, as he lifts my tear-stained face to look him in the eyes. He looks so damn offended that I would actually doubt him, that it takes my breath away. He wipes away my tears, then pulls me up so he can kiss me.

"Please don't cry, love," he says as his mouth covers mine and between kisses, "you're killing me. I don't want to see you cry."

Our kiss is open mouthed, carnal, my salty tears mixed up in the embrace.

"I'm sorry, Clayton," I whisper to him between his kisses. "I shouldn't have said any of that to you. I didn't mean anything by it, especially the part about you thinking you're better than everyone. My temper sometimes—"

I shouldn't have reminded him.

"I'm fucking wealthy, okay? It is what it is, so get used to it. I don't flaunt it in people's face. I don't judge anyone who has less than me, or more. But the fact remains that I have a lot of money, and I won't apologize for that."

I feel like the biggest ass on the planet. I nod at him, properly chastised by his words, and close my eyes. He wants me here with him proving all his actions and words. I need to believe him. I need to stop being afraid that he's going to hurt me. I need to grow up and be a big girl.

"What you said earlier—" he says.

I cringe.

"About how you were—" he doesn't finish the words.

Falling in love with you, I say silently, but there is no way I'll ever admit that.

"I don't remember," I say unconvincingly, and lightly brush my hand up his arm.

"Don't you?" He asks, his eyes bright as they stare down at me.

"No." I whisper hoping he will just let it go.

I can tell he's calmed down, but the storm is still there and I know he just needs to get it out of his system. I want to help him get back to Zen.

My hand moves down his arm then over to his stomach, then down until I find the button on his shorts. He inhales sharply, knowing what I'm about, his body reacting to my touch, instantly so hard and big that it makes my mouth water. God, he turns me on.

I push him on his back and unzip his pants. His erection springs free and I'm so ready for him that I can't even wait. I lean down and take him fully in my mouth, sucking on him so hard that he cries out in pleasure. I lick his shaft, teasing and taunting him, wanting him to lose his mind with need.

His hands grab my hair, twisting, pulling, pushing himself further in my mouth.

"God. Sophie," he moans as I take more in, working him, moving with the thrusts of his hips. My hands move around his body, under his shirt, touching, teasing, then grabbing on to his erection as I come up to look at him. He stares down at me, his eyes half-closed, lit with desire. For me. His hands caress my hair, as he waits to see what my next move will be. I hold onto the shaft and squeeze, watch him close his eyes in ecstasy, and I revel in the power I have over him.

"You're so sexy, Clayton." My voice is husky with want.

He tries to pull me up to him, but I won't let him.

"I want this to be about you," I say with passion, as I lower my head and take him fully in my mouth.

He trembles from my touch and I work him fully, completely, tasting him as he shouts my name and finds release.

Chapter Fifteen

ERIK AND ORIE SIT across from me in complete silence. Clayton and I stayed in his villa all day yesterday. I was happy that he wasn't ready to give up our time alone together. Luckily, I received a message from the hotel informing me that the boys were out on a daylong fishing trip on the hotel yacht. They wouldn't get back until really late in the evening, so I left a message telling them that I was staying at Clayton's villa and asking if we could have breakfast in the morning.

So here we are.

They are both analyzing the shit out of me, trying to see if there is any difference, and I can't wait to hear what they have to say. I pick up my glass of my fresh watermelon juice and take a sip as I wait. We've been like this now for a few minutes, in a complete stand-off. They've definitely been working on their tans because they're positively glowing. The Maldivian sun really works to their advantage.

Erik breaks the silence, as I knew he would. "This is insane." He leans in over the table to give me a look of censure, trying to be intimidating as hell. "Do you realize how fucked up this is?"

I still stay silent as my gaze moves over the both of them. Okay, part of me is enjoying this first moment I've had in my friendship with Erik—the first time I actually know more than he does. He's practically foaming at the mouth.

He looks at Orie for moral support. I know this is killing him. It takes another ten seconds before he reaches his limits with me. He says to Orie, "Are you going to tell her what a complete and utter secretive ass she's being?"

I can feel the laughter well up inside. Orie just smiles at me, winks, then looks at Erik.

"Maybe she wants to keep it all to herself. A woman's heart is sacred, after all . . ."

"Oh, fuck sacred," Erik interrupts, his voice dramatic as he dismisses Orie's defense of my silence.

"Do you want to know what sacred is? Sacred is buying this bitch tampons at two a.m., because she's bleeding like a double homicide crime scene and can't make it to the pharmacy. Sacred is waxing her armpits and bikini line so she wouldn't look like a beast at the high school graduation beach party! Sacred is driving her ass to Jerry the Fairy's and waiting down the street, in a goddamn rose bush, with thorns in my ass, by the way, just so that she wouldn't be alone when she dumped him . . ."

"Enough! I get it!" Orie says. "You've done a lot of shit for her. I understand. And so does she."

Orie tries to say this with a straight face but ends up laughing hysterically. I can't take it anymore. I crack up and double over on the table; I can barely catch my breath.

Erik looks at the two of us and shakes his head. "And the most fucked part of all of this is that I know what this bitch is doing. She is making me wait for it. She wants me to beg for the details." I look at him, unable to stop laughing, and he continues to point a finger at me. When Erik is on a rampage, it's like a goddamn runaway train. "Don't think for one moment that I don't know what this is about. This is the first goddamn time you have more information than me. I'll let you taste the feeling of knowledge, of being the one who is going to tell the story that everyone is dying to hear. Go ahead! Bask in it! Feel the glory!"

I finally pull myself together. "What would you like to know?"

"And you call yourself my best friend?" He shakes his head at me.

"Come on!" I laugh. "I'm just playing with you. It's so rare that I ever have the opportunity."

"Rare?" Erik interrupts me, his arms still crossed. "Try never."

"Agreed. And you are my best friend, the one I adore and love forever. Until the end of time," I tell him solemnly as I reach out across the table and squeeze his arm.

"So where do I fit into this equation?" a voice I know intimately says. "Should I be jealous?"

Clayton has come up to the table. Snuck up, more like, and puts his hands possessively on my shoulders. He leans down and kisses me on the head.

I blush as I look up at him, touch his hand, and then look at Erik and Orie, who are staring at the two of us with, their mouths wide open. I try my hardest not to laugh at their expressions, but it is very difficult, all things considered. Clayton is totally unfazed by their shocked looks; in fact, I feel like he is enjoying their surprise over our intimacy.

"I'm sorry for interrupting," he says politely as he brushes my shoulders. I lean into his touch. "I know you guys have a lot to catch up on."

I blush again at the reference to our time away and am thankful he's behind me.

Orie is the first to recover. "Not at all. Please, join us. Have you had breakfast?"

"Thank you, but I ate in the villa while I made some business calls. I'm actually on my way to the spa."

"Nice. What treatment are you getting?" Orie asks. I notice that Erik's arms are still crossed as he looks Clayton over. I know he's trying to find a flaw. Good luck, buddy.

"A shiatsu massage. I also took the liberty of booking the three of you a total relaxation treatment. I figured since I've dominated so much of Sophie's time, it was the least I could do for you. That way you can spend some time together. I hope you don't mind."

There he goes again with his insane generosity. I look up at Clayton again and squeeze his hand in gratitude. "You didn't have to do that." He smiles down at me.

"I won't take no for an answer, unless one of you has an aversion to relaxing spa days . . . ?" he says.

"That is so nice of you, Clayton," Orie thanks him with a genuine smile. "I can't imagine a better way to spend the day."

"Thank you, it's pretty shit hot of you," Erik finally says, and I know he's blown away by the gesture. I mean, who wouldn't be? It's one thing to be so rich, and another to share the wealth so magnanimously.

"Thanks. Your appointments are in one hour, so take your time finishing up," he tells us. "And there's one more thing I believe you all might enjoy."

"This I gotta hear," Erik responds dryly.

Clayton actually smiles at him. "My friends and I have been invited to have dinner with a colleague and his wife who is staying on a yacht not far from the resort. I would be honored if you could join us."

Not far from the resort?

"You don't have to take us," I tell him, hoping that he doesn't hear the disappointment in my voice over possibly not spending the evening with him.

His gaze meets mine possessively. He gives me a look that says, *as if it's an option for you.* I can't stop the feeling of happiness that washes over me, knowing that he wants me with him as badly as I want to go with him. He takes my hand and kisses my palm. I'm totally enamored and I know my friends can tell. And I don't even care.

"I won't take no for an answer. The helicopter is picking us up at six thirty."

My eyes open wide.

"Helicopter?" Erik is the one to ask. He literally takes the word right out of my mouth.

"The Remingtons are staying in a yacht about twenty minutes from here."

"Cool, sounds fun. We'll be there with bells and whistles," Erik agrees quickly, but then we'd have to be complete idiots not to want to experience a helicopter ride and dinner on a yacht. It's a once-in-a-lifetime opportunity. I can't get the infamous scene in *Indecent Proposal* out of my head, the one where Robert Redford whisks Demi Moore away to sleep with her for a million dollars. I know Erik has got to be thinking the same thing.

"Thank you so much for including us," Orie smiles warmly at Clayton. He's totally already planning his outfit.

"Of course." He nuzzles the top of my head, and then places a soft kiss on my cheek. I feel a shiver of pleasure. It never gets old. "Now if you'll excuse me, I'm going to get my massage."

We all say goodbye and I watch him walk away from the table and enjoy the view for a good minute until I can't see him anymore, then sigh happily to myself over his complete and utter deliciousness.

I cross my arms and meet Erik's gaze.

"Now spill the beans," he says.

If someone had told me before I came to the Maldives that I'd be flying over the Indian Ocean in a luxurious twelve-seater helicopter on my way to have dinner on a yacht, I'd have laughed right in his face. But that's my reality, believe it or not. Clayton's put me next to the window so I can look out on the view, which is so spectacular from this vantage point, especially as the sun sets over the horizon.

Erik and Orie are beyond thrilled. After telling them about my blissful two days with Clayton, and then spending the day in the spa, I think they are half in love with him, too. Erik's done a complete one eighty and is back to being his usual, chipper self. They're both in awe of him, of everything he did for me. But the best part is how happy they are for me, that he was my first, and that he is acting like a complete gentleman. They actually called me lucky.

I guess I am. I glance over at him surreptitiously. I missed him today. In fact, being apart from him for those hours was torture. When we walked back to our villas from the spa, well into the afternoon, I realized how happy I was just knowing that I was going "home" to him.

As soon as my key was in the lock, the door opened and Clayton pulled me inside, immediately pressing his lips to mine, showing me that I hadn't been alone in my misery.

"That was too damn long," he said passionately as he carried me off to bed. After, Clayton read over some work documents and held my hand the entire time.

I got ready and put on the only dress I hadn't worn yet—a simple, (hmmm . . . maybe too short?) black dress with spaghetti straps and some tall wedge heels. My best accessory was my new tan, which really made it all work. I looked good and felt sexy. I came out of the bathroom and the expression on his face was priceless. He looked handsome himself in tan pants and a navy linen shirt. The blue of the shirt made his eyes shine even more, and he'd rolled up the sleeves, exposing his browned forearms. I wanted to kiss that throat of his, run my tongue up and down that tantalizing expanse of chest. But . . . we couldn't be late for dinner.

"Change," he immediately said. I know he liked what he saw because of the way his eyes were eating me up. But clearly, I was right that the dress was too short.

"What? Not sexy?" I asked coyly, spinning around so he could see the back as well, hoping a little flirting would work to my benefit.

If anything, he got even more adamant.

"I want to rip it right off of you."

I smiled at his choice of words. "I take that as a yes?" I teased, walking up to him, totally turned on. We were running a little late but another twenty minutes wouldn't hurt anyone.

"I don't want anyone else thinking those thoughts, Sophie," he said rather possessively, as his gaze raked my body. "You belong to me."

"I'm yours," I agreed, nodding my head, the first time I said those words without him being deep inside me, demanding them. "But this is all I have to wear."

"Not true. You have an entire suitcase filled with clothes. Find something more appropriate." I really didn't appreciate his autocratic tone. I thought, *We need to lay down some rules here.* He had to understand that I would wear what I wanted, when I wanted.

"No. I want to wear this. I feel good in it. I'm not changing, Clayton."

He took a dangerous step toward me. "Care to bet on that, my angel?"

My angel? It was the first time he'd said that. I wanted to caress his cheek tenderly. . There I went again, getting distracted.

"There's no time," I said.

"The chopper will wait."

"Clayton! Please," I begged him. I can't believe I was actually begging to wear a dress I liked. It was so absurd, it made me want to laugh. Or cry, depending on how I looked at it. I was spared Clayton's response by a knock on the door. I rushed to open it, greeting Erik, Orie, and Eduard with a relieved smile. Eduard gave me an appreciative look and a low whistle.

"Nice dress, Sophie," he said. I didn't dare look at Clayton. I could only imagine the look on his face, and I knew it wasn't pretty.

"Ready girl?" Orie asked, kissing me hello. "You look hot as hell. I'm dying over the dress. It is so sexy and . . . daring. Totally unlike you, but I love it! Turn around for me so I can get the full look." I spin for Orie, still carefully avoiding Clayton's gaze.

"Is that the Dolce we bought together at the sample sale?" Erik asked me, knowing full well it was, like he's capable of forgetting anything! Especially when he's been part of the buying process.

"I knew it," Erik said.

"How much?" Orie asks.

"It was like fifty dollars. It had to have been mismarked," I explained. "But it was the perfect price for me."

I could feel the anger radiating off Clayton, but surrounded by three men who completely approved, there was nothing he could do or say without looking like a complete dickhead. He knew it. I knew it. I hoped I wouldn't pay for it later in the evening.

"Let's go." Erik grabbed my hand and pulled me out of the villa.

I looked over my shoulder and caught a glimpse of the wrath of Clayton Astor Sinclair and I almost made the sign of the cross.

And now, here we are. I look over at him as we land on the yacht's helipad and wonder if he's still pissed. Okay, yes, he is. His face has that serious, stern look on it. I wonder how pissed he is. Is it a level five, or

DEFCON one? I reach out and take his hand and his gaze is pure ice.

"Come on. Don't do this," I whisper so no one can hear, as I try to cajole the crazy out of him.

He takes my hand and caresses my thumb, then leans in close, so on the outside it looks as if he's whispering sweet nothings in my ear. I should be so lucky.

"Sophie, love. It would be wise of you to understand that I don't like to be disobeyed," he says. "If you want to know if I'm still angry the answer is no." Oh thank God, I think to myself, irritated that he used the word "disobeyed" but okay with letting it slip this once. But the sense of security walks out the door when he says, "I'm fucking livid. We'll continue the discussion when we get back to the villa."

Oh no. He pulls away from me as everyone starts to exit the helicopter, grabs a blanket from one of the seats, and hands it to me.

"Wrap this around your waist so the whole goddamn world doesn't see what belongs to me."

I do as I'm told and I'm actually really happy that he spared me the embarrassment of having my dress fly up over my head. Watching Elizabeth and Jane stumble out of the helicopter with dresses blowing in all sorts of direction makes me blush.

Once we're all safely on the deck of the yacht we're greeted by the Remington family. I kind of figured they would be English but I guess I didn't realize just *how English* they would be. They have those low, posh voices that Jane, Elizabeth, and the guys speak in, but times one hundred. Their pronunciation is exaggerated and, I'm guessing, very old school. Mr. Tom Remington is an older, distinguished looking man with blond hair and quizzical green eyes. His wife, Sheila, is a petite blonde with an amazing body that she's showing to its full advantage. Lord, I'm surprised she can even walk in that dress. She also has on about ten pounds of makeup and jewelry. She's sparkling so brightly it's almost blinding.

I notice the way her hand touches Clayton's arm like she's intimately familiar with him or something and my claws come out. She's barely civil to me but embraces everyone else like they're long-lost relatives. Including Erik and Orie, who she instantly loves. We are introduced to a man, Albert Larson. He's a good-looking guy and downer Jane immediately sets her sights on him.

The help passes trays of champagne around and I gladly take a flute. I stand with Erik, Orie, and Elizabeth watching Clayton and Sheila sipping champagne together like it's old times. She eats him up with her eyes, like a barracuda on the prowl.

I hate her.

And I wonder how long Clayton is going to ignore me.

Chapter Sixteen

"WHAT A LOVELY DRESS. Really, quite fetching." I'm startled to hear Tom Remington voice behind me.

I turn to face him and we make room for him as he joins our small circle. Tom looks at me in a way a married man should never look at another woman and I'm repelled, repulsed, and totally revolted. *Yes, those are all words that begin with the letter R but I could come up with others.*

"Thank you," I answer politely, suddenly wishing I had listened to Clayton and worn something less revealing. Not that I'd ever admit that to him, but still, he might have been right. Maybe. "Thank you for having us for dinner tonight," I go on, not sure what else to say. "It's quite an impressive yacht."

"Yes, Sheila love found the *Siren* for us. It is nice but we do find it rather small, with only ten staterooms. We're accustomed to much larger accommodations. It's really quite stuffy with all the family on board. We're practically on top of each other."

Too small? This is the biggest yacht I've ever seen! Erik and Orie stay suspiciously quiet, but I know what they must be thinking.

"I'm sorry you feel so cramped. That is not a pleasant feeling," I say lamely. "How many are on board?"

"It's Sheila and I, and our two boys, Archibald and Brentley. Albert, Sheila's business partner, has joined just for the evening."

I look at Tom Remington and smile uncomfortably. Honestly, I don't even know what to say to him. What would be the proper blue-blooded response to ten bedrooms on a yacht not being large enough for a family of four and a child who goes by the name of Brentley? *The poor kid,* I think to myself, *I thought I had it bad with my parents.*

"I've learned that sometimes you have to take on more humble accommodations to truly appreciate the gifts you have." I think I'll be struck by lightning for using that adjective to describe the yacht.

"Well said, my darling Sophie. Well said." He nods at me like I'm the Dalai Lama. *I'm not your darling anything, Tom.* But I politely smile back at him.

Before I can ask another question, the two boys come over. They are exactly as I'd picture them. Thin, blonde, with pinched, angry faces. They're both wearing coats *and cravats* and they're only about twelve or thirteen years old.

"Father," the slightly taller of the two says as he looks down his nose at Erik and Orie. I almost erupt with laughter by how offended my friends look.

"Ah, Archibald, Brentley, so good of you to join us." Tom quickly introduces us to his two sons, who nod rather arrogantly at us then cross their arms and look around the deck.

Archibald lifts his hand and motions toward an older gentleman, who I gather works for them. He comes right over.

"Yes, sir?"

"What is for dinner, Niles?" I make eye contact with Erik. I'd bet money we are both thinking the same thing. Is this entire scene for real?

"Sea bass, sir."

If possible, Archibald pinches his face even tighter.

"Is it line caught?"

Erik chokes on his drink.

Orie starts to pat him in the back, trying to cover Erik's mirth. I have to keep my face down. I can't look up. *God, please don't make me laugh. Please don't make me laugh.*

Niles doesn't answer Archibald fast enough.

"I say, Niles, *is it line caught?*" His enunciation of every word is so drawn out, so utterly English, that it's really quite unbelievable.

"Yes, sir. I dare say it is."

Archibald nods and dismisses Niles, who hurries off.

I feel a warm hand on my lower back, my very *naked* lower back, and turn to see Clayton has joined us. He still won't even look at me, just keeps his gaze on Tom, Erik, and Orie. He looks at Archibald and Brentley. "Gentlemen."

"Lord Sinclair," the boys say in unison. My gaze whips up to Clayton. *Lord* Sinclair? Clayton seems to grimace at the mention of the title. He's a lord? What the hell? Archibald turns to Erik.

"My mother tells me that you are a famous Hollywood stylist."

"Or infamous," Orie says with a smile.

"What made you want to dress men and women for a living? I find that quite odd. Is that no better than being a valet?"

"Archibald Thurston Remington the third!" Tom says, and has the decency to look mortified.

"That's a mouthful," Erik says to Tom, then looks down at the arrogant shit. "I can answer little Archie's question."

"It's Archibald."

"Archie sounds better," Erik says.

"I prefer Archibald."

Erik is enjoying ruffling his feathers.

"Alright, *Archibald*," Erik begins thoroughly enjoying himself. "A stylist chooses clothes for his or her client to make a statement. To define who you are, a trendsetter or a follower. Fashion is a powerful tool used in every part of your life. Take you, for instance. Is that a Turnbull & Asser shirt and coat you have on?" Erik asks as he looks the kid up and down, assessing every line, every detail with the eyes of a hawk.

Archibald is clearly surprised that Erik knows, and to be honest, so am I, since I don't even know who that designer is.

"Yes." He looks at Erik's wardrobe, clearly the opposite of Turnbull & Asser. "How would you know?"

"Because I know style. I actually think the cut you have on is a bit stiff. It's not hip or cool, two adjectives that I just *know* you are. Turnbull & Asser dress James Bond," Erik checks him out. "How old are you?"

"Fourteen and a half."

"Exactly. You're an adult. Dress like it. A fitted blazer. Lose the cravat. Have a crisp white shirt made that has your initials underneath your collar in the back, not on the chest pocket like the older gentlemen do. You don't need to show off. People know who you are. You're Archibald Thurston Remington the third. That's how cool you are."

Goddamnit, he's so good. Archie is instantly obsessed.

"Will you tell my mother?"

"Gladly."

"I'll go and find her. Come along, Brentley," Archibald orders his brother as he runs off. I look at Erik in awe. Lord, does the man know his stuff.

"You're very good at what you do, my friend," Clayton says as he lifts his glass in salute to Erik.

"I try," Erik says.

Tom looks from Erik to Clayton, totally uncomfortable and desperately wanting to change the subject.

"What a delightful young lady you've brought with you, Clayton. Charming. Intelligent. Gorgeous. Absolutely, gorgeous. Why have you kept her hidden for so long? Your mother would just love to see you with a nice young lady like this." I lower my gaze in embarrassment when Tom mentions Clayton's mother. "How long have the two of you been friends?" Tom's creepy gaze gives me the heebie jeebies.

I wonder what kind of business Clayton is doing with him. Or, better question, *why?*

"A short while," Clayton returns evenly, his voice revealing nothing, I'm so thankful.

I wonder how long before he lets go of being annoyed about my dress. I mean, compared to Sheila, I look like a nun. Her nipples are practically peeking out from the top of her dress!

"I missed your family name, my dear," Tom says to me. That's because I didn't give it to you, perv.

"It's Walker."

"Walker?" Tom lifts his head and thinks about this a good, long time. I'm sure he's trying to figure out if I have the right blue-blooded pedigree to eat with them. Before he can finish his assessment, a bell chimes across the deck. I look over and see a man dressed in a severe black tux standing with both hands behind his back.

"Canapés are ready to be served," he says in a deep English accent. I look around at this blatant display of over-the-top wealth and feel like I'm being Punk'd, because this is so not real life.

Clayton quietly escorts me inside, where I get a full look at the opulence. It's insane. We walk into a family room extravagantly decorated in a traditional style, with two plush crème couches, a bar, a flat screen on the wall, and fresh flowers everywhere. I feel like I'm in an episode of *Extreme Yachts*.

Three servers, dressed in white, gloves and all, pass out canapés. I take a small toast with caviar and a dollop of crème. It is divine. Appetizers at parties I usually attend consist of chips, dip, and hummus.

Clayton stands next to me in silence, probably still stewing away. I finish my champagne, and before I can even look around for a place to put it down, someone whisks by, takes it from me, and hands me a just-poured glass. One could get used to this kind of wealth, I'm not going to lie.

I look up at Clayton, who's now holding a scotch. I don't even remember seeing him ask for one. He cocks a brow.

"Enjoying yourself, love?"

I lean into him nice and close and give him a sexy smile.

"Not as much as I would enjoy being back at the villa with you. Alone."

I take a sip of my champagne and the bubbles are clearly working their magic. I'm slightly lightheaded and far more at ease, which I'm thankful for because Lord knows I'm feeling pretty out of my element. I mean, aside from the gazillion-dollar surroundings, I've literally just landed in a helicopter. Hello, when does that happen to me? I just discovered that Clayton, a man I've barely known a week, who I happen to be falling in love . . . so not going down that road tonight . . . is also, most assuredly, a lord. What is that anyway? Like, a knight? A prince? What does it even mean?

"I would prefer the privacy as well." I'm thinking he wants the privacy for a completely different reason than me. I'm about to tell him this when I'm rudely interrupted by busty galore, Sheila the she-devil.

"Clayton, daaaaarling! I'm getting you a highball of Dalmore and

Mad Love

then I want to show you something in our stateroom. We picked up this wonderful little piece of art . . . one that only you will appreciate." She looks down her nose at me (I swear she squints her eyes a little) and starts to pull him away to her stateroom. Yeah, I know it's yacht lingo for bedroom.

"Please excuse me," he says apologetically to me. "This should only take a second."

I want to wring her neck. Or his. I can't tell.

"Sheila is desperate," Elizabeth whispers. She has stealthily appeared beside me.

"Oh? I thought you all knew each other?" I ask curiously.

"Socially. I know that Tom has business with Clayton. But I've never cared for him or that trampy wife of his," Elizabeth says. Now the champagne is talking. Good. "And I know for a fact she is not Clayton's friend. My brother told me how much she annoys him. Sheila is pathetic and has been trying to sleep with him since she set eyes on him two years ago, when Tom and Clayton started doing business together. Clayton only gives her the time of day because of his business relationship with Tom."

Trying to sleep with him? Now why did she have to go and tell me that? I stare at the door anxiously, waiting for them to come back, willing them to. And suddenly, the door swings open and in walks Clayton and on his arm is . . . wait . . . it's not Sheila. It's worse. It's seriously the most beautiful woman I've ever seen in my life. She might as well have just stepped out of the pages of a Victoria's Secret catalogue, with her shimmering, jet black hair cut into a Victoria Beckham bob, her sultry, sparkling blue eyes, and bronzed legs that seem to extend right up to her perfectly shaped breasts.

I am frozen in awe of her, but then my eyes zoom into her arm, which is wrapped around Clayton's like some kind of sexy python. With her perfect white teeth gleaming, she throws her head back in gales of laughter at whatever clever thing he's just said, and the familiarity between them is utterly nauseating.

And then a thought explodes in my brain like a firework on the Fourth of July: he's sleeping with her. Or, at the very least, he *has* slept with her. Probably a thousand times. It's clear. Oh God, I'm going to puke.

Sheila walks in behind them smiling like a well-fed cat and looks over at me and practically shrugs her shoulders as if to say, *Sorry!* That bitch. I picture myself throwing her over the side of the yacht. Is this woman the "piece of art" she wanted to show Clayton? I feel like someone just punched me right in the gut.

I wonder how quickly the helicopter can take me back to the resort. Hell, how far away can it take me so I can run away and just forget that I ever thought for a second that *Lord* Clayton Astor Sinclair could possibly be mine.

My body tenses up and I turn abruptly. I've got to get out of here. I need . . . Erik and Orie each take an arm, holding me still.

"What the fuck is that face?" Erik whispers down at me, his eyes worried.

I'm so happy there's soft music in the background and people are talking loudly, paying attention to their own conversations and not ours.

"Air. I need air. Now," I manage to croak out, and the two guide me out the door, which thankfully go in the opposite direction from where Clayton is standing with Miss Universe, and onto the deck. I take deep, deep breath, clench my fists, and beg myself to get a grip. Why? Why does she have to be here right now and ruin this for me? Why am I letting her make me feel inferior? But I mean, seriously, she could make a supermodel hate herself.

"Talk to me, Goose," Erik demands as I and suck in the night air trying my hardest not to act so obvious.

But I can't form a sentence. Not yet.

"I don't mean to take away from what's obviously a serious situation but Sophie is so *not* Goose. if anything, she's Maverick and *you're* Goose," Orie breaks the silence.

"So I'm the one who can't eject himself from the seat in time?" Erik sounds annoyed.

"Yeah, I guess. If you want to put it like that."

"That's so fucked that you think so little of me." Erik goes on.

"Erik, we're talking about *Top Gun, a movie*," Orie returns. "Why do you have to be so *dramatique* all the time?"

"Art imitates real life," Erik says. "And I'm offended you think I'm Goose when I'm *so* Maverick. Or maybe even Ice-Man."

Before Orie can comment—

"Did you see her?!" I blurt out, interrupting a conversation I know they will no doubt pick up again as I turn to face them. "That . . . that . . . Helena Christensen doppelganger?"

I'm sure my face is pale, my insecurity written all over it. Erik knows me better than anyone.

Both guys look instantly pissed off. What the hell?

"Are you fucking kidding me?" Erik snaps.

Orie takes the calmer, gentler approach as he always does, and brushes back my long hair. At least her hair is shorter. It seemed thin, too. Good! A flaw! Surely there are more. Right?

"You're not going to cry, are you?" Erik looks horrified at the thought.

He quickly turns to Orie and orders, "Inside. Shots. Tequila. Pronto." Orie doesn't argue and runs inside.

"I can't do tequila. I'll get sick."

"Well, sick is better than acting like a crazy lady because Clayton is talking to some other woman," Erik says in a disappointed voice. "Jesus Sophie, for a second I thought something was really wrong with you!"

I stifle a laugh.

"She's not some other woman. Don't you dare lie to me to make me feel better! I'm not blind, for Christ's sake. She's fucking stunning."

"And?"

"She's perfect!"

"And?"

I'm suddenly furious at him. "And? And? What else would you like me to say? They know each other! Like . . . really know each other. As in they've probably slept together."

"Slept." Erik shrugs. "So what? Who fucking cares? You knew he was bound to have exes. Get over it."

"Fine, but how could I ever compete with *that?*" I whisper, hating my weakness and self-doubt. I'm a hot mess.

"Compete? What are you talking about? *You have him!*" Erik practically shouts at me. The door rattles and we look over to see Orie walk out with three shot glasses and a bottle of DeLeón Tequila. Lord, he brought the entire bottle.

"What did I miss?" he demands as he reaches us.

"I was just getting to the best part," Erik tells him as Orie pours.

"Our koo-koo bird here thinks she's got to compete with that creepy Amazon inside the yacht."

Orie laughs, looking completely relieved. "That's hilarious."

Okay, obviously they did not truly take in the goddess-like woman with her body entwined with Clayton's like some kind of succubus. That, or they just weren't paying attention.

"She has some mother eff'ing crazy eyes." Orie says.

"Fatal attraction written all over her." Am I missing something?

Erik turns to me as Orie hands us shots.

"Take it. Now."

I close my eyes, hold my breath, and swig the tequila. Holy shit! I cough, suck on the lime he hands me, and try to get a grip. The drink warms me from the inside out. I watch in horror as Orie pours another. I firmly shake my head no.

"Don't even start with me, Sophie Walker. You will take as many goddamn shots as I say, and you will listen to me and listen to me good. Comprendez?" Erik orders as he puts his hand on his hip and faces me. I can only nod. "First, you're crazy. Second, that bitch inside might be crazier than you. Third, you're stunning and Clayton knows it. You put her beauty queen looks to shame. She's taller than you, that's all! And we've already discussed how you can fix that! Clayton's had his eyes on you the whole night. Every single goddamn time I look at him, he's staring at you, eating you up. No doubt pissed off about the length of your dress . . ."

"How did you know that?" I ask in shock, but unable to disguise the delight I feel from the other things he said. Orie hands us each a second shot.

"Babe, we're men. We saw his face when you did the turn for us back at the villa. He was fucking pissed. But you should have seen it when that weirdo Tom was talking to you; he looked like he was going to kill him with his bare hands," Orie tells me with a smile.

"He did?" Hope blooms.

"Yeah. He did. He wants to take you by the hand," Orie continues, "get the hell out of Dodge, and have his way with you, but he's trying to keep it under control here." He lifts his shot glass and we do it again.

Holy mother of God! I have to bend over. The burning heat from the tequila moves through me like liquid fire.

I hear Orie start to pour another.

"I can't," I tell him. "I'm gonna die." Or throw up. I back away slowly, hoping they won't make me take down another shot.

"She's good," Erik tells Orie as he examines my face.

I'm already feeling warm and totally buzzed from the champagne, which is now definitely being amplified by the tequila. I smile at them in gratitude.

"I love you guys. Thanks for always taking care of me. You're the bestest." I'm slurring, and I know it. But it's kinda funny.

"Christ. Did we give her too much, Erik?" Orie asks in concern, as he looks me over.

"No. She'll be fine. She looks sexy. She's got the alcohol-induced flush and those fuck-me eyes. He's gonna die." Erik rubs his hands together in excitement.

He is? I'm not sure if I believe him. Orie primps my hair, Erik smoothes out my dress, pulls it down farther in the back, and then tells me to pucker my lips so Orie can put some clear lip gloss on me. I smile at them both when they step away. I feel good. Really good. My body is humming inside.

"You've been out here for a long time," I hear Clayton say in his husky way.

Crap. There goes my buzz. Not really, but slightly. He makes his way over to the three of us and takes in the scene. Orie's holding the tequila bottle and three glasses, and I know he understands what's just gone down. His gaze finds mine and I'm suddenly overcome with longing. He takes in my, according to Erik and Orie, "wanton" appearance and his eyes glow with desire. I feel warm all over because he wants me. This, I do know.

"Is it hot in here?" I ask out loud to no one in particular.

Erik and Orie find my comment vastly amusing.

"We're outside, girl," Orie answers as he grabs hold of Erik's hand.

"But it has gotten rather hot suddenly. I think it's all the energy here. We'll just go inside and wait for you two."

They run off, abandon me actually, and I'm left alone facing Clayton, who's holding a glass of scotch in one hand and looking me over possessively.

"Are you still mad?" I ask.

He smiles tightly. "What do you think?"

I cross my arms.

"Well, good, because so am I."

"And what are you mad about, Sophie?" he asks curiously.

I gather courage and tell him.

"First of all, do you think running off into Sheila Remington's room to check out a piece of art is an appropriate thing to do when you've brought a date with you?" I ask him, finding myself really angry all of a sudden. "I might not be your girlfriend, Clayton, but you did invite me to this damn yacht, and you should have the decency to show me that small respect."

His eyes narrow and he takes a minute before puts his drink down, then starts to stalk me in that wolfish way of his. Since I'm already at the railing and there's nowhere for me to go, I hold my ground. He comes up on me, putting a hand on either side of the railing, then closing in so he can pull me close. His fingers caress the skin of my lower back.

"Please." I roll my eyes at him, my desire temporarily cooled by my anger.

"You're wrong. If you're not my girlfriend, then what are you?"

Fuck buddy? Vacation . . . sex . . . friend?

"I honestly don't know."

He looks frustrated by me. "Sophie, you *are* my girlfriend. I didn't think you needed me to tell you."

I feel my chest, neck, and cheeks instantly flush, and my knees literally go weak. I lower my eyes for a second, trying to hide the pure unadulterated pleasure I feel from his words.

"And you're right. I shouldn't have gone with Sheila, but her husband is my client and I had no choice. But you're really testing me, Sophie."

"How am I testing you?" I ask, and I don't have to wait long for the answer.

"I'm furious with you, and with myself, for this lack of control I seem to have with you. This is new for me," he says, clearly feeling unnerved. "And I hate the thought of any man ogling you, lusting after what is mine."

I melt into him, holding on to his shirt, his body against his. His arms hold me close. We look into each other's eyes.

"I just have one more question. Who's the Amazon?" I ask softly.

He looks confused for a second then gives a small, serious smile.

"Amelia."

My heart thumps in my chest.

"And?"

"And what?" He definitely looks uncomfortable. I try to pull away from him, but he doesn't let me; in fact, he holds me tighter.

"I can see, Clayton. The way she was clinging to you. And looking at you, hanging on every word that came out of your mouth," I say. "You guys know each other, or at least *knew* each other. And it seems like she's still into you." I know I've revealed a lot to him, and made myself vulnerable.

He stares at me for a long while, as if deciding whether he should tell me the truth. I can tell that he doesn't want to have this conversation at all. What man would?

"What exactly are you asking, Sophie?" I know it's crystal clear what I'm asking so I guess he's trying to prolong the inevitable.

"Did you date her?" This is code for *did you sleep with her*, which I don't have the balls to ask.

"What does it matter?"

"It matters to me."

"Why?"

"Because I want to know," I tell him stubbornly. "I want to know if that beauty queen in there had been in all the same intimate scenarios with you as I have."

He silently stares at me, probably cursing the fact that he brought me with him tonight. I've blown it. But I go on.

"You get to ask me anything. You get to ask me about my past, about Jerry, about everything. Can't I have the answer to this one question?" Wow, I said that pretty well. And not a tear in sight. Must be the tequila.

"Amelia and I dated." His voice is reserved. The last thing he wants to do is give in to me. But he has no choice because the logic I've used is undeniable. He can't have it just one way. He has to give me this.

"When?"

"We broke up last month."

And I've just sustained another punch (maybe a kick this time) right to the gut. I can feel the acid rising in my esophagus—I seriously might vomit this time. My entire body tightens up with nerves, and I try to pull away from him, but then I remember . . . even though it seems like an eternity ago, Jerry and I broke up even more recently than that. Still. It's different. I never touched Jerry. We were never intimate. Oh my God. What if I'm a rebound?

"How long did you date?" I go on.

He sighs loudly.

"It doesn't matter."

"It does to me."

"A year."

A whole year? It hits me hard. Fuck. He brought *her* to the Maldives on vacation. He brought *her* to that villa he's staying in. To that bed. This time last year, she was in his arms. He grabs my chin and forces me to look at him. My gaze can barely focus on his, as I try to get a grip on my raging emotions.

"She didn't mean anything to me. It was convenient. If I actually saw her during that year, it would never have lasted longer than a month. But I was traveling a lot and she was always off on modeling jobs. We never saw each other." *Model. I knew it!*

"Why is she here?" I whisper.

"Because Sheila is a bitch and was told about you by Jane, who is Tom's cousin. She used the opportunity to invite Amelia, who was in Malaysia on a job, to create this very situation."

Jane and Tom are cousins? I definitely see the similarity. I can't believe she would be so calculating and cold because Clayton likes me. It's just so evil. And wrong.

"She went to all this trouble because she dislikes me that much?"

"I will have a word with her." Clayton is angry, I'm sure, that Jane put him in a situation in which he had to explain his past relationships to me.

My heart leaps. He looks so serious, though, and I want to wipe the frown off his face. And so I do. I take away his frown the way he's done it with me. My fingers trace their way to his soft lips, which I touch softly. He grabs my hand and kisses each one of my fingers. I rise up on my toes and his hands pull me up close and I kiss him softly on the lips.

"Clayton, darling? Dinner is about to be served."

I look over to see the beautiful Amelia staring at us, slack jawed, as she takes in the intimate scene. I try to pull away from his embrace but he won't allow it.

"Sophie and I will be right there."

She looks so hurt, I almost feel sorry for her. She spins around and disappears inside.

"Shall we go eat?" Clayton asks.

I nod slowly as he takes my hand.

"One more thing, Clayton?"

He turns to look at me.

"When were you going to tell me that you're a lord?"

Chapter Seventeen

"I HAVE SOME BAD NEWS," Clayton tells me as we lie in each other's arms the next afternoon.

My stomach sinks in dread over what it could be. My body is tense as I wait for him to tell me.

"I have to go to Singapore."

My heart stops beating. Falls to the ground, through the crust, deep into middle earth where I feel my life just being sucked out of me. He's leaving for Singapore. *He's leaving?* Is he ever coming back? I haven't prepared for this. I thought we had more time. Are we done? Is it over between us? Is this the end?

He lifts my chin so he can look at me.

"Sophie, I'm only going for the night and I'll be back the day after tomorrow. I don't want to go, but I must. And actually, I wanted to know if you'd like to come with me."

I start to breathe again. He wants me to go with him. The amount of relief I feel from those words is staggering. He's going just for one night.

We have more time. What am I going to do when we leave the Maldives and an ocean separates us for good? What will happen? How will I ever cope, if I can barely stand the thought of him leaving me for one night?

Time has gone by so fast here already. It feels like just yesterday that I arrived. And now, in a few days this dream will be over. My trip is almost coming to an end and we have yet to discuss anything beyond the here and now. Both of us intentionally avoid the topic, avoid anything that will taint the remaining time we have together. I want to go with him. I want to go with him so bad, but there's something in me that knows I shouldn't.

I need time to time to think about everything that's happened. Everything that's going to happen when I leave. I need to face reality and the future, whatever that holds for me. And the fact that he asked me to go with him is proof that he wants me with him. There's really nothing more that I could ask for.

Clayton looks at me, watching the emotions play over my face. He doesn't wait. He keeps talking. When I don't answer he goes on, "So what do you think? I would love to show you Singapore. I don't know how long I'll be working, but I can book you into one of the best spas in the city, have you pampered."

I smile at him, overwhelmed by his thoughtfulness. I'm glad he wants me to go with him; it shows he wants me beside him, near him. I have nothing to worry about. I think.

"So what will it be?"

"I'm sorry?" My runaway thoughts get in the way of staying in the moment.

He rolls his eyes in amusement. Nothing sounds more appealing to me then spending the night in Singapore with him and seeing the city, but I can't give him what he wants.

"It's so sweet of you to invite me, but you're going to be doing business and you won't want me in the way. I'll be a distraction," I tell him. "And it will give me some time to spend with Erik and Orie too."

He doesn't appear to be happy with my response.

It takes him a moment, but then he nods his head and looks almost sad.

"I want you with me, but if this is your wish, then so be it."

"So you'll spend tomorrow night with Erik and Orie and I'll be back the following day." He states the obvious and I have the feeling he's saying it to try to understand and stomach it. After all, this is a man who always gets what he wants.

"Yes. And I'll miss you."

"If you were going to miss me, you'd come with me."

"That's not really fair," I say.

"I know." He's pouting. "But I want you near me." He almost sounds childish.

It's strange how the thought of just one night away from him seems like an eternity, but it does. And I know it's because I've completely fallen in love with him. There, I said it. I can't bear the thought of not being with him. But I need to be a big girl now and be confident in who I am and the feelings I believe this man has for me. So no matter how hard it is for me to spend a night without him and considering I really don't know how much time I'll have with him, I take an adult step and relinquish all crazy neediness.

"Absence makes the heart grow fonder."

"I have no need of absence, Sophie."

My toes curl and I practically throw myself in his embrace, wanting to show him how much he means to me, how much I'll miss him when he's gone, and how I'm already obsessing about what I'm going to do without him in this villa tomorrow night.

I've spent the day drawing and tormenting myself with thoughts about Clayton. He left me early in the morning, making love to me before he quickly departed and ordered me to sleep in. I tried, honest to God, I tried, but it was just impossible without him. So I ended up getting dressed and sitting on the deck sketching. He had surprised me by having a giant sketchpad delivered to the bungalow yesterday and now I'm glad he did. It has kept my attention for hours. I opted out of a lazy beach day with Erik and Orie, wanting to give them their space and to be honest, give myself time alone. I've only stopped to have coffee delivered to the room and to shower. What's funny is that I'm not drawing the ocean in front of me, no, I'm busy sketching the ocean from our island. The one I felt and saw when he took me in the water, made me swim and face my fears. The place where I found my salvation, so to speak.

The phone rings and takes me out of my moment. I rush to answer.

"Hello?"

"Baby."

I sigh with happiness.

"Hey. How was your flight?"

"Shitty. You should be with me." His voice is gruff.

"I know." I agree with him. I wish I was with him.

"Have you had your meeting yet?" I ask him, changing the topic.

"I'm on my way." He sounds tired and especially annoyed.

"I hope it goes well."

"Thank you." He sighs. "What are you doing?"

"Using the sketchpad you got me."

"What are you drawing?"

"Our island," I tell him, wishing that we were there. Together. Now. "I really miss you, Clayton. I wish you were here. Actually, I wish you never left." I let him hear the longing in my voice.

"Fuck, Sophie," he whispers to me, his voice strained. "You're killing me."

I am?

"I wish I were there too, sweetheart. But you could have been here with me. We wouldn't have to feel this way now." His voice has a certain edge to it.

"I know. But just think about how sweet tomorrow will be," I say, wishing I could wiggle my nose and have him magically appear.

"Tomorrow is not today."

No, it is not.

"I'll call you later, baby. Enjoy your sketching."

"Good-bye, Clayton."

"Bye, baby."

We hang up and I feel overwhelmingly sad. I miss him so much it hurts. I want him here. With me. Now. That's not going to happen, I know. I'm suddenly exhausted.

Making love to Clayton all day and night takes its toll—the good kind—but still. I realize that I need to take a nap, something I'm not really used to doing, but since he's gone, I will. I'll just sleep for a little and then come right back to my sketching. Since Clayton already called, I turn the ringer off so I can sleep without any interruptions.

The second I put my head down, I'm out.

I wake up to a banging sound on my villa door. I open my eyes and am shocked to see that it's night. Crap! How long was I out? I run over to the door and find Erik and Orie, dressed for dinner, standing there looking at me annoyed. I brush the tired from my eyes as I stare at my friends. Jesus. Talk about a nap. Try, I slept the whole damn day away! I lean against the door and smile at them.

"Hi," I yawn loudly as I finally greet them.

"Hi," Erik says back to me, as he checks out my outfit. Yes, I'm wearing the Singapore Airlines pajamas top.

"We've been calling you all goddamn day. We were actually worried. I thought you might have slit your wrists or something. Were you really sleeping the whole time?" he says as he examines my face. "Or were you crying because lover boy left you for one whole day? Your eyes look kind of puffy."

I roll my puffy eyes at him.

"I was sleeping. I was really tired, I guess," I answer.

"We have dinner reservations, remember? The three of us? The way we were? Before you started fucking Clayton all day long, all day strong?" Erik's pissed.

"I'm sorry!" I tell him truthfully, trying to appease his wrath. "Just give me a second and I'll be right there!"

"Honey, you need more than a second!" he calls after me as I run into the villa.

Ten minutes later, I'm showered and we're on our way to the restaurant.

I laugh as we head down the long walkway lit by tiki torches to the main beach and restaurants.

"Fuck me. I'm going to be sick," Erik says in a shocked voice.

"What?" I ask, looking up at him in concern. He looks totally fine.

"Mother fucker," he says, his face in complete and utter disbelief as he stares ahead. Orie and I quickly follow his gaze and my heart stops. And not for a good reason.

Holy shit.

Holy mother fucking shit. It's Jerry. He's standing at the end of the pathway from the villas watching us. He looks exhausted. He's in Bermuda shorts and a polo, a look that any woman in the world would find handsome, but not me. He runs a hand through his thick brown hair and slowly makes his way to us.

I'm incapable of speaking. Of words. Of thought. I can't believe he's here. Right now. In the Maldives. What the fuck? How did he get here? Why, oh my God, *why is he here?*

"Sophie," he says quietly to me, then smiles at Erik and Orie. "Hey guys. It's nice to see you. Your tans look great."

Erik is shell-shocked and can only nod.

"Hey, Jerry," Orie says. "What are you doing here?"

"I came for Sophie," Jerry says, his eyes stay fixed on me. He looks earnest, safe, the same way he's always looked over the many years I've known him. My stomach sinks in dread.

Why? Why God? Why? I look over at my friends, begging them, pleading with my eyes. But Erik gives Jerry a once over. He grabs hold of Orie's hand, I realize so they can leave me all alone with Jerry. To face this problem by myself. Head on. With nowhere to run. Motherfucker!

Erik gives me a serious look. "We'll be waiting at the restaurant for you. Drinking. Heavily."

He comes back and gives me a quick hug and whispers in my ear before he leaves. "Just you."

I watch them leave, then turn to stare at Jerry. I don't know what to say.

"You look good, Sophie."

That makes me want to cry, because the last thing I want to do is break his heart. He's my friend. I've known him all my life. I don't want to hurt him.

"Thank you." This is my problem to face alone, I know, but I feel like I'm living a nightmare. I force myself to be a big girl.

"We broke up. You shouldn't be here. Why would you come?"

"Isn't it obvious?" he asks as he takes a step closer to me. I step back. He notices and sighs.

"I know that I've not been everything you wanted me to be. I thought about everything you said to me, I mulled it over in my mind so many times. At first I thought you were right and then I realized how wrong you are." My heart drops in fear. "I never really told you how I feel about you. I should have tried . . ."

I hold my hand up. I don't want him to go there. "Jerry, don't. It's okay," I tell him. "You don't have to say any of this. I understand, and I'm fine with it. We're friends. That's all." I try to shoulder some of the responsibility. "We never should have tried to be more, and I'm just as much to blame as you. I should never have let it last so long, the way it was."

"Don't say that, Soph," he says, using the nickname that he used to call me. "I love you. Yes, yes, I do. Don't shake your head at me and try to tell me how I feel. Because I do. I love you. I want to spend my life with you. Just you. It's always been you."

The tears fall before I can help it. I know he's mistaking them for my acquiescence, but I'm just so sad. In my moment of weakness, he pulls me into his arms and holds me tight, kissing the top of my head. It's unreal to me how I feel nothing from him. No butterflies. No electricity. Nothing.

He's just . . . Jerry.

"Let me go, Jerry," I tell him as I remain motionless in his arms, just wiping the tears from eyes. "You need to just let me go."

"I won't, I can't let you go, Sophie! Please let me make this up to you. I can't lose you. Let me," he says slowly, passionately, his brown eyes earnest as he pulls my face up to his, forcing me to look at him.

"I want to make love to you. Let me make love to you and show you how much you mean to me." He pleads desperately, but the thought of him touching me in any way that Clayton has makes me physically nauseous. In truth, I feel like it's uncomfortable for Jerry even to be having the conversation with me. I mean, one day the thought of touching me disgusts him and now it's something he can't wait to do?

All because I flew across the world? It makes no sense to me.

Before I can say a word and tell Jerry that it will never happen, someone else does and my body goes cold.

"It's a little too late for that." An angry voice I recognize cuts right into our conversation. "And I suggest you get your fucking hands off her before I rip them off your body!"

I quickly move away from a bewildered Jerry, who's gone deathly still. My eyes find Clayton, hidden in the shadow of a palm tree, arms crossed, wearing the most lethal look I've ever seen in my life. How is he here? Isn't he supposed to be in Singapore? And oh my God in the short while I've known him, I've seen many furious looks from Clayton, but this, this has got to be the worst.

He's still wearing his navy blue suit pants and white business shirt he left in, and the top buttons are undone against the brutal heat. His hair is windblown and he looks tired, but still good.

His gaze slices over me in undeniable fury then moves back to Jerry.

As Erik would say, *motherfucking shit*.

"I'm sorry, have we met?" Jerry asks him coolly, sounding offended and a bit intimidated. However athletic and tall I once thought Jerry was, Clayton absolutely puts him to shame. There is simply no comparison. Clayton outshines Jerry in every way. And Lord Almighty, why is *he* here? He should still be in Singapore!

"Clayton Sinclair. And you're Jerry," he answers him in that arrogant, condescending English voice that he likes to use sometimes. Jerry immediately stands a bit taller as he looks him over. I wonder how long it will take Jerry to figure out why Clayton is acting like he owns . . .

"Who the fuck is this, Sophie?" Jerry turns angry eyes on me.

"Watch your mouth!" Clayton roars at him.

Right, the pot calling the kettle black. Obviously this is not the time to point that out.

"Don't tell me how to talk to my girl!" Jerry snaps at Clayton, not one ever to back down in a fight. Oh no.

"Jerry . . ." I begin to say that I'm not his girlfriend, but Clayton interrupts me.

He takes a menacing step toward Jerry.

"She's *not* your girl."

"Who the fuck is this British Prick, Soph?" He gives Clayton a look of complete disdain. "And where does he get off giving me shit?" Jerry turns to look at me, pins me with his smart gaze, wanting me to tell him what I'm guessing he's already figured out. The tears continue to fall because I realize that he will never talk to me again, that this friend of mine from childhood will never want to look at me again.

"Jerry, I don't know why you came here . . ." I begin shakily.

"Who is he?!" he screams at me, enraged. I've never seen him like this in my life.

"I'm the man she's sleeping with," Clayton says in a voice that is possessive, that announces complete ownership, and I just want to die. He could have said a million other things, but he chose to say the one thing that would kill Jerry, to know that I ran away and in the course of two weeks slept with a complete stranger. It would hurt anyone, especially if they crossed the world to try and win you back.

"That's a lie."

"Ask her."

Jerry turns and looks at me, his face ashen. Childhood memories flash through my mind as I face the finality of our relationship. I wipe the tears off my face and nod.

"It's true," I whisper.

At first Jerry doesn't believe me, then he looks at Clayton's victorious face.

"*This* guy is who you choose?" he says to me. "This condescending asshole?" His voice is filled with disgust. His misguided love has turned to hate in an instant. Even though I didn't ask him to come here, even though I broke up with him, I still don't want him to look at me like I'm the most loathsome, disgusting creature he's ever laid eyes on. I still don't want him to judge me. It hurts so bad to see.

"Please don't say that," I beg him for many reasons, the main one being that Clayton Astor Sinclair happens to be advancing on him, and I'm truly afraid for my friend.

"I thought you were so innocent," he says, then shakes his head in fury. "*You flew across the world to get laid by a foreigner, Sophie?* You're nothing but a goddamn whore!"

When Jerry utters the last word, Clayton's rage bubbles over. He picks Jerry up and throws him across the sand, his fury giving him superhuman strength. Jerry tries to stand, but Clayton punches him so hard in the face that he goes flying again.

"Clayton!" I scream at him, worried that he's going to kill Jerry. He ignores me and pounces on him, and before I can jump on his back to try to pull him off, Erik, Orie, and Eduard are there, grabbing Clayton and holding him off Jerry. It takes all three men to do it.

Jerry's face is bloody, but at least he's moving. I feel so guilty. I feel like I'm responsible for this whole situation, and even though I know I'm really not, I don't want Jerry to get hurt. I take a step toward him, wanting to help him up, and explain my feelings about Clayton to him, but I stop cold in my tracks when I hear Clayton's next words.

"Take a bloody step toward him, Sophie, and I will kill him." The primal rage in Clayton's voice is frightening. I don't move. Orie runs over to Jerry and tries to help him up, but he pushes him away.

"Don't fucking touch me!" Jerry screams, stumbling in the sand as he gets up.

Erik and Eduard are still holding Clayton back as Jerry looks over at me in complete and utter disgust.

"I wanted to marry you! And you gave yourself to this animal!" He spits in Clayton's direction. "He's used you! Where do you think this is going, Sophie? You're just an object to him! I thought you were smarter than this, but clearly I was wrong."

Clayton fights against the hold the guys have on him.

"Just go, Jerry. You've said enough." I'm sick to my stomach. Sick over his words, over him being here, over the thought that he might be right.

"Gladly."

I'm lying in bed with Orie in their bungalow. We're both quiet. He's turned the television on and has given me a t-shirt to wear. Eduard and Erik pulled Clayton to the bar, adamant that he not talk to me until he calmed down, and Orie asked if I wanted to go for a walk. I asked him to take me to their villa so I could sleep and Orie gladly agreed. But to be honest, the only place I really wanted to go was home to Los Angeles. At the villa, he handed me a glass of wine and we both got into the giant bed.

I feel so empty that I don't even know what to say. I can't believe what just happened: Jerry showing up out of the blue, Clayton's unthinkable rage. Thankfully, Orie let me cry, uninterrupted. Now I'm just staring at the TV.

"How are you feeling, Sophie?" he says after a while.

"Numb."

"I don't blame you. That was pretty fucking intense."

"Yeah." I pick up the glass of wine and take another sip. "You could call it that. Or totally insane."

Orie laughs.

"Well, I guess I'm glad that Jerry finally showed us he has some balls and flew across the world to be with you. Talk about being a little too late for the party." I know he is trying to make me see the comedy in the situation, but it's so hard for me to look at it in that way. At least not yet.

"He shouldn't have come."

"No."

We hear the key card in the door and Erik walks in. I look at him with wide eyes.

"What happening?" Orie asks as Erik walks over to the bar and pours himself a giant glass of wine. He takes a long, long sip of the drink before he turns to us to answer.

"Clayton's getting fucked up, drunk as shit, and thankfully I think Jerry is hidden away somewhere on the island because he was nowhere in sight. I hope he doesn't show his face again."

Erik turns to look at me. "How are you feeling?"

I shrug as a few more tears fall. "Like shit."

"Jerry's a dickhead. What he said to you was so fucked up it makes me hate him even more. How fucking dare he judge you and call you names? If Clayton hadn't beaten his ass, I would have."

"Maybe he's right," I whisper softly.

"Fuck him. He doesn't know shit," Erik practically yells at me. "He's fucking wrong. And don't you let him get to you, the mother fucking piece of shit." Crap. Erik is really angry.

Orie reaches out and takes my hand and Erik falls into one of the chairs. "And Clayton. Holy shit. I've never seen anyone punch someone like that. I have a whole new respect for the guy. He fights like a champ." Erik takes another sip of his drink. "I thought he was going to kill him, I swear to God, I really did. Eduard told me that he's never in all his years seen Clayton act that way. He was in complete and utter shock. So you're the first, Sophie. The first to ever bring out that rage in him."

Erik lifts his drink in salute. "Congratulations. You should feel pretty honored, babe."

I don't know if that's as good a thing as Erik seems to think it is. Yes, it's flattering. But I'm still so pissed that he would say what he did to Jerry. It was so wrong. So completely *wrong*. And even though Jerry said some pretty insulting things to me the last thing I would want to ever do is hurt him and Clayton did just that. I don't even know what I will say to him when I face him. I can't even think right now.

"Do you guys mind if I sleep here tonight?" I ask in a small voice. The last thing I want to do is face Clayton. Alone. With all these emotions raging through both of us. It can't be a good idea for us to see each other tonight, even though part of me wishes I was with him, in bed, and this was all just a bad dream.

"Hell, no," Orie smiles at me. "I kind of assumed you were. I'm excited for us to snuggle up."

"Thanks."

"He's gonna come for you," Erik tells me.

"He wouldn't dare. Not tonight," I say back, as I lower myself on the pillow and close my eyes.

"Oh, he'd dare alright. He'd dare anything, that guy," Erik says, shaking his head. "He's got one hell of a fantastic temper. Who would have thought that a Brit would be so passionate?" Erik seems totally perplexed by this. It almost makes me smile, except that this display of passion isn't at all like the kind I prefer from him.

"Close your eyes, babe. And sleep. Tomorrow is another day," Orie tells me as he caresses my hair and kisses me on the forehead. "Everything will be better in the morning."

"Or in the middle of the night when he comes for you," Erik mutters.

"He's not coming for me," I say back to him as I close my eyes.

"We'll see."

Chapter Eighteen

EXACTLY ONE HOUR later, I am proven wrong. The knocking starts just after Erik and Orie got into bed and fell asleep.

"Motherfucker," Erik grumbles in annoyance as he turns on the light and walks to the door. I'm safely on the other side of the bed, the farthest away from the door, with the blankets up to my face, acting as a shield. I feel as if I'm going to have a panic attack. He came for me. I can't believe it, no that's not true, I think to myself . . . yes, you so can.

"Hey man," I hear Erik say once the door is open.

"Is Sophie here?" Clayton asks quietly.

Where else would I be, I think to myself, completely annoyed. He made sure that I didn't have any other alternative than his villa. Erik opens the door and motions toward the bed, where I'm pretending to be asleep. I close my eyes tight, hoping they think I'm dead to the world.

I should know better. As if Erik will ever let me get away with that.

"For God's sake, quit pretending. It's so obvious. We all know you're wide awake," he grumbles. I know he's exhausted but still, shouldn't he be protecting his friend?

Clayton steps in the room, crowding the bungalow with his mere presence, instantly making it seem so small. I look over at him and raise a brow, trying to act indifferent, throwing him the same type of look he's given me many times. He looks plastered. He stares at me hard.

"You're coming with me." His voice leaves no room for argument.

"Ha," I snort, turning my back to him, wanting no part in any more drama for the evening. As if I would ever go willingly with him to his villa tonight? I even pull the covers up over my head, to show him how I'm so *not* coming with him. I know it's a tad bit childish, but I could care less. He needs to get the point. I hear him whisper to Erik, then try to listen in as my friend answers him, but I can't decipher anything. I wonder what the hell they're talking about, although I'm sure it can't be good. Then before I know it, I'm yanked out of the bed, grabbed around the waist, and thrown like a bag of rice over Clayton's shoulder.

"What the hell?!" I shriek in outrage. He pulls Orie's t-shirt down to cover what would have been my bare bottom.

"See you guys at breakfast. Ten a.m."

"We'll be there," Erik tells him with a smile.

I lift my head up and scream at Erik, willing him to look me in the eyes. "How dare you betray me to him!"

Erik actually smiles at me. "Love you, babe." He waves goodbye as Clayton walks through the door. "It's for the best. Trust me. You'll thank me later," he calls after us as he closes the door, shutting me out, leaving me alone. With him.

Clayton walks with me over his shoulder in complete silence, like it's totally normal that he's carrying me around like a sack of rice. He's acting like a caveman! Who does this? Who behaves like this? Where was this guy raised? I thought he was English and posh—aren't they supposed to be a culture of impeccable manners?

"Put me down! I'm not sleeping with you tonight!" I yell up at him as I try to punch him in the back. I feel his body tense up against my chest. "Did you hear me, Clayton? I said I'm not sleeping with you tonight!"

"I think the whole resort heard you," he says dryly. He doesn't sound like he cares. "Keep your voice down. It's impolite not to think of your neighbors," he orders as he smacks my ass lightly. I'm mortified and try to twist out of his arms. Drunk Clayton is not as steady as a sober Clayton, and the more I twist, the more he sways, and before I know it we're dangerously close the edge of the pathway.

"Put me down, you Neanderthal!" I scream at him, and give him a good kick in the gut to prove my point.

Bad idea.

Clayton loses his balance, his fight, I should say, for sobriety, and before I know it the two of us go flying over the side of the wooden path, deep into the darkness of the ocean.

The water is warm but still a shock to the system. I sputter up for air and look over at Clayton who bobs up out of the water looking completely bewildered.

"Well, that was just great!" I yell at him. "You could have killed us!"

"Me?!" Clayton yells back. "If you hadn't moved around so much maybe I would been able to keep my balance."

"If you were sober—"

"Don't you dare get me started on why I wasn't sober!" he says angrily.

I flip my wet hair away from him and spot the ladder that goes up toward the path. I swim over to it.

"I have nothing more to say to you," I say over my shoulder as I reach the ladder.

"I would think twice about going back to Erik and Orie's villa."

"As if!" I huff as I climb out of the water. Clayton is fast behind me.

Two things dawn on me. One, we could have been seriously hurt flying off the dock the way we did. And two, I just *fell into the ocean at night* and didn't freak out. Talk about conquering some fears! The joy of my moment is taken away when Clayton joins me and yanks my hand and pulls me with him to his villa. We walk inside and I try and make a beeline to the guest bedroom.

"I'm sleeping in here."

He throws me over his shoulder again and walks into the master suite and sets my wet body down.

His gaze meets mine. Lord, he's still angry!

"The only place you'll put your pretty little head down to sleep is in my bed, with me. I thought we went over this already. Now. I flew twelve hours today. I had a terrible meeting because all I could think about was getting back to you. And when I finally got here, I had the pleasure of finding you in the arms of your ex-boyfriend, Jerry, who was busy offering to rid you of your virginity, I might add. I come back to the villa, thinking I'm going to find you here, but instead you're in bed with Erik and Orie, in a t-shirt that barely covers your naked ass. You made me trip and fall in the ocean at night. I'm drunk. I'm exhausted. And I'm bloody furious. Do you really want to try me right now, Sophie?" he asks in a dangerously soft voice.

I shake my head no.

"Good. Now be a good girl and go dry off or take a shower then get into this bed and go to sleep."

"Okay," I mutter.

He watches me like a hawk as I walk into the bathroom, huffing the whole time.

"You can at least use the other shower," I tell him annoyed, assuming he will be taking one.

"Gladly," he says to my utter bewilderment. "I expect to find you here when I come out. I hope I'm not disappointed," he says coolly as he leaves me in the room.

I don't know if I'm offended or what but I shower in two point five seconds, dry off, slip on a nightie, and am in bed in under five minutes.

I hear the shower still going in the guest bedroom, get up and grab three of the extra pillows on the couch, and plant them down the center of the bed, creating an effective barrier between the two of us. I'm happy with my work. I lie down on my side of the bed and the shower goes off. I hear him fussing around, then the bedroom door opens. Since the light is still on, on his side of the bed, he can see my wall. Yes, it is probably the most immature thing I've ever done in my life, but God, it felt good.

I'm pretty sure he doesn't move for a minute because I don't hear any sound, and then I feel his body sink into the bed and hear the click of the light as darkness envelopes us. The mattress creaks and he turns on his side, away from me. *What?!* He's not going to say anything about my wall? *Excuse me?!* I sit up completely furious, and scream out in the dark.

"Are you serious?!" I'm outraged.

I feel the rumbling in the bed. It shakes hard and I wonder if he's crying. No?! *Is he crying?* I lean over and flick on my light and look down at him, completely worried that I've devastated him.

No. I definitely have *not* done that.

He's so not crying. Try . . . he's laughing! At me!

"Well, that's nice!" I snap as I turn the light off again and seethe. I scootch over more to my side of the bed, my arms crossed in rage as I think about how amusing I seem to him.

He's laughing so hard, the bed is literally moving around like there's an earthquake. Then he breaks through the pillow barrier and pulls me in his arms.

"God, Sophie. You're a genius!" he tells me before the mirth overcomes him again and he falls back. I can't believe it."

"I'm happy I amuse you."

"You do, baby." He rolls on top of me, covering me with his naked body. He nuzzles my neck, distracting me from my anger. "You really do."

His licks my neck, then kisses me softly, causing shivers to race up and down my spine. I want him again, even though I'm pissed and angry that he would intentionally hurt Jerry the way he did. But my body craves him. I try to remain stiff, unaffected, but it's virtually impossible, and damn him, he knows that.

"I'm mad at you," I whisper to him as his hand moves down my body, his fingers slipping inside me, making me sigh in reaction. God, he turns me on. I can't help it. My body is so completely in tune with his, it's unnerving as hell.

"You're wet for me."

"I can't help it."

"I don't want you to," he whispers in my ear as he kisses me softly. My body arches up to him. He reaches down to pull off my t-shirt and I find myself helping him.

His body crashes down on mine and he licks my neck again, then his mouth moves down until he finds my breast, cupping it roughly as his tongue moves over my nipple, teasing, pulling, until I'm aching with desire.

"I'm fucking pissed at you too, Sophie," he says passionately, moving down my body, his mouth against my stomach, causing me to go delirious with desire. His hands hold my ass as he pulls me up to his mouth.

"I wanted to kill him for even touching you. Do you know how hard it was to control myself when I saw you in his arms?" He doesn't give me time to answer because his tongue begins to work its magic, stoking the inferno that rages inside. Within seconds, I explode, my climax rocking my body as I come against his mouth, dying a thousand slow deaths from the exquisite feeling.

He moves over me and his mouth finds mine, kissing me. I hold him close, never wanting to let him go, the force of my desire consuming me like a wildfire. He rips his mouth away from mine, breathing savagely, and I grab his face and force him to look at me.

"You hurt him." My voice shakes with the depth of my emotion. "He didn't deserve that." I need him to hear that what he did to Jerry is not okay. Hurting a man who was only trying to win me back, however misguided it might have been, was not right. Jerry hadn't done anything wrong.

Clayton's inhales sharply as his eyes blaze in anger.

"I don't give a fuck how he feels!" His voice is raw with emotion. "And I won't have you feeling an ounce of pity for him. Not a thought. Not a fucking word! Never utter his name to me again!"

Is he serious? Well, yes, Sophie, look at his face. Have you ever seen anything so serious in your life? It's ridiculous. Completely. Utterly. Ridiculous. But behind the anger, behind the insane jealous and possessiveness, behind it all, I know it's because he cares.

"Promise me!" he says as he pushes himself inside of me. My eyes close, savoring every minute, every piece of him that I can get.

"Promise me, Sophie!" I can sense the urgency, the need, and I open my eyes to give him what he wants, because I know he needs it.

"I promise you." A look of complete satisfaction and ownership comes over his face as he pushes deeper inside me, filling me fully, making me tremble from the force. Fuck. I think I'll die if don't have him like this every day, inside me, filling me with every part of his being, his arms holding me tight, his mouth brushing against mine in that sexy way he does.

"You belong to me." *I know, Clayton,* I think to myself as I hold him close, my mouth finding his, trying to show him just how much I belong to him and want to be a part of him and his world.

I never want us to end.

I'm consumed with the depth of emotion I feel, not just for the ecstasy his body gives me, but for the man he is. I feel the tears start to fall as I find my release again as he's deep inside me.

"I love you," I whisper softly, trying to fight the exhaustion that is overwhelming me. If I stay up he'll say the words back to me, I know it . . .

I lose the battle and am dead asleep within seconds.

Chapter Nineteen

I'M HAVING TROUBLE accepting the fact that I'm actually leaving the Maldives in one hour. My bags are packed and I'm waiting for Bikram to come and pick us up to take me out to the seaplane where I'll be meeting Erik and Orie. I've only been here for eleven days, but so much has happened that has irrevocably changed my life. I look over at Clayton, who's working on his computer. He's been suspiciously quiet all morning long, pensive and serious. I'm pretty sure he's still mad that I'm going.

When I started packing this morning, he asked me to stay. Last night in bed, he begged me to stay. Yesterday afternoon, again, he asked me to stay. For the past two days, he's asked at every opportunity. But I can't. It would only prolong the inevitable end of our time together here. And to stay without my friends, without their support, is too much for me to bear. I didn't tell Clayton this though, because if I did, he would surely offer to pay for the extra nights for them and I know they would probably miss work to stay longer. And I can't have that. Instead,

I used my parents as an excuse.

I don't want to think about what will happen when I leave, how I will feel without him, our future together uncertain, our lives separated by more than just an ocean. It is too much. Too painful. And as Noom's friend Dan told me yesterday at my session with him, it is not real until you are actually living it.

I'm glad I decided to see him. In many ways, the time I spent with him prepared me more for today. I was unsure when I booked it, but now I know. I met him at the spa. He stood next to the massage table and asked me to have a seat on it. After I did, I looked up at him, feeling in many ways like a little girl again.

"Tell me."

I burst out crying, my tears like a massive, neverending waterfall, my pain so acute that I didn't even know where to begin.

"Your heart is heavy with sadness, carrying a great weight of love and longing. Your tears should be those of joy, to have known a love so great and consuming, to have it change and help define who you are," he said softly to me, as he pulled me down on the table, face up, and stood above me. "It is a great gift to be given such a love in this lifetime. To know it from the moment you set eyes on your twin flame. You should be rejoicing."

"How can I rejoice when we are to be separated?" I ask him, wiping my tears away. "I'm leaving tomorrow. And then what? Do I have to live my life knowing what I do and never finding it again?"

"You do not know what tomorrow brings, Sophie. Or the next day, or the day after that," he told me. "That is your first mistake. The universe does not put things in front of us that we cannot handle. There is a great meaning in every moment, every person, every experience you have."

"So what now?" I ask him. "What are you telling me to do?"

He smiled at me as he closed my eyes. "Now you live. You be. Right now. Here. And you trust the plan. The moment. And that is all you trust. Because that is all you know."

He did his healing on me then, and it was incredible. My body tingled with energy, with life, and I felt a great sense of peace when I left him. The tears dried and somehow I knew he was right. Deep inside my soul, I felt that the universe would take care of me. It would make it right, it would make it as it should be. And there was a wonderful calm in that.

"Come here, baby," Clayton says to me, holding out his hand.

I walk over to him and sit down on his lap, cuddling up against him and breathing his scent in. Relishing the moment, his touch, trying to memorize everything about it. He holds me tight.

"Stay," he begs me.

"You know I can't."

"You can. You don't want to."

I pull away from him and let my fingers trace the soft lines of his face.

"Don't say that."

"It's the truth."

"I have to go. Please don't make this worse than it already is," I whisper to him, begging him.

"How can this get any worse?"

I close my eyes and lean against him. It really can't, I think to myself. The door rings and I know it's Bikram. All of a sudden, I feel so nauseous that I can't even think.

"Fuck," Clayton swears angrily, both of us looking at the door as if Satan himself is on the other side. I try to move out of his embrace, but he holds me tighter, not letting me move.

"I have to get it," I say.

"You don't."

I actually smile at him, shocked that I can find the courage to do that, and then I pull away from him.

"You know I do." I get up and answer the door. Bikram can sense the somber mood and quickly puts my luggage in the cart. Clayton gets up and follows me outside and gets in the cart with me.

I take my last look at the resort as we drive over the wooden walkway, past the bungalows, and I silently thank the island. The sea. Noom. I thank it all. This small piece of paradise brought me the most magical experience of my life.

We reach the dock and the plane is there, ready to take us away.

I'm happy to see Erik and Orie are waiting for me. Shit. They look like I feel. Bikram unloads my bags and helps load them on the plane. I try to get off the cart.

"Stay, goddamnit!" Clayton swears at me, holding me back. *I'm trying to be brave, damn you,* I think to myself. Don't make me shatter now! I shake my head at him and pull away from his hold. He looks angry, upset, devastated all in one. He follows me to the end of the dock, where he holds out his hand to say goodbye to Erik and Orie.

"Gentlemen, it has been a pleasure," he tells them as they shake hands. "Please, take care of her on the flight home."

Orie pulls me into his embrace, knowing I'm walking a fine line and can crumble at any minute.

"We've got her. Don't worry."

"I hope we'll see you soon," Erik says to him, voicing the longing in my heart. Like can we see you in an hour, I think? Can you get on the plane with us to LA? Can you?

"You will. Sooner than you think," Clayton responds. Erik smiles at him. I know he likes his answer.

I am handed a lifejacket from one of the men from the resort. I put it on and Clayton helps me buckle it tightly as Erik and Orie walk onto the plane. I feel so sick, I think I'm going to throw up. It's surreal, like a complete fucking circle. Here he is seeing me off, there he was, helping me arrive. My hands move up slowly and I cover his as they hold onto my safety buckles. I close my eyes, knowing the inevitable tears are going to come.

He leans down into me, putting his forehead against mine, taking a deep, heavy breath. I can feel his raging emotions, I know he's upset with me for leaving. I know he's upset at the whole situation. And I hate disappointing him.

I take his hands and kiss each palm.

"I want to thank you . . ." I begin, my voice wavering with the depth of my emotion.

"Don't you fucking dare, Sophie. Don't you fucking dare," he responds harshly, like he knows what I'm about to say to him.

He lifts my chin up and stares at me, his eyes ablaze with feeling.

"This is not the end."

I can only nod.

"Do you hear me?" he says roughly. "*This is not the fucking end!* Say it to me. Say it now!" he demands.

My voice is choked up. I can barely speak, but I give him what he wants. "This. Is. Not. The. End."

He nods at me, then grabs my face between his palms and kisses me so passionately that I think I'm going to die.

"I will see you soon. And when I do, I will punish you for making us both go through this mockery. Because it will never happen again." He says it so savagely that my toes curl. I throw myself in his arms and kiss him again. Then I pull back slowly and smile at him.

"I love you."

He doesn't say the words back, like I wish he would, but I know he's not used to emotions. It's so strange. I've never uttered these words to a man before, and yet it feels so natural right now. I love him with all that I am, and even though I know he's not ready to say the words to me, I am finally completely confident that he feels the same way, and it's okay.

"I do, you know," I tell him softly.

"I know, baby." He pulls me in and holds me close.

I cried the whole way to Male. And on the entire, four-hour trip to Singapore from Male. And just about drove Erik and Orie crazy. I don't think they could much more of it. When we got off the plane in Singapore, with a three-hour layover stretching out in front of us, Erik turned to me and really let me have it.

"One more goddamn tear and I'm going to scream."

I stared at him with wide eyes.

"But . . ."

"No fucking 'buts!' He's coming for you. He's not letting you go. So stop your whining and go have a glass of wine. Make it two," he ordered. "I'm going to Hermès in duty free to buy myself something nice. If I feel like it, maybe I'll pick up a bangle for you. But only if you stop the damn crying. If I see one tear, one damn tear when I get back to the lounge, you can kiss the bangle goodbye. Now go drink."

So here I am.

I grab my bag and turn my cell phone on, hoping that I have reception so I can connect to the Wi-Fi in the lounge. Thankfully, I do.

I have three texts from Clayton Sinclair.

When did I input his number in my phone? Um, I *never* did. I slowly smile. He must have done it himself, the sneaky bastard.

Clayton:

"SOPHIE, TEXT ME WHEN YOU LAND IN SINGAPORE."¥

The next one reads.

Clayton:

"I'M FUCKING PISSED YOU LEFT."

I start laughing.

And then there's another.

Clayton:

"I CAN'T BELIEVE YOU LEFT. I JUST CAN'T BELIEVE THIS. THE VILLA, THIS RESORT, THIS PLACE IS JUST NOT THE SAME WITHOUT YOU. I MISS YOU, GODDAMNIT. CLAYTON."

My heart soars. I feel so happy, so incredibly content, because of that text.

I write him back instantly.

Sophie:

"I JUST LANDED. I'M IN THE LOUNGE.

I FUCKING MISS YOU TOO. XO SOPHIE."

I don't even have to wait thirty seconds for his response. He must have supersonic reception in the Maldives.

Clayton:

"DON'T USE THAT LANGUAGE. IT'S UNBECOMING OF YOU. AND YOU HAVE ONLY YOURSELF
TO BLAME. PICK UP YOUR PHONE."

The phone rings a second later and I answer after one ring.

"I'm going crazy here without you." His voice is even sexier on a cell phone. He's calling me! I'm so happy I could scream.

"I'm miserable," I admit. Because I am. I want him to be with me. I want us to be together, wherever that place is, just together. And if I'm miserable now, I keep wondering how I will ever survive the rest of the separation. The time difference, the long flights? How?

"Fly back. My assistant can book you a flight right now."

"You know I can't," I whisper to him, wishing the opposite was true.

"You can drive a man mad, baby."

"I'm sorry I can't give you what you want," I tell him, because it's the honest truth.

"You will," he assures me, sounding completely confident.

"I miss you, Clayton."

"I miss you too, baby." I can feel the tears start to come again. Those dreaded tears.

"I have to get a grip. Can we talk a little later?" I ask him, not wanting him to hear me cry.

"Yes, that's fine." He sighs. "I know your layover is another couple of hours. I have a work call I'm jumping on right now that I should be off before your flight leaves. I will ring you right when I'm done, okay?"

"Okay."

"Bye, baby," he says softly, then pauses for a second. "Sophie?"

"Yes?"

He takes a moment.

"I've never felt this miserable before. I just want you to know that. I want you to know that you're responsible for this feeling of discomfort I have. I'm not used to it. And honestly, I hate it. I don't know what someone would call this . . . if it's . . ." My heart stops. Love. He wants to say it. "I don't know, because I've never experienced this before."

It's the most amazing thing he could have said to me. The sweetest, best thing—besides I love you—that he could say to make me soar.

"I understand, Clayton," I tell him.

"Do you?" He sounds annoyed.

"Yes. I make you queasy, angry, and uncomfortable." I laugh.

"Christ. I miss you," he says sharply.

"I'll talk to you after your call, Clayton," I tell him with a smile, so happy that he just told me how much he misses me.

"Count on it."

"I do."

We hang up and I'm happy to note that I am feeling a little better.

Knowing that he misses me is reassuring and gives me hope. I pick up my carry-on bag and go freshen up in the bathroom in the lounge, then make my way to the duty free.

A couple of hours later, and after blowing even more money that I don't have, I find Erik and Orie in Gucci buying aviator sunglasses that look suspiciously like the ones Clayton had. I smirk at the sight.

"Fancy you two liking those."

"That's a very English thing for you to say," Orie smiles at me. "I'm guessing lover boy called?"

"He did."

"Thank fucking God. Can you imagine a flight home listening to her cry the whole way?" Erik says to Orie with a look of pure horror. "The thought makes my skin crawl. But if that happened I'd slip an Ambien in your drink and call it a day," he admits.

"You'd drug me?" I ask him, feigning horror, even though I know he probably would; for humanity's sake, he would tell me, and for his own sanity. Shit, I'd probably welcome it under those circumstances.

"One hundred percent. No doubt." He turns to me with the aviators on his face, posing like a runway model.

"How do I look?"

"Pretty damn good."

"Could you die?" He smiles at me then tells the sales lady, "I'll take these."

"I'm going over to the newsstand. I want to pick up some magazines," I tell them.

"Grab an *US Weekly* and *People*. I feel so out of the loop with my celebrity gossip," Erik asks me as I head out.

They have a pretty impressive wall filled with about one hundred different magazines from around the world. It's so overwhelming, I don't even know where to begin. I grab the two that Erik wanted me to get, then pick up an interesting-looking magazine for artists, a *UK Vogue*, a *Bazaar*, then stop dead in my tracks when I get to *Hello* magazine. What the hell?

I can feel the bile rise in my throat.

It can't be, and yet it is. It's him. Clayton Astor Sinclair. On the cover of a magazine. And he's not alone.

The headline reads:

Lord Clayton Astor Sinclair on again with the beautiful Amelia Von Peters.

It's a picture of Clayton and Amelia taken a few days ago in Singapore. When he told me he was going for business. He's wearing the same suit he had on that day, so it can't be a picture from the past, and there's no mistaking the Maldivian tan. His arm is around her, holding her close, as they're caught on a street corner in the city. In broad daylight.

Like a lunatic, I read the article, which gives a location and time. An eyewitness even says that they were caught leaving the Ritz-Carlton Hotel arm in arm. *They look so in love. What a handsome couple they are,* another witness said of the two them. As if on cue, my phone rings and it's him. Clayton. I don't answer as I stare blindly at the magazine. Moments later, Clayton rings again. And I still don't answer.

Then again. Damn it! I grab my phone and turn it off, making sure there is no way I can hear the ringer again as I try to digest it all.

So, I was used. Thoroughly. Completely. Used.

Played.

I have to sit down.

I literally collapse on the ground in front of the stand, the magazine gripped tightly in my hand. I look at the photographs. As if I'm watching myself look at the photos of the two of them from a distance, I note how good they look together. Their height and coloring complement each other very well. According to the article, it seems they have the same pedigree. Amelia's father is some important person in Parliament or something, honestly, I can't even focus. *And his family loves her,* his friends say. I'm sure they do. What's not to love?

"Yo bitch, I think they just called for our plane," Orie says behind me.

"Do you have any idea how germ-infested airport floors are?" Erik says in a horrified voice. "Are you insane? Do you want to catch the bird flu?"

I lift my arm up, holding the magazine in my hand. No words. I just hold it up. Someone, one of them, grabs it from me and they both take it in.

"What the hell?!" Erik practically screams.

"That motherfucking piece of goddamn shit!" Orie chimes in, enraged.

A few minutes go by and the two are now completely silent. A rarity. I know they're probably staring down at me, wondering how in the hell they're going to deal with me, what they're going to say, what *can* they say, and just what they should do for me. I'm beyond pain. I'm beyond feeling. I'm in such a deep, deep state of shock that I don't know what to say to them either. So many colorful adjectives come to mind, but I don't think they would fully capture the essence of what I'm feeling inside. I actually don't know if there are any words in the English language for it.

Erik breaks the silence, as I expected. "We all need to get a grip for a second and back the fuck up."

I stand and face my friends. Erik holds the magazine in his hand and waves it around.

"Where did we go wrong?"

I'm incapable of answering him because I'm at a loss. I grab the magazine from his hand and turn to pay for it at the counter.

"Is that really necessary?" Erik asks me.

"I think it is."

I hand the woman cash then look at them with zombie eyes.

"Are we going?"

They nod and follow my lead as I make my way toward the gate. I'm methodical, robotic, it's like I'm having some type of out-of-body experience and this is not for real, none of it is, and I'm going to wake up. I'm going to wake up and I'll be at home, in my parents' place, and I'll never have gone to the Maldives, I'll still be a virgin, and I'll think about this dream lover I had who was incredible. And a lying cheat. Christ.

I hand my ticket to the stewardess and walk onto the plane, Erik and Orie behind me, speechless.

I find my seat and collapse in it. My friends come to me, both staring at my pale face, waiting for some type of reaction that will show them that I'm still breathing, living, and sane.

But something inside me has died. Something was crushed so cruelly and completely that I don't know if I'll ever be able to revive it. Recover from it.

"Are you going to say something?" Erik asks me, worried.

"What is there to say?"

"Something! *Anything*," he says frantically, searching my face for signs of life. "This is so fucked!"

"Well, I'm going to say something," Orie cuts in, with a look on his face of pure anger, a complete rarity for him. "I feel betrayed by this English asshole. What a crock of shit he is. A big, fat, motherfucking lie. From head to toe. And I hate him. I really hate him, Sophie. He's a goddamn dick. If he were here, I'd beat the living shit out of him. Actually, he's way worse than that, Sophie. *He's a cunt.* Isn't that a word the English love to use?" Erik nods in agreement, giving his boyfriend a high five.

"You couldn't have said it better. He *is* a cunt," Erik says.

I almost smile. And then I feel it coming. I think I'm . . . I think I'm . . .

"Oh shit! She's gonna barf!" Erik screams out as he pulls out the barf bag and hands it to me.

I throw up into the bag.

"First time on a plane," Erik says to someone who walks by and looks at me in disgust.

"Nerves," Orie says as he grabs another bag and I continue to vomit my guts out.

I try and take a deep breath. I hand Erik the used bags.

"You do know how to test a friendship," he says in disgust as he takes them from my hand.

Orie leans over me. "Talk to me."

"But not directly in his face, you might make him puke, too," Erik says.

I almost laugh. But then reality hits me again.

"What do you want me to say?"

"Tell us how you feel. But hold a hand to cover your breath." Erik says trying to make me smile.

Unfortunately it doesn't work.

"You're both right. We were played," I finally say. "All of us. He's really good at it. So good that we all believed him. Obviously, me more than you two. But I did believe in his sincerity and in his honesty. I thought . . ." What can I say that they don't already know? I know I sound devastated. "I guess it doesn't matter what I thought. The reality is shockingly obvious. Will you guys just go get me something to drink from that stewardess?"

"And a toothbrush. I'll get the toiletry bag." Erik says before he and Orie disappear.

I grab my phone from my bag and turn it on. It vibrates with the sound of a million voice messages and texts. I only allow myself to read his last text to me.

Clayton:

"DID YOU SEND ME TO VOICEMAIL??!"

Yes, you asshole, I did.

I think long and hard before I start texting him, but then I can't stop myself. I have to say something. I have to let him know that I *know* what he is.

Sophie:

"I DIDN'T REALIZE YOU WERE SUCH A CELEBRITY IN SINGAPORE AND LONDON. I SAW THE PICTURES OF YOU AND AMELIA ON THE NEWSSTAND. YOU KNOW, FROM THE DAY YOU CAME TO SINGAPORE FOR "BUSINESS." YOU HAVE BETRAYED ME IN THE WORST WAY POSSIBLE. THERE IS NOTHING LEFT TO SAY BETWEEN US. YOU ARE A CHEATER. EVERYTHING THAT HAPPENED BETWEEN US WAS A LIE. I WAS A FOOL. CONGRATULATIONS, CLAYTON. YOU PULLED A FAST ONE ON ME. THANK YOU FOR BEING ANOTHER FIRST FOR ME—THE FIRST TO BREAK MY HEART."

I press send then decide to text one more thing.

Sophie:

"I'M GOING TO FORGET WE EVER MET. NEVER CONTACT ME AGAIN. GOODBYE. FOREVER."

END BOOK ONE

The sequel to
MAD LOVE
by Colet Abedi

"The great question that has never been answered and which I have not yet been able to answer . . . is, "What does a woman want?"
-sigmund freud

Chapter One

"Alright Sophie, in a moment I'm going to count to three. And when I do, I want you to take a deep breath in and then slowly exhale," Dr. Goldstein, my hypnotherapist, says to me in a soothing voice. "And when you release your breath, you will let go of all your pain. All your anxiety. And you will forget you ever knew Clayton Astor Sinclair."

I take in a shaky breath and prepare myself.

"One."

My eyes flutter like a butterfly and before I can stop myself I see a flash of Clayton pulling me into his arms.

"Two."

His lips crush mine with savage intensity.

"Three."

His tongue moves into my mouth to take full ownership and—

Dr. Goldstein snaps his fingers.

"Uh-hum," Dr. Goldstein coughs loudly. "I said, *three*."

It takes me a moment to remember where I am and more importantly, *why* I'm here. And when that happens the memories hit me hard.

When I open my eyes I'm pretty sure my cheeks are on fire.

"How do you feel, Sophie?" Dr. Goldstein asks me with a raised brow.

I think about lying to him, but wonder if he's a mind reader too. He's the hypnotherapist that Erik recommended to get rid of bad habits. People usually saw him for smoking, alcohol addiction or binge eating. Not to forget sex with a man they met in the Maldives.

"Good." I hope I sound convincing.

Dr. Goldstein brushes a hand through his silver hair and stands up to walk behind his large glass desk. I sit up from the black leather couch that I've been lying down on and smooth out my grey sweat pants. I watch Dr. Goldstein pace. His office could be the poster child for minimalist perfection. The walls are winter white, with three large iconic Ansel Adams framed photos. A simple black leather sofa with single metal chair for the doctor, are placed in front of his enormous glass desk. It is sparse, but strangely comforting in a non-threatening kind of way.

I watch as Dr. Goldstein moves to stand in front of the window that overlooks Santa Monica pier. He crosses his arms and a feeling of dread washes over me as he frowns at the view.

"Honesty is a requirement in this office," he says. "Without honesty how do we know this is helping?"

I think about his words before I reluctantly answer.

"Well," I begin slowly. "I guess when you told me to forget Clayton, I saw a flash of his face. Then I thought of his arms around me and kissing him, then—" my voice starts to get choked up, the tears, those damn tears of mine are dangerously close to falling. Again.

Dr. Goldstein waves his hand in the air.

Mad Love

"I get it. You *see* Clayton even though I keep telling you to *stop* seeing him. Same way you've been seeing him for the past three weeks." He turns away from the window and sits down at his desk. He leans back in his chair and twirls his mustache between his fingers as he stares at me.

It feels like an eternity.

"I can't believe I'm going to say this, but since you've been coming here for three weeks now at three times a week no less, with no improvement whatsoever I'm going to have to say that I think you're a classic case study."

Classic case study?

I wonder what mental issue he's about to diagnose me with.

"Tell me, Dr. Goldstein," I say softly, ready to hear his conclusion and learn how to forget Clayton forever. "I can handle whatever you're going to tell me as long as there is medication for it."

I think Dr. Goldstein rolls his eyes but I can't be sure because my eyes are blurry from the tears that I'm determined not to shed. Not anymore.

"There is *no* medication for what you have, Sophie! You don't want to forget the damn guy." He throws his hands up in the air when he says the last bit.

But I'm trying. I really am.

The last *person* I want to be with is a serial philanderer, always focused on the next conquest. Someone I can never trust and will always wonder about.

But the problem is that I've not been able to forget him. *Not yet.* The man who introduced me to passion. Who introduced me to love. The most perfect man in every way—*Okay, except for one glaring flaw— okay, more than glaring, try epic flaw—oh whatever, Sophie! You're the one who fell for him!*

Clayton. *The Cheater.*

My plane ride from Singapore was like something out of a nightmare. Between the wine and the tears, I was sure I drove Erik and Orie crazy. I remember the two of them staring at me like I needed to be admitted to a mental institution. I sat in my seat in first class (not that I even noticed the luxury), cried my heart out and drank an obscene amount of red wine.

Erik, my dear beautiful best friend, tried his hardest to talk me out of the hole of darkness I had buried myself in.

"Get a goddamn grip! You need to be strong! You're a woman now in every sense of the word. This is real life, Sophie."

Real life? Was this my only choice?

"What Erik is trying to say, " Orie chimed in with his usual gentle demeanor, "is that unfortunately this is part of the ups and downs of life. Of relationships."

I turned my gaze away from Orie and stared blindly out the plane window.

"Sophie," Orie continued. "I think the best way for you to handle this is to pretend like it's a death. You can never go back because it's gone. *He's gone*. For good. It's done. It's over. It's dead—"

"I think she gets it," Erik interrupted. "But Orie's right. If you look at this like a death you can give yourself real closure. Like, pretend a shark ate him in the Maldives. Or, I don't know . . . something just as gruesome and painful because that's exactly what the bastard deserves."

But he wasn't dead, he was alive and well at the resort. And probably zeroing in on his next victim. Moving her to the villa next to his. Getting ready to wine and dine—

"Jesus. Look at your face," Erik said as he grabbed my hand. "It's not going to be easy. But we're going to be right here next to you the whole way. You *will* get over him. I promise you. You will. And one day, we'll look back on this and laugh. The way I'm silently laughing at your teeth and lips right now."

Erik put a small mirror in front of my face and I gasped in horror at how frightening I looked because of the stains from the red wine.

"You look like death becomes her," he said trying his hardest not to smile.

He did finally manage to get a giggle out of me. But it didn't last long.

And that was twenty-two days ago.

I'm all cried out now. Exhausted. Trying not to think about him even though I can't stop dreaming about him. Hoping that I wake up and the pain will at least be a bit less. Something that I can deal with. Not this horrible feeling that no one will *ever* be as perfect as him. But there is no way I can be with a man who is unfaithful. No way. I remember a girl at school whose father always had affairs. It was awful and the worst part was after twenty years of putting up with his shit, he ended up leaving her mother in the end—no way I would let myself go down that road.

When I got home from the trip I locked myself up in my apartment and refused to see anyone for two days. My parents tried to force their way over but I avoided them by claiming I had a horrible flu and just wanted to sleep. I got a two-day reprieve and then made myself go to their house, or else I knew they'd have the police breaking down my door. Thankfully my tan hid the fact that I was such a mess inside.

I sat in the family room on the couch and stared blindly at the TV. My dad was watching CNN and my mom was in the kitchen cleaning up the dishes from dinner. We had opted to stay in so we could catch up. I was grateful because I was able to wear what had become my uniform since I returned: sweats, sweatshirt, with my hair tied up in a bun. My parents were dressed casually as well, but they were wearing nice track suits that didn't have old stains on them. My dad looked relaxed sitting back on the cozy white sofa with a glass of wine in his hand. His silver hair was brushed back from his handsome face and I could tell he was enjoying the broadcast. I felt good when my dad was at ease. At least there was something in the world that could make me happy.

Dad had occasionally broken the silence by asking me a question about my vacation. My answers were abrupt and I'm sure he could tell that I didn't want to talk about it. So he had stayed silent for most of the evening. I was happy for that because it gave me the opportunity to obsess about Clayton and analyze every single moment we had together.

"God what a frightening thought," my father said out loud.

"Uh huh," I replied automatically as I relived the moments on the Remington's yacht when I first met Ameila Von Peters, the model.

"Just awful," he went on.

"Sure is," I nodded blankly as I realized I should have known from the looks she gave him that something was going on.

"To think we had the alien mother ship in our backyard this entire time and didn't know it."

"Yeah."

Huh. Aliens. Amelia's beauty reminded me of an alien. It was like something from out of this world—

"Sophie Walker have you heard a word I said?!"

Crap.

I looked over at my dad's knowing look. I was so busted.

"What's wrong, honey? Talk to me. This silence is so unlike you." The caring tone in my dad's voice was nearly my undoing. He looked so genuinely concerned about me. I wanted to tell him. A big part of me wanted to throw myself in his loving arms and hear him say that it would be okay, that he would keep me safe, as he had when I was a child. But I was so afraid of the disappointment I thought I would see when I told him everything that I couldn't bring myself to.

Mad Love

"Nothing, dad."

"Don't lie to me," he said. "You know I can tell. Something is wrong. You've seemed off all day. Didn't you have fun in the Maldives, honey?"

Fun? Try it was the time of my life until I found out—ugh, I didn't want to go there again.

"It was great, dad."

"Is it a financial thing? Are you in trouble because of the trip?"

I almost laughed. Even though we had paid for the villas in advance, Clayton had gone behind our backs and taken care of our entire bill. He had paid for our villas, our meals, activities, spa- the whole trip. I guess I could thank him for giving me a month of financial freedom that I didn't think I had when I left on my vacation.

But now I needed to start making money. And fast. There was no way I would ever ask my parents for any help because that would lead to them arguing that I needed to go back to law school.

"I'm okay, dad." I lied. "It's just jet lag. I'm tired, that's all."

"Is it a boy thing?"

I almost started hyperventilating. My dad, being the perceptive lawyer, could see it on my face.

"It's Jerry isn't it, Sophie?"

Jerry?

I had almost forgotten about him.

"It's not a relationship thing, dad. I told you, I'm just tired."

I knew my dad didn't believe me but I also knew that he would let up for a while and probably call me the next day to see what was going on. Thankfully, I'd be able to fake happiness on the phone much better than in person.

"Sophie?" Dr. Goldstein's voice interrupts my reverie. "Have you heard anything I've said?"

"Yes," I lie then shake my head. "No. No, I haven't heard a word."

"I asked if he was still calling you from an anonymous number."

Right. Since Clayton wouldn't stop calling me I blocked his cell. Then I started to get calls from a private number. I never picked up. And then he stopped leaving text messages. The last one he left was one week ago. It was simple. To the point. And final.

It appears that my desire to speak to you and explain what you saw means absolutely nothing to you. There's nothing left to say then except goodbye, Sophie.

"No. He has stopped calling me."

"How does that make you feel?"

Like my life is over.

"It's getting easier," I say. "I know this is going to take time."

Dr. Goldstein gives me a sympathetic smile.

"Heartbreak is the hardest experience to go through, especially the first time. But chin up, Sophie. Life is long. You're bound to have your heart broken at least a dozen more times."

I will never date again. Never.

Made in the USA
Coppell, TX
02 September 2021